Forever, my Love

Fran McNabb

Prologue

April 1862
New Orleans

This was war.

Confederate Captain Hilliard McDougle knew all about war. He'd been fighting one for six months, and the tiny woman sitting stiffly on the carriage seat next to him had declared one loud and clear.

He knew how to deal with the enemy in blue uniforms, but by God, what do you do with an angry pregnant wife? The black barrel of a Yank's rifle paled in comparison to the verbal storm that brewed beneath her blonde curls.

He gripped the soft leather reins in his gloved hands and spoke to the pair of matched grays.

"Giddee up, girls. You'll feel better in your own stall tonight." Then under his breath, he whispered, "Me, too."

The rumble of distant thunder couldn't stop him from reaching River's Bend, his beloved plantation on the Mississippi River. Come hell or high water, he was going to make it home tonight.

He sneaked a quick glance at his young wife. "Are you tired? Do you need to rest?"

He ignored the fact she hadn't spoken a word since they sat for breakfast in the dining room of The Crystal

Bell, that is, unless the grunts she used to answer his questions could actually be called speaking. Even without words she let him know how she felt about his having a little fun with the men the night before.

"I'm fine."

He sighed at her terse reply. Tension and exasperation bubbled in his chest. Inhaling deeply, he reminded himself the pregnancy had her temper flaring so he squelched his own irritation.

"I told you last night that nothing happened," he tried to explain again. "The men and I were having a little fun in the gambling hall, got carried away and stayed a little too long. That's all, just a little fun.

It sounded reasonable to him. Getting together with the men last night hadn't been planned. He deserved a little fun after being on the battlefield for the last few months.

Ula McDougle snapped her head around. "And the perfume on your clothes? Am I to assume that was 'just fun' too?"

Hilliard rolled his green eyes. "I'm not explaining that again," he said, but continued anyway. "One of the ladies got a little too friendly with the whole group. We played along with her, but no one did anything wrong. She was nothing more than one of the fixtures in the saloon."

Ula grunted.

Outwardly Hilliard ignored her anger, but sweat formed under his hat in his mass of bright red hair. It trickled down his scalp. The woman had the keenest sense of smell in the county. He bent his face closer to his shoulder and sniffed. He couldn't smell a thing.

The two sat in silence for several more minutes, each in deep thought.

With his troops only a few days away from his plantation, Hilliard took the opportunity for this little getaway to New Orleans, where life was still relatively peaceful. Picking up the newly completed portrait of Ula was supposed to give her a much-needed outing. Since the war had begun, no social life existed. He thought he was doing his marriage a favor.

The portrait that was supposed to be a truly beautiful addition to the family estate would now be a constant reminder of their first argument, but Hilliard's Irish stubbornness refused to let him apologize. He'd done nothing wrong. She could seethe all she wanted.

Suddenly, Ula grabbed Hilliard's leg. "What's that noise?"

Hilliard had already heard the thunderous roar of hooves ahead of them. His military training took over. Without having to think, he whipped the carriage off the dirt road to avoid the inevitable onslaught heading their way, but a thick growth of twisted vines and low hanging branches blocked their path. Rearing up, the horses refused to go forward. Muddy slush beneath them sucked in the wheels of the carriage.

"Hilliard, we'll sink!" Ula screamed.

He didn't answer, but concentrated at working the reins until the horses were back on the higher, hard road. The thunder on the road, closer now, blended in with the storm's thunder overhead.

He looked over at his pale wife. Panic as he had never felt before closed his throat. She didn't deserve this.

He cracked the reins and screamed his order. "Get-up." The horses reared again, nearly toppling the carriage.

Ula grabbed her husband's arm, shrieking loudly, but he couldn't comfort her.

Pulling against the reins, he tried to soften his voice. "Whoa, girls. Settle down. It'll be okay."

But Hilliard knew it wasn't okay. A cloud of dust erupted around the bend, and within seconds he and his young wife of fewer than two years stared into the barrels of Union rifles. As he reached for his own weapon, a red flash exploded from one of the barrels and sent him flying over the edge of the carriage.

More screams filled his ears as he floated in slow motion to the ground below. With a thud, his body landed on the dirt road, filling his mouth and eyes with mud and leaves. He struggled to move, but nothing worked. Through a fog, he saw one of the soldiers grab for his wife. He tried to reach out to her, but nothing happened.

"I'm sorry," he screamed, but he knew that the words never made it to his mouth. "I'm so sorry."

Chapter 1

The present

Jewel Ferguson bolted upright in her bed. Thunder crashed in the distance. With knees pulled to her chest, she grabbed the edge of the blanket and pressed it to her chin. Except for her heavy breathing, nothing stirred in the room.

The central air kicked on, sending a soothing stream of cool over her sweat-soaked body just as the first drops of rain hit her bedroom window. She closed her eyes and let the breeze from the vents above her bed settle around her and the first patter of drops on the windowpane calm her shattered nerves.

It had happened again. For the past several weeks when she'd least expected it, a debilitating sensation immobilized her. Sometimes it pulled her out of a deep sleep and left her shaken and weak. Sometimes it was nothing more than a feeling that gave her pause during her busy day.

The sensations had become more frequent, more disturbing, almost frightening. Even with thousands of students surrounding her every day on campus, she felt totally alone. There was no one to share her experiences with, no one to talk with while she decided what to do.

Jewel glanced over at the clock. 4:45. She exhaled a loud ragged breath, then rested her head against her knees.

Was she losing her mind? Should she see a psychiatrist?

No, she wasn't ready for that—at least she hoped she wasn't. Something was happening to her she couldn't pinpoint, and even though she couldn't put it in words, she could feel it taking shape.

If she did see a shrink, what would she tell him? She was having dreams? Of what? She sat up and shrugged. That would give a doctor a lot to go on.

No, she wasn't ready to share her experiences because they were nothing more than vague disturbances, and there had to be a logical explanation.

As the cool air dried her perspiration and the light of her lamp took away the night's demons, Jewel tossed the covers aside and started her day a little earlier than the rest of the world.

By eight o'clock, a bright sun had replaced the rain. With only a small satchel, she headed across her college campus for appointments with two of her doctoral students. She loved teaching her science classes during the regular semesters, but her small workload in the summer gave her time to devote to her second love, writing. For several years she'd been working on a book concerning the role of Southern plantations during the Civil War and Reconstruction. Like her colleagues, she worked on science papers during their time away from the hectic teaching schedule, but she always found time to do research about the plantations, a subject dear to her heart.

"Morning, Dr. Ferguson."

"Morning, Sandi. Beautiful day, isn't it?"

"Yes, ma'am."

Jewel smiled at her student as she continued down the shaded sidewalk to her office. The campus in the sprawling city of Houston had become her home for the last six years. Nothing could suit her better. She loved being in a city so near to the Gulf of Mexico, a location with all the amenities that came with a city of its size could offer. If she chose to lose herself in her studies, she could work for weeks without leaving the three mile radius from her office to her apartment, but she always had the option of taking in the city's shopping districts and cultural centers. What more could she ask for in a university?

She stepped up on the brick stairs leading to the building that housed her department, biochemistry. It was one of the many science buildings on campus. Everything around her soothed the soul and opened the minds of those that were fortunate enough to attend.

Today she needed a little of that soothing. She carried with her a slip of paper with a name, Bryce Cameron, a name resounding with character, age, and wisdom. In her mind she saw an older, distinguished gentleman with long gray hair pulled back behind his head, maybe an old hippie who refused to move into the Twenty-first Century, or a graying scientist who searched for answers for the future by studying the past.

She admired people who wanted to preserve and learn from the past. Studying the plantations from another century was not in her line of work at the university, but it gave her an appreciation for what people like Mr. Cameron did. In a way, she guessed the two of them had a lot in common. As an architectural engineer he studied the construction of old structures to restore and preserve them. She studied and taught the science of living organisms in a sterile lab so that she could help preserve human life.

She knew they would understand each other so even though he was a stranger, when Mr. Cameron extended an invitation for her to visit the fort he was restoring on an island in the Gulf of Mexico, she accepted without hesitation. He said he had information about one of her ancestors, and even though he didn't offer a lot of details, Jewel knew she had to talk with him. In her own research over the years, she'd discovered that her great-great-grandfather had died while being held on the island by Union forces

The conversation with Mr. Cameron had taken place yesterday afternoon. This morning she hurried through a few office duties, talked with the two students she'd scheduled for appointments and even saw another of her students who was in a panic. Before noon she sat in the window seat of a commuter plane as it sped down the runway about as fast as her mind spun. Everything had happened so quickly.

It had all seemed logical and rational at the time that she'd talked with this man, but now that she sat in the plane, she felt as skittish as some of her students as they faced their doctoral committee to defend their dissertation.

What had possessed her to drop what she was doing to go gallivanting across the Gulf Coast to meet Mr. Cameron, a man she didn't know and for reasons she didn't understand?

Jumping into a situation without completely understanding it was not like her, but as though she'd been waiting all her life for that telephone call, she packed a small bag and headed out. She simply knew that traveling out to the island was the right thing to do.

Now she sat strapped in the seat of the aircraft watching the ground *and* her bravado fly by. What had she gotten herself into?

Dropping her head against the neck rest a little too quickly, she groaned.

The man sitting next to her turned. "You okay?"

She forced a smile. "Yes, thank you."

Embarrassed that he had heard her, Jewel rolled her eyes and stared at the clear blue outside her window. She needed her head examined. That's what one of her associates told her. That's what the head of her department told her, and that's what she'd told herself.

But something in the voice of the man on the phone yesterday morning touched her deeply. He didn't give her much to go on, only that he had information about Captain Hilliard McDougle. As a child Jewel remembered sitting on her grandmother's big porch, listening to her tell the love story that had been passed down through generations about the red-haired Hilliard and his young wife Ula. Jewel had lived those stories in her mind countless times until she felt she knew the captain and his wife.

The socially-conscious, politically-correct part of the family who took her in after her mother and father died ignored her connection to that part of history, but she couldn't. How could she not be intrigued when the color of her own hair connected her to the infamous McDougle?

Her pragmatic world of science gave her a good understanding of the logic behind the genes that produced her red hair, but her fascination didn't end with the science of the color of her hair. There was a connection to her past she longed to find—needed to find.

She couldn't get enough information about that period to satisfy that longing, and what Mr. Cameron could add was like a magnet drawing her into the past.

She had taken all precautions. She called the headquarters of the restoration company to find out if the site was a legitimate reconstruction project and if this Mr. Cameron was one of the co-owners of the company. After feeling confident that all was on the up-and-up, she spent a whirlwind afternoon getting ready to go, not giving herself time to think about what she was doing.

As the plane rolled to a stop at the Biloxi-Gulfport Airport, Jewel pushed away her doubts and found strength in the knowledge that she was doing the right thing. This part of her history couldn't be ignored. She picked up her small travel bag and headed down the ramp.

The helicopter ride out to the island took Jewel over the sparkling blue waters of the Mississippi Sound. Tiny boats that had appeared as only dots from the jet now became larger and more distinct. The pilot pointed out different points of interest including a small school of sharks that swam near the tip of one of the islands.

"Hammerheads," he informed her.

She strained to see the sharks from her window. Even though marine biology wasn't her field, she'd always had

9

an appreciation for that branch of science.

"I didn't expect to see so many big sharks that close to the islands," she said.

"Oh, yes, ma'am. We have all kinds of sharks in these waters—not like the Great Whites in other places—but quite a few none the less."

"I'll have to remember that if I take a dip."

He laughed, then turned his attention back to flying the helicopter.

The crystal blue sky, the sparkling water below—minus the hammerhead sharks—and a smooth ride in a helicopter had to be a good sign for what was to come.

When they flew over the fort, she leaned as close to the window as possible. Over a hundred years ago it had been a hub of activity for soldiers. Now the fort stood stoically silent and the activity on the island reverently still.

The imposing brick structure still looked formidable, but deep within its walls, Mr. Cameron had told her that the last century had not been kind to it, but from the air, the symmetrical lines and circular patterns created a work of art that she would appreciate.

The helicopter landed on a newly constructed pad near the fort. Except for several big piles of lumber and pilings where buildings had once stood before the last hurricane, Jewel saw nothing but miles and miles of white sand and thin stretches of brownish green grass.

Barren and empty, yet exquisitely beautiful and pristine. She had never seen anything like it.

"That's Mr. Cameron on the pier," offered the pilot as the helicopter hovered close to the makeshift landing pad near the fort.

Jewel's optimistic bubble about this trip immediately burst. The man was about her age, and no way did he fit the earlier image of a scholarly gentleman and the old hippie she had conjured up.

Instead Bryce Cameron stood at least six feet tall with

broad shoulders stretching his black T-shirt. His brown chestnut hair shone in the sun and hung down onto a chiseled countenance. And the jeans. Even from the helicopter she could see they clung to every inch of his muscular legs.

She swallowed hard. This wasn't the way it was supposed to be. She turned to the pilot. "Are you sure that's Mr. Cameron?"

"Yes. I fly in and out here quite a bit. I know Bryce personally."

Jewel's insides tightened. "Is there any way you can wait to take me back today?"

"No, I'm afraid not. I have another delivery this afternoon." He glanced in her direction. "I thought you were staying until tomorrow."

Jewel tried to smile. "I thought I was, but I've just remembered something I have to do on the mainland tonight."

The pilot looked at her as if he knew she wasn't telling the truth, but it was better to tell a little white lie than to find herself in an uncomfortable position by staying any longer than necessary with someone who looked like this man.

The helicopter touched the landing platform. Sand swirled around the windows before the blades came to a slow stop.

Jewel swallowed and looked at Bryce Cameron on the pier. A few months ago she would've clambered out of the helicopter to introduce herself. Not anymore.

She'd never met this Mr. Cameron, but she knew his type. Tall, menacingly dark, and brutally handsome. The Greek god type who crumpled those around him like the fabric in a royal cloak.

Her excitement over her fort adventure quickly disappeared, but before the familiar ache sent her into the proverbial black hole, she swiped the hurt aside and forced a smile.

That man who stood on the pier wasn't her former fiancé and was probably married with a gorgeous wife and four perfect kids. He couldn't help that he was handsome.

Still, after the shock of not finding her pony-tailed older gentleman, she'd feel more comfortable finding a room on the mainland tonight.

"Ms. Ferguson?" The pilot pulled her attention back inside. "If my staff hasn't scheduled another run since I was in the office, I can come back later this evening after my next delivery if that will work for you?"

Jewel breathed easier. "Yes, thank you. That would be great."

"If your cell phone doesn't pick up out here, I'll call Bryce."

When the blades stopped turning, Bryce Cameron opened the door.

She lifted her bag. "Mr. Cameron?"

"Yes, that's me, and I'm guessing you're Miss Fergusen."

"Yes, Jewel Fergusen."

Up close, the man might not be her grandfatherly type she first expected, but he certainly wasn't menacing.

Her upbringing kicked in and she smiled. "Thank you for inviting me. I hope you got the message I was coming out on the helicopter instead of waiting for the boat. I was a little excited about hearing the news you have for me."

He extended his hand. "Yes, I got the message."

The man smiled, but it didn't reach his eyes. He gave her a "society smile," – a name her aunt used when she wanted to appear to be cordial. Jewel simply called it "fake." In fact, he seemed to stare at her as if he saw someone familiar but someone he couldn't place.

They shook hands. "Call me Bryce. We're not very formal around here." Finally, the society smile turned into a warm one that showed straight white teeth against his dark tan. "Sometimes our chopper's schedule can't be relied on so I wasn't sure when you'd get here."

The pilot leaned over and spoke around Jewel. "Hey, watch how you talk about my company, Bryce. Have I ever left you stranded out here?"

"Just a few times." Bryce reached over and shook the pilot's hand. "How're doing, Buddy?"

"Fine, but I have to get back. See you two later." He looked at Jewel. "I'll call about picking you up."

Jewel offered Bryce her bag, then accepted his outstretched hand, callused but smelling of a fresh soaping. He helped her step out onto the landing platform.

Now that she was closer to him, she could see he wasn't the perfect specimen as she first thought. His tan couldn't hide a scar near his left eye and a bruise and a smudge mark on his upper arm—all signs of hard manual labor. The muscles in his arms were toned, but the calluses and short nails were nothing like someone who sat in an office all day and worked out at the local gym.

Bending down away from the blades, she followed him to the make-shift walkway that led to a pier. Once there, Bryce lifted his hand in a farewell salute as the helicopter flew over the top of the fort and out over the Mississippi Sound, leaving them standing in the quiet of the island.

For several seconds neither said a word. A case of nerves twisted Jewel's insides, her excitement over her day of researching her ancestor gone. Bryce Cameron was a stranger, someone who offered her information she longed to have, but standing next to him she sensed as much hesitation and distrust on his part as she felt herself.

She almost laughed. She's the one whose stomach twisted from being on an island with a stranger, especially one who reminded her of her ex. She wasn't sure why he seemed distrusting of her, but that wasn't her concern. He had information about Captain McDougle. She'd listen to what he had discovered, then climb back onto that helicopter as soon as Buddy landed.

Bryce cleared his throat. "Let's get in the fort where it's cooler. We can talk in a little more comfort."

She nodded, keeping her reservations to herself. "Great. I can't wait to see inside this structure."

"I think you'll be impressed."

She followed him, but felt an explanation was in order. "I know you extended an invitation for me to stay a day or so, but I can't. Buddy is coming back out this evening."

Bryce looked down at her bag in his hand and raised an eyebrow.

"I haven't had time to check into a hotel."

"Well, you do whatever makes you comfortable. We'll get right to business so your trip will have been worthwhile."

"Thank you. I'm eager to hear what you've uncovered about Captain McDougle."

Bryce offered her his hand once again as they stepped around a pile of lumber stacked against the wall of the fort. "Sorry about the obstacle courses around here. Things aren't back to normal after the last big storm."

"No problem." She accepted his hand once more, then feeling a little better, walked alongside of him.

She threw her shoulders back and fell into step next to him. "I've been reading about the damage that storm did down here."

"Yeah. The surge undermined some of the structure and messed up some of the wooden beams. We're trying to keep it intact for another hundred years or so."

Jewel stretched her neck and looked up at the massive brick wall. "It's amazing."

"Yes it is." He brushed sand from his jeans, then looked at her in her capris and sandals. "I'm glad you dressed for the island. We're pretty casual around her, and you'll find sand's a way of life out here. You either cover up to keep it off your body," he said, "or give in and discard the shoes and most of the clothes all together. Because of our working conditions, we stay pretty much covered during the day, but after the work is done, a bathing suit is about all we need. Hope you brought one to enjoy this beautiful beach while you're here."

"I did, but I don't imagine I'll have time for a swim." She wished there was a way she could enjoy this pristine island, but that would never happen—not on this trip.

"Have you restored many of these forts?" she asked.

"This is our third one." As he talked about his company's work, he squinted against the sun, creating little lines around his eye. Mid to late thirties, she guessed. His eyes were gentle eyes, looking as if they should be in a face of a big teddy bear rather than the face of a ruggedly handsome six-footer.

"And you say you have information here in this fort about Captain McDougle?"

He nodded and touched her elbow as he led her into the fort's massive entranceway with its high arched ceiling and intricately worked brick walls. "This is called a sally port. If you're going to be our guest here for the afternoon, you might as well get to know the parts of the structure."

Letting down her guard for a second, she took in the workmanship surrounding her. The brickwork was exquisite, perfectly lined along the bottom and walls, then creating a breathtaking curved ceiling.

"Beautiful, isn't it?" he said as they walked through the sally port.

"Yes, you certainly don't see workmanship like this in our modern buildings."

She looked around as she followed him.

"Soon, I'll explain everything about why I brought you out here, I swear. First, though, my crew is working, and I'd like to introduce you to them and show you around a bit. My partner is around here."

He continued to point out different architectural elements with an air of appreciation she couldn't ignore. He didn't look like the sort who would see the beauty in delicate carvings— her ex never saw the beauty in anything but expensive jewels and beautiful women—but in just the few steps that they had taken together, she realized the man next to her saw more than just a wall of old bricks.

While still determined to keep her emotional as well as a physical distance from him, she had to admit it was refreshing to see a man who appreciated the beauty of things from the past.

As soon as they had stepped out of the sun, the temperature inside the bricked structure dropped at least ten degrees. At first Jewel inhaled deeply and enjoyed the coolness touching her skin. After being on the island for only a few moments, the heat of the sun and its reflection from the water and the sand had made her hot and clammy.

But the cool lasted only momentarily. The farther she stepped into the sally port, the warmer she became. A spark ignited within her. Bolts of energy surged through her veins. Her face flushed.

She tried to listen to what the man was telling her, but her head spun. Panic struck. White spots floated in front of her eyes. Her skin felt clammy.

This wasn't the heat of the sun or the effect of man walking next to her. This was something much, much more. The same feeling she'd been fighting for weeks now.

"You'll find it stays rather comfortable inside the walls of these forts in the summer," he said as she grabbed for his arm. "Are you okay?"

She tried to nod.

A powerful arm scooped her to his side and sat down on a bench along the entranceway. He deposited her unceremoniously in his lap. With one arm on her stomach and one on her back, he bent her forward.

"Breathe. Take a deep breath. I'm sure the heat's just gotten to you. Happens to a lot of people their first trip out here. Breathe."

His words floated in and out of her consciousness. Jewel hung over the man's arm and tried to breathe as he instructed. In. Out. In. Out.

She concentrated on inhaling and exhaling as if it were the most complicated thing in the world. Nothing mattered but breathing the precious air that swirled around her head, teasing and tempting but evading her lungs.

Soon the heat within her subsided and breathing took place without too much effort. Several huge gulps of air cleared her head.

Bryce still held his one arm around her stomach. Placing her hand over his, she planned to gently move it away, but with each movement, another wave of weakness racked her body. Instead of pushing his arm away, she clung to it.

"Take a few more deep breaths before you try to sit up. I've got you. You won't fall."

She nodded. Yes, he did have her. Pressed against his body in the most awkward position she'd ever been in with a stranger, but for the moment she wasn't embarrassed. Having him wrapped around her body was comforting, a feeling she hadn't experienced in a long, long time.

But she couldn't hang over the man's lap forever. Taking another second to make sure she was steady, she inhaled deeply and sat up, now with her back plastered against his chest. She tried to pull away, but he kept his arm clamped around her midriff.

"Whoa, girl. Don't you go collapsing on me again. Sit here a little longer. We're in no hurry."

She nodded and was tempted to close her eyes and let the feeling of contentment last forever, but she knew it couldn't last.

"Thank you for helping me," she said between several long breaths, then slowly moved away from him and slid onto the bench next to him. "I'm a little embarrassed. I've never passed out in my life, but I think I was about to."

She closed her eyes and trembled. She'd never passed

out, but she knew this feeling. What was happening to her? She might not be ready to talk with a psychiatrist, but she definitely would make an appointment with her primary physician as soon as she flew back home. She was convinced that something was medically wrong. Normal, healthy women didn't go around swooning.

"Don't apologize. I've seen grown men collapse because of the heat." His eyes studied her face. The creases in his brow this time showed concerned. If he thought her a complete wimp, he didn't show it.

He spoke a little too fast, probably nervous because a female visitor was going to cause his men trouble. "It's pretty comfortable in here, though. It's amazing how these brick structures can stay so cool even out here under the unrelenting sun."

Jewel didn't want to be a bother, especially to this man, but as hard as she tried to concentrate on his words, they kept fading.

"You're still not okay, are you?"

Frustrated that her body would do this to her, she tried to lie, but in the end confessed. "I'm not sure."

"Sit here as long as you want." He fidgeted. "Uh, I'll go get you some water."

"No. No, I'm okay." This time she lied. Her head still spun, but not as fast, so she plastered a smile on her face. "Let's go on in."

Bryce stood up and put his arm around her for support. She didn't refuse. Ever so slowly she stood up, and even though she hated to lean against any stranger, but especially one who reminded her of her ex, she had no choice. Now wasn't the time to show her independence. She allowed him to guide her, and with each step, she felt stronger.

Jewel had never been in a fort, in fact, had never even been on an island, so as he led her through the entranceway and out into the open courtyard, her curiosity took control and pushed the remains of the weakness away. His arm still lay against her back. As good as it felt to be encircled by his strength, she gently pulled away.

"You sure you're not going to collapse again?"

She shook her head. "I'll give you plenty of warning if I think I am."

His laugh eased her misgivings.

The interior of the fort had an awesome silence. Several groups of men worked together, nestled quietly in different areas of the courtyard, but mostly the large structure stood empty.

Cool. Quiet and solemn. She remembered having this same feeling when she followed her grandmother into their neighborhood church. Only a child at the time, she still whispered and tiptoed without being told.

As if the man next to her understood, he allowed her time to experience the feeling without interruptions. Except for the wing-beat of a small black bird that flew through the arches of the walkway, no sound disturbed them.

"It's awe-inspiring, isn't it?"

She nodded dumbly and swallowed. Something here, something bigger than herself, touched her deeply. It was as though the past called out to her. Awareness surfaced within her, an awareness that actual men from another age lived and breathed and possibly died right here where she stood.

"As I told you earlier, this is our third lady that we've restored, and each one has me as impressed as the last." His voice was soft. "I never tire of being here at moments like this."

She turned to see him scanning the expanse, taking in the surroundings as if it were his first time.

He was the first to break the spell. "Let's go put your bags down, and I'll introduce you to the men, unless, of course, you'd like to lie down."

"No. I'm fine, but that glass of water would be nice."

"Then water it is." He escorted her into a large room

with the smell of new wooden floors. "This is it. It's not much, but it's our sleeping quarters, the storage area, the pantry. You name it. You'll find it in here."

Leaving her standing alone by the door, he walked over to a large water barrel and filled a cup of water. "It's not spring, but it's nice and cool."

Jewel savored its coolness as she sipped from the metal cup. "Thank you. I think I'll make it now."

Now that she had her wits back, she looked around the room. Several beds and pile after pile of boxes, tools and equipment she didn't recognize took up over half of the room. A makeshift screen was propped up against the back wall. She wondered if this is where she would've spent the night had she stayed.

He caught her staring at the screen. "It's the only room that's fit for us to stay in. The storm pretty much destroyed the wood flooring in the other rooms. This is the only one we've had chance to redo."

She sipped the water, then turned when the door opened.

"Jewel, this is my partner, Marcus Tillman."

Marcus wasn't as tall or as handsome as Bryce, but he walked with the same confident air about him that again made Jewel think of her ex. His thick wavy hair and stout body could have made him one of her Irish cousins.

He grabbed a cloth and cleaned his hands before extending one to her. "You must be Jewel."

Manners. She liked that.

"Welcome to our stately lady," he said as he shook.

"Thank you. I couldn't stay away. Mr. Cameron told me only enough to whet my interest, and now that I'm here," she looked at Bryce then back at Marcus, "I can't wait to hear what he has to say."

Bryce shuffled a foot. "We're glad you came, Jewel. Let's get a cup of coffee and sit outside in the courtyard. This might take a while."

Chapter 2

Bryce picked up a box from a table, then led Jewel outside to a concrete bench in the shade of the western wall of the fort. Marcus followed balancing three cups of coffee.

"Here we go. Couldn't find any sweetener, but I was easy on the sugar."

Jewel took the cup and inhaled the rich scent. "Thanks. Now, I'm about as ready as I can get to hear what you two have for me."

The two men looked at one another, but it was Bryce who spoke up. "We found a few artifacts in one of the cells where some of the prisoners had been housed during the Civil War. I asked a friend in Jackson to do a little research, and we're pretty confident that several of the things we found can be traced to your great-great grandfather, Captain Hilliard McDougle."

"You found something that actually belonged to him?"

Again, the men looked at each other, then Bryce ran his hand along the container. "Yes. Records show that he was captured in Louisiana, somewhere between his plantation in St. Marks and New Orleans. He was brought here, but wasn't here long before he tried to escape." Bryce looked up into her eyes. "But I guess you know that already."

She nodded. "When I was a little girl, I listened to

stories my grandmother told about Hilliard and his wife Ula. I was never sure how much was truth and how much was embellishments from being told over generations, but I know the part about his being killed trying to escape was real. I did some research on my own years ago."

Bryce let out a loud exhale of breath. "That's what I found out as well." He opened the box and carefully pulled out several sheets of papers. The first was a photocopy of her family tree dating back to the time of the Civil War, but ended with her mother's generation.

"I haven't seen the exact lineage in ages, but I recognize them." She ran her finger down through the years, finding Ula and Hilliard's space, hesitating on some of the other names she recognized, then stopped on the bottom of the tree where the names of her mother Mary, her mother's two sisters Leslie and Jodi, and a brother George ended the chart. She inhaled deeply, then looked up.

"I first contacted your Uncle George because I knew he'd still have the family name and would be easier to track down since this chart didn't include who your aunts married, but he told me that you would be the person most interested in this information."

"Uncle George is the oldest sibling and isn't in good health."

"He had a little trouble finding the information, but he eventually found your Aunt Leslie's number. He said she raised you, but when I told her what I had, she didn't seem very interested. She did, however, give me your number."

"Humph, I'm surprised she even talked with you. I hope she wasn't too unpleasant. Like Uncle George told you, she and her husband were my guardians. She's my mother's sister. My real mother and father died in a car accident when I was only seven. Aunt Leslie married into money and could afford to take me in, but she's not real impressed with our family history."

"Yeah, I could tell."

"She has always discouraged me from digging too deeply into the past. She never understood my need to find out about my ancestors." She shrugged. "Maybe because I grew up without my real mother and father, I needed those facts to feel whole. Aunt Leslie laughed one day when I told her that, but I understood. She had her parents until they were pretty old, and she still has other sisters and a brother."

Jewel got quiet remembering how she wanted what Aunt Leslie's children had—a mother and a father who loved them and a place to call her own.

She shook away that feeling. "After Aunt Leslie laughed at me, I never told her anything I found out about Captain McDougle and his wife."

Bryce stared at her for a moment making Jewel wish she hadn't said anything about her past and her search for belonging, but then he surprised her by what he said. "I think the past can make a world of difference in anyone's present, especially if you didn't have a solid family around during their childhood."

He smiled, then slipped his hand back into the box and pulled out another photocopy. "Maybe this will help. This is a letter written in 1864 by a fellow prisoner of Captain McDougle. It mentions a red-haired captain who'd been brought in with a shoulder wound. It didn't take much to pinpoint that prisoner as your ancestor."

Jewel held her breath and took the photocopy. In the crude longhand of a Confederate prisoner, a piece of her history came to life. She trembled as she read out loud. "The wretched man didn't have a chance to escape this hell-hole of an island. His wounds were as bad as my own, dear wife, but he said he had to get to his beloved Ula. Maybe he was mad from the fever or just crazy in love."

The words of the letter took away Jewel's breath. "I've always thought about Captain McDougle like that. Even though I was a child when I heard the stories, I never forgot his love for Ula. Yes, this prisoner knew him. Crazy in love," she repeated in a soft voice, then read the rest of the letter even though they didn't mention any more about the captain.

"I wonder if this man survived the war."

"Yes, his name's on the documents where the prisoners were mustered out."

"Good." She smiled.

Bryce reached back into the box. "Jewel, this is what we found in the wall of the fort. It's what got us wondering about this man." He pulled out a bundle of neatly folded tissue paper, then carefully spread the sheets to reveal a piece of yellowed fabric.

For a moment Jewel only stared at it, unable to touch it. Had this piece of cloth actually existed in this fort for over one hundred years?

She put her fingers around the fabric and closed her eyes. The years fell away as she held it to her heart. "It's as if I'm holding a piece of the captain." But then she opened her eyes. "How do you know that this was his?"

Bryce touched her hand and turned the fabric over. There in small crude letters was a message from Hilliard to his wife Ula, simple words of eternal love written by a desperate man who knew he'd probably never see his family again. "My dear Ula, you and our child will have my love forever."

Another sentence was illegible, but the signature was clear enough to read the name Hilliard.

Closing her eyes again, she ran her hand over the fabric. For over a century this message had sat unread.

"This is amazing," she whispered. "This is more than amazing. I didn't know it existed, of course, but I knew one day I'd find something that told me Hilliard's stories were real. Now I know I wasn't crazy."

"You're not crazy, Jewel."

Again she pulled the cloth to her chest, smelled the musty scent. "I can almost see him. I've never seen a picture of him, but in my mind I see him."

When she looked up, Marcus and Bryce were looking at each other as if they wanted to say more. Neither did.

***

A huge generator, loudly grinding out electricity, drowned out all other noise as Jewel sat on a cot in the privacy of a partition in the living area. The rest of the crew had left the island about four in the afternoon, leaving Jewel alone with Bryce and Marcus.

Had it not been for the information Bryce had shared with her earlier, she would've questioned her sanity for making the quick trip and being on an island with two strange men.

Earlier in the afternoon when Buddy called to tell her the chopper was having mechanical problems, and he couldn't get another one until tomorrow, she still knew she'd made the right decision in coming. For some reason, everything seemed right, even being here alone in a fort with two men she didn't know.

The outside door opened and she listened as the footsteps reached her partition. With a quick knock, Bryce stuck his head around it. "You up for a walk?"

"A walk?"

"Yep, we still have an hour or so of sunlight. This is the best time of the day out here. It'd be a shame if you missed it sitting in this dark room." His gaze dropped to the paper in her hands. "It's a lot to absorb, isn't it?"

Jewel nodded and looked down at the papers as well. "There're so many questions to answer. I'm not sure what to ask first."

"I know what you mean. Believe me, I know."

Their gazes locked. Did he really understand her longing, her need to know more?

With a loud sigh, she put the papers down. "I'd love that walk. Should I change?"

"If you have a pair of shorts or a swimsuit, you'd probably be more comfortable. I'll meet you out on the pier."

The late afternoon sun had begun its slow descent by the time Jewel stepped outside the fort. She'd changed into a comfortable pair of shorts and tennis shoes.

Silhouetted against the reddening western sky, Bryce stood at the end of the pier with his back to her. He, too, had changed into shorts and a T-shirt and had removed his shoes. His deeply tanned skin glistened in the afternoon sunlight. Jewel swallowed before she could take another step.

Bryce could have been her former fiancé David waiting for her. His stance, his stature, everything about his mannerism made her think of her ex.

She hated herself for letting David invade her thoughts now that she'd moved on, but because he had, she didn't think she could take this walk.

Bryce turned before she spun around and headed back to her room. "Hi. Looks like we have a flock of egrets settling in at the point down there. If we're lucky, we can see some skimmers with them. Feel like walking that far?"

She nodded. "Sure," she said, ignoring her moment of hesitation. "Sounds fine."

"You might want to take off your shoes. You'll be carrying them before you get halfway there."

When she'd first arrived on the island, she had a feeling his smile hid misgivings about having her here. Now his quirky smile seemed genuine. Even if it wasn't, she was glad he was trying to make her feel at ease after all he and Marcus had thrown at her.

She sat on the edge of the sun-warmed pier and removed the socks and shoes. When she looked up he was staring at her.

"Is something wrong?"

He shook his head. "No, I'm sorry. I didn't mean to stare, but there's something about you that looks familiar."

"Maybe you knew someone in the past with red hair," she said as she let him help her off the pier and into the sand.

"Maybe that's it."

But, his look told her the red hair probably wasn't the only reason he was staring. She didn't ask any more questions and he didn't elaborate as he led her away from the fort.

A gentle curve in the shoreline took them around the fort and out to the western tip of the island. She walked on the firm sand near the water's edge with Bryce at her side. At first neither talked.

Bits and pieces of what Bryce had told her shot through her brain. Over and over she saw the words that Captain McDougle had written to his wife. She could almost hear McDougle's fellow prisoner call him "crazy in love." So much had been revealed to her in the last few hours, too much for her to comprehend.

She looked up at Bryce. Deep in thought, he stared into the distance. Was his mind still on the happenings from over a century ago? Did he feel the connection?

Several small waves rippled onto the shore tickling her feet with warm foam. Instead of jumping away from it, she let it lap against her ankle, then waded out a few steps into the blue water.

"Nice, huh?" Bryce stepped into the water beside her.

"Yes, it is. This is absolutely wonderful. So peaceful."

She stooped down to examine a hermit crab as it clumsily crawled to the water. Its spider-like legs disappeared inside its shell as she placed her hand on it.

Bryce stooped down and turned the shell over in her hand. "They're like turtles. They use their shells for protection, but hermit crabs borrow their shells. When they outgrow them, they simply move out of the old one and find another, larger one."

Jewel rubbed her fingers along the shell then tried to

peek into the opening. "They're ugly little creatures on the inside, aren't they?"

Bryce nodded. "Pretty on the outside though. Kind of like some people." He laughed, then rose. "Look, there're our egrets."

Several large white birds ambled along the beach, stretching their necks and searching for just the right tidbits of food.

Jewel smiled. "They're beautiful."

"Yeah. They're pulling up their supper. They move through the tidal pools stirring up the sand then they return and grab up the tiny fish and worms that surface. I guess it works. They do it every day."

Jewel watched the family of birds work one small pool then move on to the next. When one spotted her and Bryce, it lifted its big body, spread its wings and gracefully glided above them. Soon, the rest of the flock followed.

"Look over there. Those black birds are skimmers. If they have nests, they'll fly toward us then detour away to make us walk away from their nesting grounds. They're graceful birds. If you remind me, right at dusk we can go out on the pier and watch. That's when they feed. They'll pass right next to the fort with their lower beak in the water literally skimming for tiny fish along the surface. It's amazing to watch them."

Jewel followed the flight of the graceful swoop of the bird. "I think it's coming this way."

"Let's turn around. I really don't like to disturb them."

Bryce placed his hand on her elbow. This time a warmth spread through her body as she allowed him to gently escort her back along the shoreline.

"You know a lot about the islands, don't you?"

Bryce shrugged. "It's kind of hard not to be when I've spent my last five years on one island or another or at least along a coastline. My job is fort restoration, and a lot of forts are built on islands."

"I guess you have a point there." She walked a few feet through the water, then stepped up on the hardened sand. "This is all so beautiful, but it's hard to imagine men like Captain McDougle being imprisoned in a place like this. Did he have a window in his cell?"

Bryce nodded. "Yes. I'll show it to you when we get back if there's still daylight. Most of the prisoners were held outside in wooden buildings in fenced areas, but some of the ones who tried to escape or who were trouble-makers or maybe wounded were held inside the fort. According to that letter, our captain wasn't content to sit out the war on this island. I guess that's why he was in the dungeon as my men refer to it."

Jewel grimaced. "Dungeon. Ooh, that's an awful connotation. Sounds barbaric."

"I don't know how barbaric it was, but it was crude."

She dug her foot in the sand. "I wonder what he saw when he looked out. Did he see the beauty in the sunrise? Did he see the moon and stars and know his Ula was seeing the same sky? I wonder if it made him feel closer to her."

Bryce walked up alongside of her nearer to the water. "You and I think alike." He kicked at couple of small waves, then stepped back. "I've thought those same thoughts every time I restore one of these forts. They all have some sort of prisoner cell in them, and even the forts that weren't used as prisons, you imagine the men who were stationed in them during the war. They had to be lonely."

"You mentioned St. Marks in Louisiana. Captain McDougle had a plantation on the Mississippi River called River's Bend."

Bryce nodded. "Have you seen it?"

"No, Aunt Leslie simply doesn't acknowledge the existence of the plantation. For the last one hundred and fifty years, her husband's family has lived in the lap of luxury in Boston's elite financial section. She never speaks of her Confederate connection. She and my mother's other sister never acknowledge the fact that their ancestor had been an officer on the 'other' side as her other children say."

"I see. So they wouldn't be too thrilled that you're down here?"

"That's an understatement," she said and laughed, but noticed that Bryce wasn't smiling.

Not wanting to pry into his thoughts, she continued. "When I was doing my research on Captain McDougle, I found out all sorts of information. The plantation in St. Marks isn't too far from here. It must've been hard on the man wondering if the Union troops had gotten to it, and if Ula had survived."

"I think not knowing would've been the hard part." Bryce picked up a shell and tossed it into the water. "So you haven't been to the plantation?"

She shook her head. "In my free time I collect research on Southern plantations that survived the war. I got interested in the homes when I started digging around my own family's history. River's Bend is no longer in my family, of course. I want to see it, but there's something that keeps me from going there." She looked down. "I'm not sure why, but I have a feeling seeing River's Bend would bring me sadness."

"You never know. You ought to get the courage up to visit it one day. Come on. Let's get back before it gets too dark." After a few steps, Bryce turned to her. "I take it from our conversation on the phone that you aren't married."

With those words, the peace she'd been enjoying vanished. She nodded, but didn't elaborate. David and her devastating engagement were the last two subjects she wanted to talk about now.

"But you have been?" he asked.

She looked up at him over her sunglasses. "No."

"Oh, I got the impression that you had been. Sorry."

"No need to be sorry."

"I mean sorry I had the wrong impression, not sorry that you had never been married."

She laughed, but she was sure he could tell it wasn't genuine. "Okay. Maybe it's a subject I'm a little touchy with right now."

He stopped walking. "Umm. Well, maybe I ought to be sorry I brought up the conversation at all."

This time she laughed out loud. "It's okay. I'd rather we talk about something different, that's all."

The setting sun, the sparkling water, and the crystal white sand beneath her feet called for anything but depressing talk about her past.

She took a few steps and he followed, but he didn't change the subject.

"It's okay to have had a rocky romance," he said, "if that's what you had. I don't know anyone with a perfect record, do you?"

She didn't know how to answer that. Rocky romance? That's not what she had. As far as she was concerned, she thought she'd had the perfect romance until...

He reached out and touched her arm. She stopped.

"I really am sorry this time. I'll change the subject if you're too uncomfortable to talk about it."

She knew she was overreacting. She sighed and twitched her lips. "Thank you. I'd appreciate that. My past romantic life and subsequent black hole just doesn't seem to fit in with this wonderful walk we're having."

His look told her he was thinking about what she'd said. "Okay. I'll accept that. The fact you're enjoying yourself on my little end of the island makes me feel better. We'll change the subject. Come on. I'll race you to the fort."

She opened her mouth to tell him she didn't think that would be a good idea, but he was already sprinting ahead of her.

She laughed. "Okay. You asked for it."

Her words vanished in the wind as she stretched her legs and lifted her face to the open sky. The afternoon sun warmed her back and the southern breeze eased the weight off her shoulders. She sprinted alongside of him.

He tossed his head back and grinned. She took a deep breath and for the rest of the run, matched Bryce's strides, ending up at the foot of the pier together.

With hands placed on his knees, Bryce lifted his face to her. "That was quite a run, lady. You must do this a lot."

Jewel's heart pumped and her breaths came in short gulps, but she hadn't felt this good in a long time. She, too, grabbed her knees, dropped her head, and tried to regain her normal breathing rhythm.

Finally she looked up at him. His bright smile warmed her as much as the setting sun had.

She took another second to regain her composure. "I do run often. It's a nice break from sitting in my office grading papers or working on records. I can't tell you the last time I've run on sand though. I have a feeling I'll be sore tomorrow."

"No, I'm the one who'll be sore."

After a short cool-down walk, they entered the fort and nearly barged into Marcus in the sally port as he turned the corner.

"Well, it's about time. I thought I'd have to put on my hiking shoes and go after you two."

"Sorry. We just took a little longer than we thought we would."

"I warmed us up some stew." Marcus spoke directly to Jewel. "Our meals are simple, but they're filling."

"After that run your partner just had me on, I'm sure I won't have any trouble finding my appetite."

"Good, we like our guests to feel comfortable."

Bryce pointed to the living quarters. "If you need time to freshen up, we'll wait outside for you."

"No, I'm fine. I'd rather see the prisoner cell if there's still enough light."

"You want to go to the dungeon?" Marcus raised an eyebrow.

"She wants to see where we found McDougle's message. Why don't you grab a couple of lights? That stew can wait a few minutes."

Jewel followed Bryce and Marcus through the courtyard, then into a darkened alcove under the top level of the fort.

"Watch your step. The stone floors are cracked and lifting in places."

Bryce took her by the elbow and guided her to a gated passageway. A few hours ago when she'd first arrived on the island, she would've pulled away from Bryce, but now that she was getting to know him, his gentle touch offered her a bit of reassurance.

Marcus pulled open an iron gate. "You sure you don't want to wait until morning to do see this place. At least you'd have a little sunlight to brighten the room. It's kind of depressing right now."

"I'd like to see it now and again tomorrow morning. I want to see what the prisoners experienced."

Marcus nodded, and Jewel had a feeling he understood. He aimed his light into the narrow, short hallway that led to a set of three steps. She and Bryce followed, walked down the steps, then ducked to enter the cell through a small door where another iron door had been propped open.

Once he was inside, Marcus stepped aside. "Well, here it is in all its glory."

It took a moment for Jewel's eyes to adjust to the darkness inside the room. Even with the beams from the two lights, there was a depressing gloom, just as Marcus had said.

The room was a small octagon shaped room. Except

for a ladder and a wooden workbench, there was nothing but a stone floor and brick walls. The only redeeming factor was a small window high on the wall with iron bars on the outside.

"How could the men survive in a place like this?" she asked as she ran her hand against the damp bricks. "No wonder some of them took their chance and tried to escape."

"It wasn't a very pleasant place to spend the war, but I'm told in comparison to Andersonville and some of the prison camps, this wasn't so bad. I think boredom was the prisoners' worst enemy."

Bryce stepped away and took a few steps toward a corner. "This is where I removed a brick to find the message. I was trying to reach a beam on the other side that we were sure needed replacing."

Jewel followed him to the far corner of the room. Bryce reached up and pulled out a loose brick. "This is the spot I found it. At first I thought it was nothing more than a clump of dust and mortar, but when I brushed it out of the hole, it hit the floor and some of the dust flew off."

Jewel reached out and took the brick. In her hand it lay as it probably did in Captain McDougle's hand over a century ago. She closed her eyes and inhaled. Nothing stirred around her. Bryce and Marcus said nothing.

At first the cool, rough brick was all she felt, but then the same flush she'd felt earlier in the day warmed her face and neck. Her skin tingled. Her head felt light.

She opened her eyes. Blinked hard. Inhaled deeply.

"You okay?" Bryce touched her shoulder. "You're not going to pass out on me again, are you?"

She inhaled again. "No, but I started feeling that way again." She shook her head. "I don't know what's happening to me, but something strange is going on. As soon as I get back home, I'll make an appointment with my doctor."

"Maybe it's not a physical condition that's making you feel this way."

"What do you mean?"

Marcus and Bryce looked at each other.

"You going to tell her, or do I have to?" Marcus crossed his arms in front of his chest and stared at his partner.

"Me."

The strained looked on Bryce's face told her there was more than just a piece of fabric with a message.

"Don't tell me you think something beyond the normal is happening here." Jewel surprised herself with her statement.

Again Bryce and Marcus jerked their heads and looked at each other. She watched Bryce swallow.

"We're not sure. Marcus and I kind of felt something the night that I found the message. Now don't laugh when I say this, but it felt like there was something in the courtyard with us. At first I thought I was dreaming sitting up on my bench, but then I looked at Marcus. His face couldn't have been any paler, and he was staring in the same direction that I was. Neither of us wanted to admit anything, but after a few prying questions, we realized we'd both felt a presence."

"You saw a ghost?" she asked, trying not to laugh.

"Not really. We didn't see an image. Nothing. It was a feeling. That's all."

"And an odor," Marcus threw in.

Jewel shook her head. "I don't think I'm following you. Are you saying you think McDougle's spirit was here with you?"

Both men shrugged.

Again she shook her head. "I'm sorry, but I can't grasp that notion. Spirits and ghosts aren't something I believe in. I believe the stories of Captain McDougle, but I can't bring myself to believe he's actually here."

Bryce spoke up. "We're not saying that he is here. It's simply a feeling we both experienced that night."

"Is that why you wanted me to spend the night?"

"We weren't sure we should involve you, but the more we thought about it, the more sense it made. Is it possible he's here? Don't know. Do we want to find the answer? That's another big 'don't know.' We simply couldn't ignore it since we found the note and both felt something strange."

She handed the brick back to Marcus who inserted it in the wall. "I wonder why Captain McDougle stuck the note in the wall and didn't give it to another prisoner."

"Don't know that either. Maybe the prisoner was supposed to extract it if he ever got out."

Jewel watched Marcus rub his hand over the brick now sitting in its resting place in the wall.

"I'm glad I came out to the island. Knowing where Hilliard was incarcerated makes him so much more real to me, but I have to say that I think your theory about his spirit being here is wrong."

"We hope it is," Marcus said. "Neither of us is eager to run into some poor prisoner's spirit in the forts we restore, but..."

"But what?" she asked.

Marcus shrugged. "Nothing."

She watched the two men as they looked at each other. Marcus twisted his lip. Bryce bit his.

"Come on, you guys. What aren't you telling me?"

Bryce shifted his stance. "Nothing. Really. But I guess after you've worked in these structures for as long as we have, things start playing with your mind. Spending time alone in these places, thinking about what happened in forts like this all along the coast, it does things to you."

Jewel was about to tell him that some of her fellow professors from the literature department seemed to float along in their make-believe worlds, but it didn't mean they ran into any of their characters, but Bryce spoke up.

"Maybe we've opened a Pandora's box, but it's too late to close it." Bryce looked serious as he turned to leave. "I think we need to do a little more research on this."

"Now you're talking my language," she said. "Research is something I understand. There's got to be an explanation for all of this."

Bryce threw out an I-doubt-it look, then took her by the arm. "Come on. Let's go eat that stew."

Marcus led the way. "Our food might not be fancy but you won't find a grander setting to eat it in. Maybe Captain McDougle will join us."

Bryce nudged him playfully. "That's not funny, Marcus."

Jewel saw the humor in his statement, but didn't want to make Bryce feel awkward.

She walked quietly with the two men, listening to them chatter.

"Besides the fact that we might not be alone, what do you think of our lady?"

Marcus's words pulled her to the present. She ignored his reference to McDougle. "Your lady? Oh, you mean the fort."

"Yeah, this beauty is our lady for the time being."

"I've heard boats referred to in the feminine, but I don't think I've heard it used for a fort."

Bryce spoke up. "Oh, she's a lady, all right. She's graceful and beautiful, but strong and willful. She can nestle you safely in the womb of her bricks."

"Or destroy you with one misguided step." Marcus added. "Just like a woman."

Jewel laughed. "Sounds as if you speak from experience."

The two men looked at each other, but it was Marcus who answered. "You might say that." Bryce didn't say anything.

They didn't offer an explanation so Jewel didn't ask, but she assumed that like her, they had been through some disturbing relationships. That's the last thing she wanted to hear about right now. She had her own past to deal with at the moment.

Of the two men, Marcus was the talker. Bryce was quieter, more sedate, but when he spoke it was with authority and quiet strength. She guessed that the two of them made a good, workable partnership.

"How did you two get into fort restoration? That's not a very common job."

"No," Marcus said as he opened the door to the living quarters. They followed him in where he gave them plastic bowls, then each heated stew in a microwave. "Got to love modern technology," he said.

They took their supper into the courtyard where she hoped she'd hear more about the two men.

"Well, it definitely wasn't planned. We met each other in college. Same major. Same fraternity. It just seemed destined that we'd wind up working together on projects after we graduated. Then we formed a small company and *voila*, here we are today. I'd have to say that Bryce is the brains behind the company. I'm the brawn if you want to think about it that way."

Bryce crossed his arms. "He always says that, but it's amazing how these brains manage to get dirtier than the brawn on the projects."

Marcus laughed, but Jewel had no doubts that Bryce was right. She had pegged him as the lead man of the company from the beginning. Even though the secretary had named him as co-owner of the company, she recognized right away where the strength in the company rested. His way of carrying himself. His walk. His talk.

She had seen all those traits before in men like David.

And it was that something that she didn't like or trust. She hoped these men were different, but in her lifetime watching her guardians' powerful friends, she had a feeling that they weren't. David's and her family's friends had a way of manipulating people to get what they wanted, and she knew when and if she ever let herself fall in love again, it would be to someone totally different.

"But you didn't start out to restore forts, did you?" she asked, pushing aside the ugly comparison of the men.

Bryce spoke up. "No, we started on older houses. Even now we have three crews usually working on several smaller projects while we have this fort going. We still do homes, mostly estates and other historical buildings."

"I see," Jewel said, "but you like doing these fort projects?"

Marcus jumped in. "Oh definitely. They're messy, dirty, and back breaking, but damned enjoyable."

"Someone has to do it, and our company was at the right place at the right time when the first one came along," Bryce explained. "If someone didn't take the initiative to watch over these relics, they wouldn't be with us for very much longer."

"Who oversees this?" she asked.

That's when Bryce broke into an oration about the part different organizations had in the preservation effort. From historical societies and communities to government grants and agencies, he knew the workings. He was totally wrapped up in the information, animated and excited about the information.

Bryce stopped his exposition. "I'm sorry. I'm probably boring you."

"Oh, no. I love old structures. I spend my spare time researching southern plantations. In fact, I'm working on a book on the subject."

Marcus stopped eating. "You're writing a book? That's cool."

She laughed. "It's a book that I'll probably never finish, but I'm having a good time working on it. I actually thought about majoring in history at one point, but I couldn't stay out of the science labs to give the other subject the attention it needed."

"What else do you do?" Marcus asked.

"I teach biology in Houston. I've taken a really light load this summer to do some research on my book and to give myself a break. That's why I was able to fly down here on such short notice."

Marcus raised an eyebrow and nodded. "I'm impressed."

Finally Bryce stood up. "We all have something in common then, don't we?"

"You're right," she said pointedly. "We're all involved with history in one way or the other. That's why I'm here. Couldn't stay away when you said we'd dig into my family's past."

Then in a small voice she added, "It's as if I've waited for this moment my entire adult life."

Chapter 3

Behind the partitioned wall, Jewel lay quietly and listened to Bryce get ready for the night. He and Marcus had been perfect gentlemen for the entire evening so even being in the same room with them felt comfortable.

Her lantern had already been put out, but light from the men's lantern flickered above her partition. The intricate brickwork on the ceiling and walls intrigued her. She admired the workmanship, knowing how hard it must've been to build something this large on an island so far away from the mainland. The simple task of getting the bricks to the island would've been a feat in itself. After she found out she was coming to the island, she did some research on the internet and learned the government had the bricks shipped from New England around Florida. Now looking at the amount of bricks used, it was hard to believe they had to be shipped in from so far.

Lying on the cot with her hands behind her head, she tried to concentrate on the physical structure rather the men on the other side of the partition. She thought they were getting ready for bed, but instead she heard the heavy door to the courtyard squeak open, then close, taking her light with them. With the generator shut down, the dark room was eerily quiet. Feeling more alone than she had in a long time, she turned on her side and squeezed her eyes shut.

told them. Me? David or his family members got the word around that he was the poor soul who was jilted and I was the bad guy."

"Jewel..."

"No," she raised her hand and said politely before he could continue, "you asked for this so you're getting the whole story. My aunt even called me. She was devastated. She thought the sun rose and set with David. I still don't think she believes he was the one having the affair."

She inhaled deeply. "I guess I was too stupid to see that David only wanted me because of my adoptive family. I guess he liked the idea of having connections to stay on the top of his game like his father had done. Maybe he was feeling trapped into marrying someone he didn't love as the time got closer."

With her eyes closed and her voice a little more than a whisper, she asked, "Okay, that's my story, and I have to tell you. I can't believe all that came out. I'm not sure I've ever told anyone all of that."

"I said I was sorry I asked, and I am. I can tell you're still very upset over the whole ordeal. Nobody should have to go through something like that."

"I'm managing. I think now I'm in the anger stage. They say you go through stages just like when you have to face a death. I think I'm doing pretty good if you ask me."

"Good for you."

Surprised to find her heart pounding and her breath coming in short gulps, she placed her head back on her knees until she regained her composure. When she turned her head to look at Bryce, his stare made her breath hitch. It was a look of sincerity and empathy. Even though he was a stranger, that look told her that he was in no way like David.

After a long moment, she sat up and with a lilt in her voice said, "Now, it's your turn. What's your story?"

Bryce was quiet and pulled his hand across the back

of his neck. "Why don't we turn in? I'll fill you in on my unexciting life the next time we sit together." He stood up.

"Bryce Cameron, don't you dare do this to me. I can't believe you. Here I've embarrassed myself by telling a perfect stranger about the most horrible experience I've ever gone through and now you want to go to sleep? That's not fair."

"There's not much to tell."

"I disagree. Obviously, there's something there."

"I swear. I'm not trying to keep anything from you."

"Are you married?"

His voice was soft. "Not any more. Was once."

"Oh, I see." A little lift of relief danced across her chest. She wasn't sure why, but she was glad he wasn't married.

Jewel crossed her arms. "Oh, come on. You didn't just appear on this island last week. You have a history."

Bryce stretched his arms. "Okay. My dad was in sales and he traveled a lot. My mom dragged us children all over to follow him. It wasn't a normal childhood, but it was a good one. I made lots of friends I still keep in touch with. Went to what seemed like a million different schools. I have one brother who made his home in Indiana so when I want to go someplace with the family, we usually meet there."

"Your parents are still alive?"

He nodded. "Yes. You'd think they had traveled enough during their lifetime to satisfy anyone, but they're still on the road. Now it's in one of those monster motor homes. They travel with two cats and a small, aggravating, yappy dog."

Jewel laughed. "They sound interesting."

"That's a good way to describe them."

"And your marriage. What happened with it?"

Bryce looked up at the heavens, then back at her. "Look, it's just not the time to talk right now. You've pretty much told enough for both of us tonight." He reached out his hand to hers. "Come on, I'll walk you inside and I swear, the rest of my story will be all yours the next time you ask."

Jewel's guard went up. She didn't believe him, but she nodded. "All mine, huh?"

He chuckled. "Yeah. All yours."

His eyes didn't reflect the humor his words hinted. In fact, for a second, Jewel detected a hint of sadness. She had a feeling she'd never know all there was to know about this man. She'd learned her lesson. Men were strange creatures who never revealed their true selves.

Yep, she'd learned her lesson the hard way, but she didn't tell Bryce she knew he'd never tell her what she wanted to know. Instead she forced a smile.

"I'll remind you of that promise one day."

She stood up to leave, trying to image what his story was. Maybe it was worse than hers. Had his wife cheated on him? Was he trying to move on with his life too? Maybe that's why she suspected distrust in his eyes when he'd first opened the helicopter door, but then she only had to remind herself that she'd be gone from this island tomorrow and probably never see him again.

Marcus joined them before any more was said. "I decided I wasn't as sleepy as I thought I was so I thought I'd join you two. You're not turning in, are you?"

"I thought I might," she answered. "I think I hear my leg muscles screaming. Your friend here had me running down the beach."

Marcus grinned. "I'm surprised he's still standing. He's so out of shape."

Bryce gave him a playful shove, then turned to Jewel. "If you want to turn in, make yourself at home. We'll be in shortly."

"Thank you. It's early, but I really am tired."

"Early and late has nothing to do with going to bed out here," Marcus reflected in a cool, low voice. "When it's dark and you've done all there is to do, when you've taken in as much of the wonderful stars that you can handle, then you go to bed. It's that simple."

"Why, Marcus, that was terribly poetic," she said with a lilt in her voice.

Bryce shook his head. "I'd say just plain terrible."

Feeling a little playful, Jewel joined in. "Now, Mr. Cameron, you don't strike me as being someone who doesn't see the beauty in the stars overhead."

"Oh, I see the beauty of the stars. I just don't have the appreciation for my friend's poetic wisdom."

Marcus laughed and lifted his head high. "Thank you, Ms. Ferguson. It's nice to have someone out here with a little intelligence and refinement."

Bryce held out his hand to Jewel. "Let me walk you back to the room. We'll make sure you have a light with fresh batteries." He looked over at Marcus who was now stretched out on the grass. "On second thought, I might turn in as well."

Then he surprised her. "I promise I'll give you some privacy. Just let me make sure you have everything, then I'll wait outside the room until you're in bed."

Thankful that he was still being the gentleman, she smiled. "Thank you."

"Marcus and I will be on the other side of the partition tonight if you need anything. Don't hesitate to call." He hesitated, then added, "I know you don't believe we might've felt the presence of Captain McDougle, but just in case we think we might have a visitor, we'll call you."

Jewel laughed. "I won't wait up, but do call me if he comes for a visit."

He lifted his hand and waved goodnight to his partner. "Humor us, Ms. Ferguson. At least give us a chance."

"You've got it.

"You'll need to light a kerosene lantern along with having a flashlight nearby."

When they had reached the room, he opened the door for her. "Let me light a couple lanterns. You can take one behind the partition. If you feel uncomfortable at all back there alone, you're more than welcome to drag your cot out here with us. I promise you can trust us. A fort can be a pretty creepy place in the middle of the night."

"Thank you for your concern, but I'll be fine."

He lit one lantern and placed it on a small table, then lit the other one and handed it to her. "Call us if you need anything. We'll always be in shouting distance."

Bryce smiled and the light of the lantern caught the twinkle in his eyes. His carefree, nonchalant manner unnerved her. With a quick goodnight, she ducked behind the partition.

The lantern's yellow glow sent shadows dancing across the wall. She wrapped her arms around her body.

For a long moment she stood unmoving. The quiet of the fort was deafening. She looked around her small area and pulled her arms tighter around her body.

She did not believe in spirits or ghosts or any other paranormal creature, but being here in this fort where men lived and died gave her pause.

You're being silly, Jewel Ferguson. Anything that exists can be found and studied.

She pulled the cover down on her cot, then stopped short of sitting. What had Bryce and Marcus experienced and what had she felt when she walked into the fort?

Were the two incidents connected?

She shook her head.

No.

Never.

Chapter 4

The morning sun sent streams of light through the tiny slits in the metal slatted window coverings. Quiet contentment settled over Jewel, knowing that Captain McDougle hadn't appeared. Her logical thinking and science-based background told her there was no way he could have appeared.

But then unexpectedly, she felt a tiny sting of disappointment settle around her heart.

She lay in the quiet of her partitioned room and thought about the night. Both trepidation and excitement had kept her awake for hours before falling into a deep but fitful sleep. Once during the night she'd heard Marcus and Bryce talking softly. She slipped from her cot, but didn't make her presence known. Instead, she watched the two men, hoping to find out more about the man who had so easily convinced her to come to the island alone.

At first glance, Bryce Cameron embodied everything from which she had so recently escaped. He owned a successful business. He had an aura of power that reminded her all too much of David. His perfectly well toned body shouted strength and energy and probably a massive male ego—just like David's. David had gone to the gym everyday to keep his body in shape, but he had nothing on Bryce Cameron with a physique that could capture the interest of any unsuspecting female.

But Jewel Ferguson wasn't unsuspecting. At least not anymore. She now considered herself well schooled in what men could do to someone they claimed to love. She would never again allow a male to totally disrupt her world.

Just thinking about how stupid she'd been in her relationship with David infuriated her. How could she have been so naïve?

Infuriated at herself for thinking about her ex, she let her thoughts return to the night. As she'd stood in the dimness of her room, she watched Bryce. His profile intrigued her. She could neither hear what Bryce or Marcus was saying nor see their expressions, but she was sure they spoke about things surrounding the subject of Captain McDougle, things that baffled all of them. Sitting quietly in the dark of the room, the men spun an aura of mystique.

At one point Bryce turned his head slightly. A single beam of light from a low flame in the lantern touched his face. Even in the semi-dark, his eyes looked kind and gentle. She frowned. Maybe it had been unfair to throw him into the same class as David, but to get on with her life she couldn't let her guard down for one second.

As far as she knew, Bryce could be nothing more than a self-centered, ladder-climbing jerk who used anyone and everyone to get what he wanted. Wasn't that what David told her? To make it to the top, you couldn't think about the people you stepped on. Everybody did it.

Jewel always thought he'd been joking. People she associated with in her world would never hurt anyone for their own gain. The concept of someone using others was completely incomprehensible to her.

Boy, did she have a lot to learn!

An almost inaudible remark by Marcus pulled her attention back to the men in the fort and she watched it produce a smile from Bryce. It was a warm smile that pulled at Jewel's heart. Without thinking, she lay her head against the corner of the partition. It squeaked.

Bryce turned his head in her direction, but she slid back into bed before he saw her. Darkness and solitude became her companion once more.

Now that the morning sun had pushed the darkness away, she inhaled deeply and looked forward to seeing what her day in fort held for her.

***

"Well, good morning." Bryce greeted Jewel with a smile he hoped would set the mood for her day. He sat with Marcus outside the door of the room sipping a mug of coffee, waiting for her to come out. It surprised him to feel excited anticipation when he realized she was up. "I see you found our crude kitchen facilities and served yourself."

The morning sun highlighted golden hues streaked through Jewel's dark red hair. She squinted in their direction.

"Yes, I did. Thank you. I couldn't resist the aroma. I love the smell of coffee in the morning, especially when it's waiting for me when I get up. This is a treat."

Bryce watched her rub her fingers around the mug and inhale deeply. The motion was nothing more than what Marcus had just done moments ago and he had probably done himself, but Jewel's fingers caressed the cup seductively. Her eyelids closed slightly, and she unwittingly rolled her head.

Bryce looked away. Jewel Ferguson, in her shorts, white sleeveless shirt, and hair that appeared to have seen only the mere touch of a comb, looked more tempting than all the women who tried to get him into their beds. He shifted uncomfortably.

It wasn't like him to think about a woman like he was thinking about Jewel, at least not after knowing her for less than a day, and especially knowing her background.

Women from rich families with connections that could keep them out of trouble were definitely not the kind he wanted to get too close to. He'd seen their kind and he wanted no part of them.

Marcus got up and offered her his place on the bench. "I need to get a few things started before the crew boat gets here. I'll see you two around."

"I'll be with you in a minute. I want to talk to Jewel first."

"Sure thing." Marcus smiled at Jewel. "See you around."

She waved to him, then took her seat next to Bryce on the bench.

"Did you sleep okay?" Bryce asked.

She hugged the coffee mug close to her body. "I have to admit I didn't think I would, but surprisingly, I slept most of the night."

"Marcus and I took turns getting up. I'm surprised you didn't hear us."

"I did hear you during the night, but it didn't bother me. Did you expect Captain McDougle to visit?"

Bryce chuckled and took a sip of coffee. "No one ruled that out."

"Come on, Bryce. You don't really believe his spirit could still be here?"

He shrugged. "I don't know what to believe any more. I wish I could say for certain that his spirit wasn't here. That would be easy to do, but" – he shook his head – "I'm not so sure."

Her bluish-green eyes caught the morning sun. Clear and bright, they reminded Bryce of the sparkling water that surrounded the fort. Her flawless skin shone clean, uncluttered by heavy makeup, but it was the red hair, hair the color of autumn leaves that made him swallow hard. Captain McDougle's gene had been passed down for one hundred and fifty years. Generation to generation, his contribution to the human race lived on whether he did or not.

She took another sip of coffee. "I've read about people who believe they saw something or felt something unusual, but I've never been able to swallow any of it."

"I can't say I blame you. It's not something I've ever admitted before."

"So you've never heard of anything like this happening before in one of these forts?"

He shook his head. "You mean, have any of my crew ever run into something unexplainable?" He still couldn't bring himself to verbalize the word "ghost."

She nodded.

"No, nothing unusual has ever happened. But, like we said the other night, working in these places makes you think. Gets the imagination going, and I have to tell you that Marcus and I do believe we felt something that night."

Even after revealing his moment's weakness to her, Bryce felt at ease and continued. He nodded ahead of them. "Right there by the stairwell. This morning in the bright sunlight, it doesn't seem possible, but no one can ever convince me we didn't feel some presence. And like we said last night, there was an odor too. It wasn't much of one, but we both detected it. Old and musty."

With a concentrated effort, Jewel stared at the spot where he pointed.

"I'm a scientist. It's hard for me to believe something like this, but I don't doubt you might've felt something. The imagination can produce strong sensations, I'm sure." Turning, she looked directly into his eyes.

He remembered the sensation he'd felt. It hadn't been his imagination, but he wouldn't push the subject. "Well, thanks for believing I did feel something, even though I don't think it was my imagination," he said. "I'm glad you accepted my invitation and came out here. I think you can relate more to what we've found by being in the fort."

"I'm thrilled to be here. Just being able to hold that

piece of cloth from the captain is the most meaningful thing I've done in a long, long time. That part of my history seems so much more real to me now."

"Good. At least your trip isn't a total waste."

"You really thought I might feel something while I was here, didn't you?"

"Yes, Marcus and I talked about it and we really did want you to spend some time out here. Who can say the captain wouldn't come back again." He looked away, then took a chance to tell her what he'd been thinking. "And maybe you already have felt something."

She gave him an I-doubt-it look.

"When you first came into the sally port, you had a spell of some sort. Who's to say that wasn't Captain McDougle's hello to you."

She laughed. "I doubt that, but you do have my interest up. What would you say if I canceled the helicopter this morning and stayed for one more night? I could do a little more research in the fort itself. This structure really fascinates me. Would that interfere with any of your plans? I don't want to impose," she threw in quickly.

"No. We'd love to have your company. Maybe you can enjoy more of the island today while we do some work."

Jewel sat quietly for a few minutes taking in her surroundings. Bryce left her alone with her thoughts. There was something familiar about her but he couldn't put his finger on it. Finally he said, "You have his hair, you know."

She nodded and reached up and stroked one of the long strands that hung down on her neck. "Yes. In all the stories that I've ever heard about the 'lovers,'—as my grandmother called them—the red hair has always been there. The stories were never the same. I guess no one will ever know what really happened back then, but in all the stories Captain McDougle always had red hair." She smiled. "I think the more stories that were told, the redder his got. Naturally, I've always been intrigued. No one else in the family that I know of has had this color but me."

An urge to reach out and touch her hair surged through Bryce, but he held back. "It's beautiful. You were blessed."

She rolled her eyes and chuckled.

"That's a compliment, Jewel. It's unusual."

"Unusual maybe," she agreed, "but for years I didn't consider myself blessed. It hasn't always been this color. When I was younger, it was more orange than red, bright orange. In elementary school kids used to call me names." She twisted her face and wrinkled her nose. "Carrot top. Flaming rooster. Bozo. For so long I just hated it."

Surprised, Bryce listened to her open up. She leaned against the brick wall, her hair spread out behind her like a swirling, tumultuous cloud. Unexpected, a hot belt of desire hit him, almost took his breath. He turned his head away as she continued.

Finally he turned back to her. "I know you won't believe this, but I do think there's a connection between all these happenings—the note we found, you being here, the way you felt when you came into the fort—everything just seems to tie in together." He shook his head. "I can't explain what I feel, but something's going on."

Jewel just stared at him.

Now it was his turn to chuckle. "You don't have to answer. I know how you feel."

She sat a moment before answering. "Assuming that something *is* happening with all this, do you think others have felt it? I know you said no one in your crews have ever said anything, but there are other people working in forts around the country. I wonder if others have had unexplained happenings."

"Who knows? I don't know why Marcus and I had that experience. Why us? Why now? Or then again, maybe things have happened before and no one said anything."

He watched Jewel think about what he'd just said. If

she agreed with him, it would mean she believed something out of the ordinary happened.

"Maybe just being in a structure like this makes the mind do strange things."

Bryce chuckled. "Yeah, I agree with that. You're the only one Marcus and I told about how we felt that night. We certainly didn't let on to our crews. They would've laughed us off the island." He put his empty cup down. "I guess we'll never know if we really felt something or not, but after doing my research, then seeing you and that gorgeous head of hair of yours, I know I haven't lost my mind. Everything just fell in place. I feel certain what we felt had to be something to do with Hilliard McDougle's spirit."

"Okay, I'll admit that things *seem* to be connected."

He laughed again. "Spoken like a true scientist." He waited a moment then continued. "You talked about Hilliard's plantation yesterday. Did you know he built it for Ula?"

Jewel smiled. "Yes, for a wedding gift. Isn't that the most romantic thing you've ever heard of?"

Bryce nodded. "According to the records, his family owned that land as well as other acres south of St. Marks in Louisiana. Hilliard built the home shortly before the war began. For years his family had worked the land around it with cotton and some sugar cane. Made tons of money until the war moved to the South."

"You seem to know a lot more about the home and the family than I do, and they're my ancestors."

"After finding his message, I did a lot of quick research. It wasn't hard to find out the plantation fell into the hands of the Union army and after the war a northern family by the name of Smyth bought it. According to the last reports my secretaries dug up, it's been in that same family for the last one hundred and fifty years."

"I read those same reports, but I never found any

record of what happened to Ula," Jewel added. "If she remarried, there's no records. A lot of the records were lost during a fire in town shortly after the war if she even stayed here. We've had the family tree and know my mother's family can be traced to him, but other than that, we really don't have a lot of details. I guess the only thing for sure is that Ula lost everything to the war."

Jewel's eyes showed a sadness he too felt when he thought about the young couple whose lives were torn apart by something out of their control.

Bryce felt a kinship with Jewel. They shared an interest in a piece of history, and if Captain McDougle's spirit was actually here, they could be part of that history together as well—that is, if he could get Jewel to open up her mind a little.

Bryce stood up and slapped his leg. "Come on. I'll show you around the rest of the fort you didn't see yesterday, if you're interested."

The two of them walked comfortably around the alcove of the fort. Jewel was a good listener. He liked that. Bryce regaled her with his knowledge of Civil War history and the early uses of the forts. She seemed genuinely interested and fascinated with the facts he'd collected over the past few years.

It felt good to walk with a female and share a common interest. How long had it been for him to really enjoy a woman's company?

As they reached the darkened area of the south wing he'd worked yesterday, he placed his arm on hers to help her get around some of the construction debris. She wasn't the same woman he thought he'd met when he'd opened the helicopter door. This was a warm individual, and yes, he had to admit for a moment it felt good to be able to help her around the fort.

But then, that thought tore across his chest. Nan's memory would never let him help another woman again without thinking about her. He took his arm away.

"Bryce, are you okay?'

Bryce snapped his head up, embarrassed that he'd been caught lost in his horrible nightmare.

"Yes. I guess sometimes I get caught up in the happenings of the past."

He smiled, but in his heart he knew she didn't understand. She had no idea the past he meant didn't belong to Hilliard and Ula or to any soldier who walked through this fort. He didn't try to explain. His past wrapped around him and imprisoned him like the cold bricks in the dungeon.

At least Hilliard was able to escape his, even if it was by dying.

"Well," Jewel said, oblivious to his real reasons, "I can certainly understand losing yourself in this history. It would be hard to work in these forts and not get emotionally involved in what happened to these men."

Jewel spent the rest of the day along the beaches at the western end of the island where she'd walked with Bryce the day before. She picked up shells, walked across to the Gulf side to play in the surf, then sat quietly along the shoreline to watch the birds. The many species fascinated her, but it was the family of egrets with their huge white bodies and beautiful plumes that intrigued her the most.

She'd watched families of these birds around her Houston apartment complex, but today they seemed to have a special draw. Just as with so many other things that had happened to her recently, she couldn't put a finger on what she felt.

She looked around the island with its barren sand dunes, scattered clumps of wind-blown sea oats, and miles of white sand, and assumed that the beauty and solitude of the place was playing tricks with her mind.

Finally, when sunscreen could no longer keep her skin from turning red, she gave one last look at the egrets and walked back to the fort, excited that she was going to spend another night. If anything, another uneventful night would cinch her argument that nothing beyond the normal was happening on this island.

As she stepped up on the pier, the crew, including Marcus, was getting ready to leave the island.

"Marcus, where are you going?" she shouted.

"I got a call and have to get back to shore to check on one of our other projects. I'll be back in the morning."

She opened her mouth to tell him she was going with them, but Marcus waved and the boat pulled away from the pier.

Bryce walked out of the fort as she stood staring at the boat.

"Jewel, you weren't here when Marcus got a call. I tried to call on your cell phone, but you didn't answer. He had to get back to shore, and the boat couldn't wait any longer. I told him if you felt uncomfortable with just me out here, you could call Buddy for the helicopter."

She stared at him, then at the boat, then back at him. "Uh, I'm not sure. I wanted to spend the night, but..."

"You won't offend me if you call Buddy, but, I swear, you can trust me. I'm not an ax murderer." His smile showed his concern for her.

"Okay, I'll take your word for it, but I have to warn you. I know karate and wouldn't think twice about using it."

He laughed. "I bet you would."

Chapter 5

White streaks of light flashed through her subconscious. Jewel tossed her head from side to side on the pillow and struggled to lose herself once more in sleep. The hair on the back of her neck stiffened and her heart raced in her chest.

Her eyes refused to open.

She felt—no, she knew—something stood next to her bed at her back. Deep within the subliminal she knew it was beyond the natural. Instinctively she wanted to curl up into a protective ball, pretend it wasn't there, and refuse to acknowledge it. But there was no way she could do that.

As much as she tried to hang onto the last remnants of sleep, it left her and she found herself awake and much too conscious, vulnerable, and horribly exposed. Terror closed the wind passages in her throat. There would be no screams.

Painstakingly slow, she forced the lids of her eyes to open ever so slightly, but she didn't have to see to know Captain McDougle was with her. She felt him and smelled something she couldn't identify, but it was strong, nauseating.

She lay perfectly still, trying to calm her breathing, staring into the darkness. Her fingers spasmed. How long had she been clutching the covers? Now, fully awake, she had to do something.

Squeezing her eyes a little tighter, she held her breath.

Where was Bryce? Was he awake? Did he know she was terrified? She tried to call out to him, but she couldn't make a sound.

She tried to remember the name of a saint from her old catechism days that might give her the courage to turn over and face her fear. Nothing. Praying wasn't going to help. Even in her jumbled mind, she knew she would have to face this thing on her own. She exhaled and tried to calm the trembles spreading throughout her body.

Every charged iota of her body opened in expectation as she shifted her head. There, just inches from her body, stood the image of Captain Hilliard McDougle.

Just as she had anticipated, screams didn't come. Nothing worked but her mind's awareness that he was there.

Nothing about him looked alive except for his eyes, sad eyes that immobilized her. There was no movement on his part either. He simply stood and stared. His gaze devoured her, reaching down within the very depths of her being until her soul fluttered with elation and love.

The terror that had gripped her only moments before vanished as a sensation of tenderness and caring caressed her and erased the fear. Her taut muscles eased. Her body relaxed.

Instinctive, Jewel knew Captain McDougle wanted something from her and wouldn't hurt her. For whatever reason, he stood silently and waited, but not knowing what he wanted or needed, there was nothing she could do. Helplessness and panic once more slipped into her senses.

She closed her eyes tightly to allow the creeping panic to dissipate. With her eyes still closed she prayed to know what to do. She inhaled deeply and waited.

Then it happened. A totally different sensation came over her, and for a brief moment she didn't feel like Jewel Fergusen at all. She knew she was in the fort. She knew that Captain McDougle was with her, but something wasn't normal. A definite connection to McDougle pulled her toward him. An aura of peace settled around her again. Calmed her. Soothed her. Something within wanted to reach out to him, maybe not physically, but spiritually and emotionally. Nothing within her wanted to fight the sensation.

With heavy eyelids and dulling senses, her mind reached out toward the spirit by her bed. As she let herself go, though, everything changed. A violent pain and grievous sorrow engulfed her with a feeling that weighted her down, stabbed her in the heart, and took away her breath. Her head began to spin with incredible swirling energy, just as it had done when she had first walked into the fort.

Somewhere from deep within her consciousness, the awareness that she was being pulled between his world and her own shook her to the core. With the last shred of control within her, she jammed her body against the back wall and forced her eyes to open fully.

Captain McDougle still hovered near her, but she now saw him in a different light. For the first time she saw that his Confederate uniform was smeared with blood around a gaping hole in the shoulder that stood grotesque against his pallor state.

He moved toward her. Jewel's breath caught in her chest as his limp, airy hand reached out to her, nearly touching her face with its long sinewy fingers.

This time her throat muscles worked. She screamed and covered her face, then screamed some more. Moments before, she could not find her voice. Now she couldn't make the screams stop. They reverberated against the walls of the fort and inside of her head, but she continued to scream.

Powerful hands grabbed her shoulders and she screamed louder, backed harder against the partition, and fought to get the hands off. She scratched and clawed until the hands shook her hard and a familiar voice spoke to her.

"Jewel, Jewel, it's me. Bryce. You're okay."

Still fighting, she heard the words, but it took a moment

for them to register. It was Bryce. The hands pulled her close to his warm chest and held her head tightly. Throwing her arms around his hard body, she collapsed against him.

His words came and went through a fog. "It's okay. I've got you. Nothing can hurt you. You're okay. You're okay."

Her body trembled. She clung to Bryce Cameron as if her life depended on it. Held him, burrowed her face in his neck and finally cried, deep wrenching sobs.

Bryce said nothing, but held her close to his body. She melted against him, gradually losing the tension that had wracked her body. Finally, she relaxed and let herself be enveloped in the comfort of his arms.

"You okay?" With his head close to her ear, his voice was soft, not much more than a whisper.

She nodded into his neck.

"What can I do?"

"Just hold me for a minute." A shiver ran along her spine and her whole body followed with a violent shake.

"Did you have a bad dream?" he asked.

"A dream?" Jewel pulled away, sat on her knees on the bed and faced him. "I don't know. I know it had to be, but it didn't feel like a dream. I can't believe I'm going to say this, but I swear it felt like Captain McDougle was here. Right there inches from me."

Bryce scanned the room, wrinkled his brow, then stared at her. "If you saw him, you weren't dreaming."

Jewel shook her head. "No, it can't be. I know he can't be here"— she put her head in her hands—"but he was so real. If it was a dream, it was the most real dream I've ever had." She lifted her head and looked up into his eyes and ignored the tears that gathered in her eyes. "Am I crazy? Was I thinking too hard about all this before I fell asleep? That's got to be the reason. I conjured it up in my brain."

"Maybe you did conjure it up or maybe you actually

saw something." He wiped the tears away from her cheeks. "I didn't see anything on my side of the room. I was awake. I heard you move, but I thought you were just turning. I didn't want to bother you. Now I wish I would have."

Jewel wrapped her arms around her body. "What I saw—or dreamed—was a man in a uniform. It was bloody with the huge hole in his shoulder, and there was an odor just like when you and Marcus felt something. I didn't recognize the smell, but it was there, almost like a wet-dog smell or maybe old moldy wool. I wanted to hold my nose, but I couldn't lift my hand." She laughed to herself. "I know what the old saying means when someone says they're frozen in fear. To say the least, I was frozen in place."

Bryce said nothing, just sat and listened.

She stared into his eyes, surprised to find that she wanted him to hold her again, but instead of falling into his arms, she said quietly. "He reached out for me."

He sat perfectly still, his brow creased in thought. "He touched you?"

"No, but he tried. He looked me right in the eyes. I swear it was like the Ancient Mariner. I couldn't move. He held me frozen as if my body—and my mind," she threw in, "weren't my own."

Bryce sat on the side of the bed next to her and rubbed his hand across his chin. "That's incredible."

"He definitely saw me," Jewel reiterated. "I felt like he wanted to tell me something or get something from me. I had this feeling—" she sniffled—"the strangest feeling I've ever had. I felt as if I was in someone else's body."

"What made you scream?"

"Right before he reached out to me, I had this horribly sad sensation. I wanted to cry. I don't think I've ever felt so despondent and mournful before. Ever. That's when he tried to touch me."

She sat back on her knees and hugged herself. "This is all so strange. So incredible." She looked up at him. "I had to be dreaming. I went to sleep thinking about all you and Marcus said. It was nothing more than a dream. A damned vivid dream, but a dream."

"I don't think so. To be honest with you, I really didn't expect anything to happen, but I truly believe he was here." He stood up and scanned the room. "I wish I could've seen him."

"I wish you would've too. Then I wouldn't feel so confused."

"Well, confused or not, you experienced something and now we can't drop the subject. We have to do something."

Jewel's mind raced. "But what? Where do we go from here? Spend another night to see if he comes back? We still wouldn't know if I were dreaming unless you saw him too. Then what? He might not ever come back."

Bryce rubbed his hand across his lower chin. "Do you believe in mediums?"

His question startled her. "A medium? Absolutely not. I think they're all just actors."

"Yeah, me too, but after Marcus and I had those feelings and found the captain's things, we talked about seeing one. Right now I'm not sure it wouldn't be such a bad idea to talk with one—you know—just to see what he says."

"A medium? You want me to go to someone who says he can communicate with ghosts?"

"Hey, I'm open to other suggestions if you have one."

Jewel's mind flew from one idea to the next, but in the end she blew out a deep breath. "I don't have another suggestion." She sat up straight. "But if we go to someone like this, you have to promise me we'll never tell anyone. If this got back to my faculty, I'd be the laughing stock."

Bryce laughed. "I don't think I'll be running into anyone from your department anytime soon and I certainly won't tell my crews." Then he got serious. "Jewel, I didn't think it would come to this, but we can't ignore what happened to you."

She nodded. "I agree. Even if it was a dream, Captain McDougle looked so sad, and I felt as if he wanted to tell me something or to do something. I have to find out if what I saw was real. Maybe I should go see a doctor instead, maybe a psychiatrist."

"No, I think what you saw was more real than what either of us want to believe. Tomorrow we'll go back to shore and try to locate someone who might help us."

"And tonight," she added with resolution, "you're not leaving me alone. You're going to pile up on this cot with me, or we can sit up all night with a light on. I can't lie back here by myself again."

Bryce looked down at the cot. "You think we're going to fit in here together, do you?"

"We'll make it fit."

Bryce smiled big.

"Don't you laugh at me. I'm not a wimp. I've never really been scared in my life, but I don't mind telling you I'm terrified right now."

Bryce stroked her hair. "I'm not laughing. I understand perfectly. Remember I think I felt him too. That night Marcus and I felt something, we sat up the rest of the night with the kerosene lantern burning. Believe me, I'm not laughing."

"Then you'll stay with me?"

Bryce raised an eyebrow and tilted his head. "I'll stay with you, but will you respect me in the morning?"

It took Jewel a second for his dry humor to sink in. She fought the urge to laugh. "I don't know if I can promise you that."

At that, they both laughed.

He stood up. "Let me get my pillow."

She stood up also. "Oh, no. You're not leaving me alone. I'll help you."

***

Bryce lay with his back against the walled partition holding Jewel again his body. She snuggled against him, her curve fitting into his perfectly. Outwardly he didn't protest when she asked him to stay by her, but inwardly he doubted it was such a good idea. He had promised her she could trust him. Fulfilling that promise would be the hardest thing he had done in a long time, but it would be kept.

Emotionally drained from her encounter with Captain McDougle, Jewel had fallen asleep almost immediately after she scooted against him. When her soft breathing told him she was asleep, he closed his eyes. *Thank you, God, for small favors.* Now he simply held her in his arms and relished the feel of her against him.

Her long, lean body had curves in all the right spots. His hand trailed lightly down her length. Exceptionally firm and athletic, she would be an active partner in bed.

Instantly his mind and body reeled with desire. Blood surged through him, hot and swift, and his heart pounded against his chest.

He stilled his hand. Took a deep breath.

This wasn't like him at all. For the three years since Nan's death, he hadn't been with another woman, not like this. Not this intimately close.

He tried to ignore the flood of memories that eased over him. His mind refused to be stilled. Once the flood of memories took over, it couldn't be dammed.

Lying next to Jewel and holding her dredged up memories of snuggling against Nan in their little cabin they'd rent every year or of stretching out next to her on the floor in front of the TV—all small moments from a monumental time in his life with her, but memories big enough to stagger his present.

Nothing had to be elaborate or fancy with Nan. It was always the simple things that made her the happiest, a trait that probably set her apart from Jewel. This lady was from a different society. She'd been raised in a family of extreme wealth and now she lived her life amongst an elite class of professionals who couldn't possibly understand the joys of simple living.

Unfortunately, he'd run into her kind, but he wouldn't—couldn't—think about that.

Tonight he'd let his mind simply wander on its own. He smiled. Nan appreciated the simpler things in life and now, even years after Nan's death, it was the simple things that would trigger his memories of her, crash into his normal life, and create massive voids.

But, tonight even though her memory had sneaked into his consciousness, something was different.

For the last two days being with Jewel had kept his mind and body vitalized. Living. Normally, thoughts of what he and Nan once shared would crush him into a hole by an emotional juggernaut. At those times, his body went through the motions of living, but his mind ceased to be stimulated by anything. Food, work, beer, a good looking woman. Nothing did it for him.

Nothing but Nan could save him from his debilitating depression, and that was impossible. Nan was gone. He promised himself never to become so deeply involved with another woman that he'd have to endure more sorrow and heartache. How well he knew that, in an instant, lives could be torn apart.

He pulled Jewel close and inhaled the soft scent of the beach that still clung to her hair.

Since Jewel arrived on the island, he had stayed above ground, out of the hole and in the real world of the living. For the first time in a long time, he had enjoyed being around another woman. He looked forward to seeing Jewel, and now he definitely was enjoying her in his arms.

He might not be looking for an involvement with this woman, but there was no law that said he couldn't enjoy the presence of her.

She groaned. Pulling her closer to him, he let her snuggle against his chest.

It had been a long time since he had held a woman, but that was nothing compared with how long this night was going to seem.

***

In the dim light of the morning, Jewel lay snuggled against Byrce's hard body in the tiny cot and watched him sleep. Moments earlier she had opened her eyes to the most sensational feeling she had experienced in a very long time. It took her a moment to realize where she was and whose arms she was in, and to realize that it felt wonderful. Even with the image of Captain McDougle still vivid in her mind, she knew she was safe and secure in Bryce's arms. She languished in the comfort of that feeling, totally aware that he was a stranger she had vowed not to let invade her life.

For the moment, though, she couldn't deny having him next to her spread relief throughout her body. Ever since she'd stepped off the helicopter, Bryce had been nothing but kind to her, and right now she couldn't think of anyone else better to have holding her.

Inhaling a deep breath, he opened his eyes. "Good morning." He smiled as he said it.

"Good morning to you, though, I really don't think it's technically morning. It's hardly daylight yet."

He stretched his body under the covers and nearly knocked her off the cot. Instantly, they grabbed each other in a tangle of arms and legs.

"Whoa. I didn't mean to nearly knock you out."

Laughing, she clung to him, but inside she wasn't laughing at all. Being this near to him was too much for her to handle. Gently, she tried to ease her body away. Her voice was soft, almost breathless. "Maybe I'd better get up."

Bryce got quiet, then spoke. "Don't go. There's not

much we can do this early, and we didn't get much sleep last night."

Jewel closed her eyes, remembering the terror of Captain McDougle's ghost. No, she wouldn't call it a ghost. It was a presence, maybe something in her head or her dreams, but not a ghost.

"I fell right to sleep with you next to me, but I kept having these awful dreams. Thank you for staying with me."

"My pleasure, I can assure you."

A shiver ran through her body. Bryce pulled her even closer.

"It's okay to think about what happened last night, Jewel," he whispered. "It's not going to go away, but I don't think we need to fear him. After you went to sleep, I had a hard time drifting off myself. I thought about this spirit, and if he's really real, I think he must be stuck here somewhere between this world and whatever else is out there. I think he's trying to find a way out of here."

She shook her head. "Bryce, the more I think about this, the more I believe I dreamed it."

With his arm around her, he began to gently massage her back. He spoke into her ear with a soft voice. "I don't think you did."

"I can't believe you think the captain actually was here. It's not possible."

She heard him let out a long breath. "There're a lot of questions we need to answer. I hope you didn't change your mind about looking for a medium. I really think that should be our next logical step."

Jewel grimaced. "Logical? Nothing's logical about all of this. I'm not sure talking to a medium will do any good, but since I don't have any answers, I'll go along."

He chuckled, and in the dim light of the morning, she detected a smile that went all the way to his eyes. "Good. We probably need to head out to New Orleans. I think we'd have better luck over there."

She thought about it a second. "New Orleans sounds like a plan. I haven't been there in a long time."

He pulled her even closer to him and pressed her head against his chest. She didn't protest. The rapid thumping of his heart kept pace with her own and the full length of his body touched her all the way down to her toes sending tiny shock waves reverberating throughout her body.

For a moment she allowed herself to relish the tenderness he was offering, but she knew it had to end.

This wasn't why she was out on this island.

This wasn't what she needed, even though her body screamed a different story.

And Bryce Cameron wasn't going to steal her trust at a time when she was vulnerable.

No, if she could control the hot surge of desire that threatened to turn her body to mush, she could keep control over her life, at least for the moment. She wasn't sure how she had allowed herself to succumb to the whims of David, but the experience had taught her a lot.

Jewel placed an opened hand on Bryce's chest and gently pushed herself away. "Let's try to make some of that awful coffee you served yesterday morning."

The starting of a frown creased his brow, but it quickly vanished. "Hey. You said my coffee was wonderful."

"I lied."

"Well, how about you making me coffee this morning? Let's see if yours is any better."

Bryce allowed her to slide her legs off the bed, but the confusion she saw in his face seconds before told her he knew she didn't trust him. Words were not necessary to know that he wanted more from her.

He sat up next to her and stretched. "Tell you what. I'll go get things ready and give you a few minutes to yourself."

He slid off the cot then reached over to the kerosene lantern. With precise efficiency, he produced a brilliant orange flame.

"I'll get the generator kicked up in a minute and we'll be back in the Twenty-first Century."

"And I'll see if I can come up with the courage to actually go with you to New Orleans."

Chapter 6

The night air, heavy with a late summer fog, settled around Jewel and Bryce as they walked along the unusually quiet sidewalk of Canal Street leading to the riverfront. Tonight, New Orleans's busiest street lacked its usual hustle and bustle. Only an occasional burst of traffic, moving from one traffic light to the next, broke the calm but then quickly moved on to leave periods of blessed quiet.

"I've never seen the city this quiet. Nice, huh?" Bryce placed his hand on Jewel's elbow, then stepped down from a curb and onto a side street.

"Yes, it is. I haven't been here since I was a teenager, but this isn't what I remember at all."

She stepped down with him, letting him lead the way. Could it be just three days ago that she had landed on the island and saw a man on the pier she was determined not to like? She was getting to know more about him each day, but there was something about him she couldn't pinpoint, something she wasn't sure she should trust.

Now, she was traveling the coastline with him looking for someone to help explain what was happening to her. He believed it was beyond the natural, a ghost of all things. She wasn't sure what she believed, but if she followed him, she could at least prove he was wrong.

For weeks she had dealt with dreams and unexplained

occurrences—waking up in the middle of the night in a sweat, lying in the dark wondering what was happening to her.

At least sharing her experience with Bryce had lifted some of the tension she carried. On campus she hadn't told anyone. Who was there to tell?

If she were honest with herself, except for other faculty members, she hadn't had much contact with anyone since her broken engagement eight months ago. Had she buried herself in researching her book and in her classes on campus to avoid getting involved with anyone?

She'd always been an independent person, but never a recluse. A glance up at Bryce reminded her of her self-inflicted isolation. She interacted with other faculty members, but only on a professional level, sharing grades and observations of her students—never anything personal or intimate. Her engagement to David had taken her away from her previous social groups. Now she realized how alone she was.

Bryce walked alongside of her in silence, probably deep in thought as she was. How had he become so involved with her life in such a short time?

She smiled to herself. *I guess sharing a ghost story brings people together, whether they want to be or not.* But it took only a brief moment of letting her guard down to remember the ache of rejection and the horror of knowing she had been so close to giving her life to a man who really didn't love her.

She stepped over several paper cups that had washed down the street and jammed themselves against the curb. Could she ever allow herself to be washed along in someone else's life again? She knew the answer to that. No.

Still, having Bryce next to her and understanding what she was going through was certainly comforting.

"Now this is more the way New Orleans really is. I like it when there's not much traffic."

His words drew her back to the present, but she

realized the thinner crowds were not to be continued. They had gotten closer to the river, where more traffic crowded onto the street. Stopping at a congested intersection, both of them stared at the front of New Orleans's glitzy casino. Hoards of people milled around the two-storied entrance, some going in, some waiting for their cars to be brought around by busy valets.

"Do you feel like slipping a few bills into the slots?" he asked as they waited for the traffic light to change.

"No, not really. Usually I'd say 'yes,' but I'm not much in the mood." She prayed he didn't want to go. The busy casino wouldn't offer her a place to think, and she definitely needed to think.

As if reading her mind, he nodded. "That's fine with me. I'm enjoying this quiet too much to get in the crowds."

Letting out a breath of relief, she smiled up at him. "And as nice as the River Walk is, I'm not into that tonight either." She laughed. "I can't believe I just said that. Shopping is usually a way of relaxing for me."

From the look on Bryce's face, Jewel sensed he didn't want to get mixed up in the crowds of tourists who browsed through several levels of specialty shops and eateries within the River Walk.

He nodded, looked around, then pointed to a smaller side street. "Okay, then let's turn here. I know a neat little restaurant and lounge down near the French Market if you'd like to walk a little ways."

She nodded and together they walked along quietly, once more getting away from the noisy traffic.

Jewel was pleased, given the fact they had just left the leading medium in the South and she had a lot to think about. After explaining the happenings to Mr. Bourgois, they sat and listened as he explained the spirits of lost souls from the Civil War Period weren't uncommon. He believed that the sighting of Captain McDougle was as real as any of the other spirits of soldiers who still walked the battlefields of Gettysburg or the hallowed grounds of Andersonville.

Now as they walked along the sidewalk, Jewel felt Bryce looking at her, his eyes squinting in concern. "Thinking about what Mr. Bourgois laid on us?"

"Yes, I guess I am."

"You okay with it?" he asked.

"Not really. Something happened, but I can't say I believe a ghost appeared to me just because that man with a sign in his front yard said I did." She pulled a deep breath. "But it's something I can't completely ignore right now. I have a lot to think about."

She was uneasy about her experience, but after talking with Mr. Bourgois, it was getting harder to deny what she'd seen and felt. And if she did admit the Captain was really still on the island, she knew she couldn't turn her back on him.

"You look like you still have something to get off your chest?"

Jewel smiled. "I guess I'm experiencing something similar to what you and Marcus felt that night in the fort. You know, not expecting anything to really come of our encounter. I wanted Mr. Bourgois to tell us it really was our imaginations. Maybe that I just thought I had seen him because you told me what you had felt. That it wasn't possible for this spirit to still be here."

Jewel heard Bryce inhale deeply before he spoke. "But now I think we have to deal with the fact that if he really is there, we need to do something. I don't think you or I could go on living with the knowledge that he's still out there and maybe we can help him."

Jewel nodded and together they walked along side by side.

"Now, I'm not saying I believe he's there, but if he is, it's sad." Jewel stopped and turned to Bryce. Her mind was reeling, her heart heavy. "It's horrible to die in wartime away from your home and friends and family."

"Nobody will disagree with you there."

Jewel chose her words carefully. "If he does exist, and if that's the way he died, it would be bad enough, but this situation makes it all the more horrible. Spending eternity looking for a way to depart this earth makes it more heart breaking and so unfair, especially after what that soldier said about him trying to get to his wife."

Unexplained sadness as heavy as the sorrow she felt the night in the fort now weighed on her shoulders.

Bryce placed an understanding arm around her. "What war was ever fair to those who fought in it? Who knows how many lost spirits are wandering this earth trying to find that peace. We've had a lot of wars since the beginning of time. Think about it. Man has been fighting man since time began."

Jewel blinked. "Thanks. That really makes me feel better."

Bryce chuckled and his arm dropped away from her shoulder. "Sorry, but that's the truth. Who knows what spirits are not at rest?"

"So, I hope my theory is right and yours and Mr. Bourgois's is wrong."

"We'll see."

Once again, they began to walk along the narrow sidewalk, slowly as before, but each in his own deep thoughts. Like any big city, the streets of New Orleans weren't the safest at night, but she felt secure walking them with Bryce. Protected and safe, just as she had felt in his arms as they lay on her small cot in the dark of the fort.

For an instant, the remembrance of his hard body pressed against hers sent a surprising warmth through her veins. Fear had kept her from succumbing to the temptation of his body last night, but fear didn't keep her from dreaming of what it would have been like to let herself make love to the man.

Jewel's eyes widened, not believing she let herself think such a thought. Bryce was a stranger, someone who wouldn't even tell her about his personal life.

"Let's turn here," he said, and Jewel breathed a sigh of relief to have something to think about besides beds and hard bodies.

Soon the sights and sounds of the French Market surrounded her. On a smaller side street, Bryce opened a wrought-ironed gate that led to a long dark hallway. Its worn stone floor took them to an open courtyard dimly lit with only the flicker of a few table candles and wall sconces.

"This is nice," Jewel said as Bryce pulled out a chair near a small flowing fountain.

Shiny stone floors, balconies overlooking the courtyard, lush flora with delicately scented flowers—all quietly pulled the few seated guests into a magically, romantic world. Candles in heavy silver holders and the light from a sliver of a moon that peaked through the clouds above them offered just enough light to sit comfortably with a companion.

"This is so New Orleans," she said.

"There's a reason for that."

Bryce's smile crashed into her heart. She said nothing.

He then nodded in the direction of a rather dark corner. "Look."

There, almost completely hidden from the view of those in the courtyard, were two musicians. One drummed the keys of his piano and sang a melancholy song Jewel recognized as part of the Blues genre. The other keyed the melody on a wailing sax, not loud, but low and lonely.

How fitting, she thought.

Bryce ordered them each a small cup of gumbo and a glass of wine. Jewel then settled back to enjoy the moment.

"You think he knows?" Bryce asked softly.

Jewel looked up. "Who?"

"The sax player. He's playing as if he knows how we feel and what we've been through. His sax sounds like it's calling to the lost souls out there, dead or alive I guess, who need someone to release them."

Jewel blinked, amazed that Bryce had shared with her such a personal observation. The men she knew would keep such thoughts to themselves, afraid that someone would laugh at them. The more she was with Bryce, the more he surprised her.

She listened to the sad, low wail. "I agree. Music like that can only be written, or sung, by someone who knows about suffering and heartache."

Bryce grinned. "We're awfully philosophical tonight, aren't we?"

Jewel watched as Bryce placed his elbows on the table and his chin on his hands and listened to the two musicians as they finished the number.

She wondered what Bryce's story was. Had he known heartache? Suffering? Was he hurting inside or was he just a private person and didn't like to talk about himself?

Bryce applauded lightly with several other guests as the men left the bandstand for a break. "They're good. I hope they don't stay gone too long."

Jewel clapped also, but her mind was on Bryce, not the musicians.

The waiter interrupted her thoughts with their drinks. When they were left alone again, she sipped her wine, then took a chance. "On the island that day after we walked on the beach and you got me to embarrass myself by pouring out my romantic disaster story, you said you'd tell me yours one day."

"Yes, I guess I did, didn't I?" Bryce leaned back in his chair. "But not today."

Jewel couldn't believe her ears. "That's not fair. You know about my baggage. I think it's only right that you share yours."

He shook his head. "Not today."

Slightly irritated, Jewel placed her glass down hard and crossed her arms in front of her chest. "Wait a minute. It's okay for me to embarrass myself, but not for you. I don't think so."

Bryce squinted and swallowed. "It's not baggage that I have."

"Then what is it? I call everyone's past life baggage if it interferes with the present." And it's the baggage—his past, his story—that she needed to know. For some reason, she needed to trust this man, but how could she if he hid part of who he was?

Trusting David had been so easy and look where it got her.

Bryce said nothing. He took a big swallow of his wine and looked directly at Jewel. "You might be right, but I don't think this is the time to talk about it. I'm having a nice time sitting with you and that could change if I start talking."

Was he being honest with her? Was that the real reason he didn't want to open up?

"I'm having a nice time too," she admitted, "but I still think you ought to share with me. I'm not just anyone any more, you know. We've shared a ghost and not many people have that in common."

Bryce chuckled. "Hey, you've actually admitted you've seen a ghost."

"Watch it, Mr. Cameron. I was trying to make a joke."

"But it's not a joke, is it? If Captain McDougle is really out there, then you've got a point there. Not many people can say they share that with anyone." He got serious and took her hand unexpectedly.

Jewel's breath caught in her throat. He turned her hand over gently as if he were trying to find the words to speak.

"I don't have any deep, dark secrets I'm hiding from you." His gaze stayed on their joined hands for several seconds, then he looked back up at Jewel. "My wife died in a car accident, but I'm really not up to talking about it right now. I'll share when the time is right, okay?"

A vice grip clutched Jewel's throat. How could she

have been so insensitive?

"I'm so sorry I pried. I understand if you don't want to talk about her, but when you feel comfortable with me, I really would like to know something about you. Whether you want to share your wife with me is entirely up to you."

"Thank you. I really do appreciate your understanding. I promise I'll talk with you. I just don't want to call up a black cloud of gloom over our evening."

His smile was devastating.

"Okay, if I don't have a choice, I'll wait."

He squeezed her hand once before letting go, then shook his head. "Nope. No choice in the matter."

"Well, then, I guess I'll have to wait until you feel the time is right." She tried to lighten his mood. "When you feel I'm trustworthy enough to share something personal with me. That I'm intelligent enough to understand. That I'm. . ."

"Okay, already. I get the picture, but I'm still putting you off. Let's enjoy this night out on the town. We'll even forget it started out with a medium and a possible ghost."

"I agree."

Jewel had to console herself with the knowledge he was enjoying her company, though deep inside she was surprised to feel a twist of hurt around her heart. Having him trust her enough to share his past became important to her, but looking at him she had a feeling that he still loved this woman too much to talk about her to someone else.

Her heart went out to him for his loss.

By the time their second drink and gumbo arrived, the two-piece band had returned and started with a nice dance number.

Bryce touched her hand. "Want to try it?"

No one else had gotten up, but she nodded. "Sure, why not?"

Like a gentleman, he helped her with her chair, then escorted her to a small dance floor in front of the piano. His hand touched her lower back gently, but with enough pressure Jewel knew he was there. As he turned her to him, she inhaled deeply. She had been with this man for three days now. Slept next to him in the same small cot. Poured out her life story to him, but now as he pulled her body to his, conflicting emotions collided within her body. Two seconds before she wanted to hold him close to her breast and console him, let him know that she cared about his grief.

Now, though, the tables were turning and the urge to run topped the list. All of a sudden Bryce Cameron had become too familiar for her comfort. The last thing she needed right now was for a man to needle his way into her life.

She needed time to live her own life again, not someone else's. For sure, she didn't need this man whose warmth, understanding, strength and everything else about him fit the image of Mr. Perfect. Jewel knew there was no such thing. Men might come packaged like Mr. Perfect, but once inside the wrappings, Mr. Perfects really didn't exist.

Still, every part of her body gravitated toward Bryce. She longed to melt against him, feel his warmth against her thighs, and listen to his heartbeat thump against her ears. It was hard to keep her brain from being taken over by her baser instincts, but she knew she would be inviting trouble if she allowed it.

Inhaling deeply, she inched away from him, just enough to have some breathing room.

Looking up into his face and hoping he hadn't noticed she had spaced herself a safe distance from him, she smiled. He smiled back, but it was a smile that said he had read her mind.

Bryce was a strong, smooth dancer. Why wouldn't he be? He had been a good, strong everything since she met him. She swallowed, relaxed, and let him lead her around the floor.

"You're a good dancer," he said quietly into her ear,

surprising her that he was thinking the same thing as she was. "I like a woman who doesn't try to lead."

His words slammed into her brain. David didn't like a woman to lead—in anything, not just on the dance floor. He didn't even want her to lead her own life, at least not until she couldn't offer him a fortune.

"Thank you, I think."

He laughed. "It was a compliment."

"Well, thank you, but there are times I like to lead," she answered.

A wicked smile creased his face. "Really? And will I be warned when you might decide to do that?"

Jewel wasn't referring to dancing, and by the smile on his face she had a feeling he wasn't either. She didn't explain. "I don't know if you'll be warned or not. Maybe I'll grab the moment when you're least expecting it."

He raised an eyebrow. "That might be nice."

"Thought you didn't like a woman who led," she threw back at him.

But he was quick to reply. "Only on the dance floor."

She opened her mouth to answer, but before she could, he pulled her close and swung her around to the wail of the sax.

"Sometimes leading is a two-way street," he said as he captured her head in the curve of his neck. "Life isn't always as easy as a dance. Sometimes the one who thinks he's leading is only really following and isn't even aware of it."

Jewel didn't answer. Whatever he was thinking about didn't really matter, because his words pegged her relationship with David perfectly. The man had led her into his little trap, and she hadn't even been aware of it. In fact, she thought she had matters totally under control. *How could she have been so stupid!*

If life were as easy as a dance, she would have known David was totally out of step with her. Now that she looked back, they hadn't even been dancing to the same song.

Again she reminded herself that Bryce wasn't David.

The clear tones of the sax enveloped her like a warm blanket on a cold night. Jewel sighed and totally gave in to Bryce's lead. Why fight it?

The music was good. The ambiance was great, and the man who held her was being a gentleman. Why not enjoy a good dance? She could be on guard later.

***

Jewel fumbled for her room key card as Bryce stood patiently behind her. When she'd retrieved it from the bottom of her purse, he took the card and opened the door.

Jewel was about to break the news to him that he wasn't invited in, but when she turned, he had stepped back.

"Get a good night's sleep, Jewel. We've got a lot to do tomorrow."

Before she could say anything, he had turned and was heading for his own room. Disappointment surprised her. *Mr. Perfect had done it again.*

As he opened his own door, he turned and looked her way. "Call me if you need anything. See you in the morning."

"Good night, Bryce, and thank you for a nice evening."

He smiled, but didn't respond.

As she lay in bed, alone, trying to put together the pieces of the last three days, several things stood out. Captain McDougle, of course, took center stage, but it wasn't just his appearance that bothered her. It was the fact that whether he actually appeared to her or was only in her mind, he wanted to communicate with her and not with Bryce. Why? Was it possible that his spirit recognized her as a descendent? Someone with family ties? Was there something she could do for him?

Forever, My Love

So many questions remained that even the medium couldn't answer, but they were questions that had to be answered. The medium suggested they visit the old family plantation on the river. Something there might give them a clue as to their next move, or maybe something would help them understand her connection with this man from her past who might or might not still roam the place where he had died.

She hoped something there would point her in the right direction with her life. Leaving David had been a big step for her, but she couldn't stop now. Too many things had to be done before she'd feel she had recaptured all those lost years she'd given to a dead-end engagement.

Finding a connection with an ancestor from the Civil War Period hadn't been on her list of things to do, but she had to admit it did liven up her life a little.

Finding that connection with a good looking guy didn't hurt, either.

Her thoughts wandered to his room on the other side of the wall. Had he gone right to sleep? Was he thinking of her or was he worried about the restoration project at the fort?

Whatever he was doing wasn't any of her business. Soon he'd be back on Ship Island, and she'd be back on campus and all of this supernatural business would be behind them. The way it should be.

Other than that, Bryce Cameron was just someone with whom she shared a part of her history.

She grabbed the remote and flipped through channels. The events of the day had her on edge and she knew sleep wouldn't come easily. She tried hard to convince herself that her jitters came from the situation with her ancestors and definitely not from the man in the other room who was probably stepping out of the shower naked.

Realizing the rapidly changing channels on the TV were nothing but a blur, she lifted her fingers and stopped long enough on each channel to see the program. Cartoons. A rerun of "The Practice." A chef chopping onions for an okra gumbo.

Before hitting the off button, she scanned the news network. With the Presidential campaigns gearing up, she knew what she'd find. She was right. Black suits and smiling faces with lots of red, white and blue banners gave her the evening's allotment of election rhetoric. She propped herself against the headboard and watched. Keeping up with what was going on in the national scene was necessary to talk with the other professors in her department, though politics normally didn't raise her interest. This year's election was no different, but since she found herself sitting with nothing to do, she tuned into one of the prospective candidates, Jason LeBreaux.

Jewel relaxed against her pillow and listened. She'd followed the campaign enough to know that LeBreaux had Louisiana connections, and since they were in New Orleans and heading to St. Marks, his spot on the news interested her. She watched intently. He spoke about Southern values and caring for his constituents.

Nice smile, she thought. His clean-cut look would get him lots of votes. This country could use someone like him.

***

Jason LeBreaux ripped the tie from around his neck and threw it on the arm of the hotel chair with his free hand while he held his cell phone to his ear with the other. He was tired, hot, and aggravated. He'd been on the campaign trail for days and now he had to put out another fire, a personal problem that should've been solved a long time ago.

"What do you mean all the paperwork isn't ready?" he spoke into the cell phone, his voice unable to hide his irritation. "You've been working on this project for the last six months. Now, either you get things ready for this auction or I'll find someone who can."

Jason listened to the man on the other end of the line.

His excuses were getting old and time was running out. He dug in the pocket of his pants for an antacid, but only found an empty wrapper. "Damn."

"Mr. LeBreaux, it's like I said all along. Your grandmother's family has had possession of the property since Reconstruction, but no one has ever traced the title. Why would they need to? It's never been sold. Someone in your family has been living there from one generation to the next."

"Yeah, well, someone somewhere along the line in the last one hundred and fifty years must have done something legally right. Go find the papers."

"Yes, sir," the words came through the receiver, but there was no resolve in them.

"Look, Lester. Everything has to be in order before that auction in a few weeks. I don't care who buys that piece of run-down crap or what they do with it. I want it out of my family's name before I officially announce my candidacy. There're too many nosy reporters out there to keep it out of the news for long."

"Yes, sir. I know those realtors down there have located several interested parties. One of them wants to tear down the house and sub-divide it. That would be a shame, but that buyer is the best of the prospects."

"Like I said, I don't care what happens to the property. I just don't want my name attached to it in any way."

"Yes, sir. I understand."

Jason didn't think the man really understood his problem, but he'd told him enough to make him know the importance of what he needed to do.

"And, Lester, don't go digging around on the grounds. If some excavation crew happens to find a few treasures, let them rejoice at their good fortune, but I don't want your goons out there creating a scene."

LeBreaux jammed his finger against the off button,

then stared out the window of the twenty-second floor. He wasn't even sure which city this hotel was in.

"Damn plantation," he said out loud. "I don't have enough to worry about without some dilapidated piece of crap coming back to haunt me."

His tie slid to the floor as he cursed his grandfather's land. His hands trembled. He stepped to the small bar and poured himself a straight shot of bourbon. After downing it, he poured another one then walked to the window and stared out at the lights of the city of New Orleans. Memories of staying with his grandparents at River Bend should've calmed him on his hectic campaign trail. Instead, thoughts of what happened there ate at his insides now as they'd done for the last twenty years.

He emptied his glass. Nothing good could come from that piece of land on the Mississippi River. It was a thorn in his side and he had to get it out of the family name.

Why didn't Grandmother Smyth just sell the damn place when Grandad died?

Chapter 7

Moss covered cypress trees jutted up out of black swamp water as Jewel looked out the window of Bryce's SUV. The ride from New Orleans to St. Marks had been quiet. Bryce wasn't very talkative and that suited Jewel just fine. Her mind was a tangle of cobwebs after another sleepless night.

The day had begun with beignets in the French Quarter at a sidewalk cafe, where rich, dark coffee *au lait* helped to get her eyes opened in the early morning hours. Sitting in the open-air restaurant, Jewel sipped her hot coffee and let Bryce do the talking because her brain hadn't quite connected with her vocal cords.

Her night in the hotel room had been anything but relaxing. Her thoughts had run the gamut. At first dreams of ghosts and dead soldiers ripped into her sleep. Staring into the black room, she sensed they were there with her, reaching out to her as Captain McDougle had done, touching her with airy hands. Even with Mr. Bourgeois telling her what she felt and seen was entirely possible, she still wasn't convinced that Captain McDougle's ghost was with her. But, even if his visit had been a dream, it had been so vivid she would never forget the feeling she had that night.

In her hotel room she'd torn herself out of the remnants of her nightmare and lay perfectly still, trying to calm her breathing. Her chest heaved and sounds of her gulping air filled the room. Flipping on the bedside lamp, she found a couple of aspirin in her purse and pushed aside the feeling that something was there with her.

Then when she thought she had the images of ghosts under control, she awoke in another sweat, but this time it wasn't a sweat caused from fear. Sensual and real, her body tingled remembering the arms of a tall man who crushed her against his hard body on the dance floor. In her dream, she had melted against him, swayed with him until they both glistened from their heat.

For what seemed like endless hours, she lay alone in her hotel room sweating and breathing hard again. As much as she hated to admit it, she wanted to be in Bryce's arms.

This morning as Bryce had cleared away the tray from their table, Jewel licked her lips to remove the last remnants of powdered sugar from the beignets and made a quick retreat to the car. The strong coffee had awakened her, but now she was nothing more than a fully alert bundle of nerves.

Now, a half hour into their trip, Bryce glanced away from the road. "You feeling better?"

She nodded. "Yes, I do now."

With his arm propped up on the sunny window, Bryce looked relaxed and content. "Good. I was beginning to wonder."

"Did it show that much?"

"Well, except for a few grunts about the beignets, I wouldn't call you the brilliant conversationalist this morning. I thought I was going to have to get one of those nice young waitresses to listen to the great stories I was telling."

She put her cup down and smiled. "I'm sorry. I really tried to listen, but I didn't sleep well last night."

"I know what you mean," he answered. "I guess seeing the medium on top of everything else that has happened didn't lend itself to a peaceful night's sleep."

Feeling your arms around my body on the dance floor didn't help either.

She kept that thought to herself. "Mr. Bourgois gave us a lot to think about, didn't he? I just wish he could've had something more concrete. I'm still as confused as I was before." Then she threw in, "And you know how I feel about the existence of ghosts."

Bryce glanced at Jewel. "Yes, I know, but after all you've been through, you have to think that something has to be real in all this."

"I haven't ruled it out, but I simply can't ignore everything I've learned and taught and believed in for all my career. It's not easy to throw it all out the window just because I *think* I've seen a ghost."

This time it was Bryce's turn to grunt. "I know," he said in a soft voice.

She watched him quietly concentrate on the road for the next few miles.

"I wonder if the plantation house is still standing." Her soft words were really thoughts spoken out loud, but Bryce heard and answered her.

"According to the records it is, but we'll know for sure in a couple of hours. If someone still lives there, maybe we can convince them to let us get in to see the place."

Pushing aside the turmoil of the existence of ghosts, Jewel nodded. Excitement bubbled in her chest. "It's hard to believe I'm finally going to see this home I've heard about for so long. I never tried before. I wanted to," she corrected herself, "but there always seemed to be something else more important to do. I guess nobody in the family wanted to go since it didn't belong to us anymore."

"I'm glad Mr. Bourgois convinced you to go. I have a feeling something there will help us understand what's going on with Captain McDougle."

Jewel only nodded. More than anything she wanted to find something that might help her make sense of all that she'd experienced in the last few days.

***

River's Bend Estate stood magnificently on a gentle slope overlooking the Mississippi River. The road to the estate followed the curve of the river and at one point the road offered an unobstructed glimpse of the home. Bryce slowed the car to a near-crawl for them to take in the view. From a distance the large Antebellum home still shouted power and wealth.

Jewel's breath caught in her throat. "It's lovely."

"That it is. Just as magnificent as any of the old mansions on the river."

"And it's exactly how I dreamed it would be."

Bryce reached across the seat and touched her hand in understanding, but said nothing. After a few minutes of quiet, he eased the car back onto the pavement.

The view of the house was lost to the curve in the road, but Jewel knew she would never forget the thrill of seeing the McDougle estate for the first time. Even if closer inspection showed that time had not been kind to the structure, she knew the view she'd just witnessed would be with her forever.

Shortly, two stone columns announced the entrance to the estate. Jewel's heart thumped against her chest, but her excitement turned to disappointment quickly. There, attached to the locked gate was a sign announcing a sealed bidding for the property and a possible auction of the contents of the home.

Jewel jerked her attention from the sign to Bryce. "What does that mean?"

Bryce stopped the car. "It means the owners are getting rid of the property, and they have a feeling whoever

Forever, My Love

buys it won't want the contents. Whoever they have in mind is probably planning to demolish the home."

"No way. That can't be." A helpless, sinking feeling struck Jewel. "Why would someone want to get rid of such a wonderful piece of history?"

"Progress, my dear. Progress."

"That's not progress." She ignored his attempt at humor. Her words poured out as fast as her heart was beating. "That's disregard for the past. That's an abomination of a family's heritage. That's. . ."

"Whoa, girl." Bryce reached out and touched her cheek. "We don't know for sure that it will be torn down. Let's keep our senses until we know something for sure. Maybe someone will buy it with an appreciation for that era."

Jewel looked back at the sign then up at the house. "You're right. I guess I'm more a bundle of nerves than I wanted to admit. Can we still go up to the house?" After a quick survey of the fence line, she looked at Bryce with a wicked grin. "We can crawl under the fence."

After his inspection of both the fence line and of Jewel, he scratched his chin. "Normally, I'd say no. I'm not into trespassing, but I think we have a valid reason." He opened the door. "Come on. I'm game if you are."

Tall grass and twisted vines grew along the once whitewashed fence. Large sections of the fence were down making it easy for the two of them to find a spot to enter the property.

Jewel stepped across a small ditch to get to the fence. Bryce stood close behind her and gave her a hand. "Thanks," she said over her shoulder.

"Be careful. I wouldn't be surprised to see a few snakes since we're this close to the river."

Jewel slowed her pace and fell into step with him, thankful that she hadn't decided to wear a pair of shorts. The khaki pants and tennis shoes and socks were perfect protection against the briars. She wouldn't even think about the snakes.

95

"Come over here." He nearly lifted her across a low spot in the lawn and held her to his side as they made their way to the gravel driveway. She tried to ignore the shot of electricity that heated her body where he touched her. Finally, as they got to shorter grass, he let her go. She breathed again.

"Wow. You'd think someone would have cut the grass if there's going to be an auction."

"You'd think, but again, the owners, who I'm supposing are still the Smyths, aren't interested in what people think of the yard. They're getting their money for other reasons."

A heavy weight settled around Jewel's heart. "You really think the home's going to be torn down, don't you?"

"I don't know, but the auction of the contents points in that direction."

"Looks like the historical society around here would step in and save a place like this," she grumbled under her breath.

"We may be wrong, you know. Then again, the house may not be worth saving. It could be beyond repair."

"I can't believe you'd say that. I thought any structure could be repaired. Look what you do with those forts."

"That's a different matter. Working with brick and working with rotten boards are two different animals all together. The place may be eaten up with termites."

Jewel grunted again and tramped along the grassy drive, refusing to believe the worse, but the closer they got to the house, the more evidence of neglect and lack of repair stood out. The few remaining shutters barely hung on their hinges. The others lay half-buried in the tall weeds along the house.

The exterior was in dire need of paint, and the wood along the outside of the home as well as the porch was rotted out in places.

Jewel stopped. "This is so sad. I just can't believe this is happening."

"Don't get too upset yet. Come on. Let's try to get in."

Jewel's spirits lifted.

Bryce helped her up onto the long expanse of the front porch. Even in its desperate state of ill repair, the stately columns of the Greek Revival period and tall front entrance still stood proud. Jewel saw beyond the rot to a time when this entrance greeted ladies in long, ruffled gowns and men in properly tailored suits. She could almost see the richly upholstered carriages with their fine horses pulling up to the steps for afternoon tea or for a weekend ball.

She stopped on the porch. "If I tell you something, will you promise not to laugh?"

Nodding, he looked as if he fought to keep back a smile.

"I feel as if I've lived here all my life. I feel as if I know this house." Sharing that feeling should've flushed her face with embarrassment. Instead, when she looked up to Bryce, his eyes told her he understood. "Thank you."

"For what?"

"For not laughing."

He smiled and touched her shoulders. "I wouldn't think of laughing, not after what I've told you. Anyway, you belong in a place like this. It suits you."

She turned. "Look at that river." There from the elevated porch was an unobstructed view of the river in the distance. "It must be magnificent in the spring when the azaleas are blooming. Look at the camellias. They'll be in bloom soon. Oh, can you believe the beauty of this place?"

Bryce put his arm around her and gently pulled her to him. "It's a piece of heaven, isn't it?"

With her back leaning against him, she nodded and rested her head against his chest. A feeling she had never experienced before wrapped around her. Closing her eyes, she imagined the chatter of plantation workers and children playing. She smelled the blooming bushes and freshly tilled soil, and heard the shrill whistle of a riverboat as it churned along the water with its cargo of cotton, lumber, and passengers going up the river to Vicksburg or even onto Memphis. She could almost see them standing against the white railing waving to the plantations workers along the river's banks.

"You ready to see if we can get into this house?"

Bryce's words brought her back into the present. As he removed his arms from around her body, Jewel felt disoriented and off-balanced. She stood still and watched Bryce jiggle the huge door handle.

He turned to look at her with a grin on his face. "That was silly to think the door would be left unlocked."

On the front door was another sign announcing the sealed-bid auction in three weeks. Bryce tried in vain to pry open three of the tall front windows, but on the fourth try, the window budged.

"Lady Luck is with us today. Come, my lady. Would you like to enter my mansion?"

She'd stood quietly as Bryce tried to find an entrance, but now she wasted no time in letting him help her through the window. Once inside, she stopped to find her breath.

Standing in a nearly bare room that must've once been a parlor, her heart pounded and her blood ran warm as a feeling of coming home washed over her.

"This is just unbelievable." She wrapped her arms across her chest and closed her eyes. "I can't believe I'm actually standing in Ula and Hilliard's house."

"Yes, ma'am, you are." Bryce walked over to a large, intricately carved sideboard that shone from a recent polishing. Jewel walked up alongside of Bryce and picked up a small card with the auctioneer's name and the description of the item.

Bryce looked at the card over her shoulder. "Someone's taken time to do a little research. They're pretty serious about selling the contents. Not a good sign. I'm going into the other room. Don't wander too far alone and watch your step."

Bryce stepped past her, leaving her alone with her thoughts. She ran her hand along the surface of the sideboard, wondering how many times Captain McDougle had used this piece to entertain his gentlemen guests after a late night meal. Handsomely clad men in black frockcoats and linen shirts would have stood in this parlor, puffed their cigars, and sipped brandy from crystal decanters strategically placed on this sideboard. Again she ran her hand across the smooth mahogany top, then let her fingers follow the intricate carvings along its side.

Closing her eyes, she heard the clinking of crystal and smelled the sweet aroma of aged whiskey. Jumbled words and snippets of conversations about cotton prices, lack of rain, and a possible war came in and out of her consciousness. Acrid cigar smoke and strong cologne stung her nostrils. Deep laughter and throaty words filled her ears.

In the background the shrill screams of children running past the open windows reminded her this was a family gathering and that she should still be in the dining area sipping tea, not here with the men in the parlor.

"Jewel, come in here."

Jewel opened her eyes and blinked, her hand still on the sidebar.

"Jewel? You hear me?" Bryce stuck his head into the parlor. "You've got to see this. You're not going to believe it."

Jewel nodded and put down the card she still held in one of her hands. "I'm coming."

She stepped away from the massive piece of furniture and looked around the room, knowing no one else shared the room with her. She'd been alone, but the presence of Hilliard's male guests had felt real to her.

Bryce stepped into the room. "Cross the hall with me. This is unbelievable." He took her hand, his face animated with excitement.

"Right now I'd believe anything."

Bryce glanced at her. "Did something happen?"

Fran McNabb

She smiled. "I'll explain later."

They entered a large hallway that ran almost the entire length of the house. Quickly she took in the high ceilings with its ornate frieze and the several large pieces of furniture. It was hard to pass any of it by without examining it, but Bryce didn't slow down.

"In here," he said as he led her into another room directly across from the parlor.

As she crossed the threshold, her breath caught in her throat. There, hanging over a large dining room set was a magnificent painting of a woman. Jewel knew instantly that the woman was Ula McDougle, but accept for the blonde hair, everything about the woman in the painting was a mirror image of herself. Her breath hitched. She took a step closer to examine the woman whom she'd heard stories about for her entire life.

The eyes were her greenish-blue eyes. The full lips. The small straight nose. Even the quirky smile. The portrait of Ula McDougle could've been her.

"How can that be possible? It's me with blonde hair."

Bryce put his arms around her. "It's uncanny, isn't it?"

He turned her around to face him. "I know you're not convinced you didn't just dream McDougle coming to you in the fort, but consider this. Obviously you look just like Ula did when she and Hilliard were married. If it was his spirit that came to you, maybe he thought he was seeing his wife. Maybe he saw Ula and not you in the fort."

Jewel didn't have a reply. She turned back to the portrait. "This is really freaky. After all these years, her genes have surfaced in me."

"Not just hers, but his as well. You're the spitting image of her with McDougle's red hair. It's amazing."

"It's spooky."

Bryce didn't answer.

Jewel faced him again. "This is the time when a little

reassurance wouldn't hurt. You're supposed to say it's just a coincident. That these things happen in science. That it's not spooky at all." She gulped a breath of air. "Uh, you're not helping me out here by keeping quiet."

He raised an eyebrow. His voice was flat, monotone. "These things happen in science. It's just a coincidence."

"Oh, hush," she said playfully. "That doesn't help."

His voice got serious. "These things really do happen. Genes appear all the time in people that can't be traced to anyone in their immediate family, but if they go back, they find a long lost relative with that trait. It really does happen."

Jewel looked back up at the picture and swallowed. "I'm the one who should be explaining that stuff to you. I work with things like this all the time, but when it's your genes, then it gets weird." She looked back up at Ula McDougle. "I'm her twin. That could be me up there."

Bryce stooped down and picked up the auctioneer's card that had fallen onto to floor. "They don't even name her. The picture is simply called, The Planter's Wife."

Jewel stared at the card. "How sad. If they had checked, someone could have found her name. What kind of price do you think the portrait will bring?"

"I have no idea. That frame has to be worth a pretty penny. Looks like real gold leafing on it. I'm surprised it's still here after all these years, especially now that the house is pretty much abandoned." He looked at her. "But you know what? That portrait shouldn't be taken out of your family. We won't let anyone outbid us if it comes to an actual bid."

Jewel fought back a lump that threatened to break forth into sobs of joy, something that had been building inside of her since she saw the mansion sitting on the hill. Without thinking, she threw her arms around Bryce's neck. "Thank you. Thank you. I don't know how much money we're talking about here, but I have some money saved and

I could probably dip into my trust. If not and if you have to help me get it, I swear you'll get it back."

He turned into her and pulled her to him. His gaze burned into her brain. A thousand sparks shot through her body as he lowered his head and placed his lips on hers, gently at first, then crushing his mouth on hers.

Her brain reeled. The heat of his kiss shot through her body. Instinctively her body stiffened. Her hand went up against his chest to ward him off, but she realized she wasn't pushing at all. Instead, she leaned into his embrace, shifted her hand to cup his neck and opened her lips to accept him.

Her head spun as she felt his body hardened against her. She met his ravenous kisses with an insatiable hunger of her own. For a moment, she was his and the ugly world of rejection and deception and loneliness didn't exist. Being in this man's arms lifted her beyond the crusted barrier that she'd built for protection. For the moment, she soared above that need, and had he taken her down to the floor to make love to her, she would not have resisted.

Instead, he moved his lips from hers and cradled her head against his chest. His chest heaved with agitated breaths. His heart pounded against her ears, and as she lay against his body, the realization of what she was about to do hit her.

"You okay?" he asked in a whisper.

She nodded a lie.

"I'm not going to say I'm sorry I did that, but I am going to say I'm sorry that I stopped."

Jewel pulled away and looked into his darkened gray eyes. "I'm glad you did."

"I don't think you are. If you're honest with yourself, you'd see you wanted us to continue. You enjoyed it as much as I did."

She ignored that last statement. "This is not what we need to be doing. I'm sorry I lost control." She pulled away and turned from him.

He reached out and pulled her around. "Why? Do you think because David hurt you, all men are like him?"

"It's not that simple."

"Sure it is," Bryce said, let her go. "I know exactly how you see me. I'm a predator just like David. I'll take advantage of you like David. I'll use you."

"No, you have it all wrong."

"Do I, Jewel? I think that's exactly how you see me and all men right now, and maybe it's the only way you can see men right now. Maybe the time isn't right for you to let yourself trust another man."

Jewel turned away again. His words hit home, but listening to him say it, she wanted to protest, to scream he had her all wrong, but she knew she couldn't. She didn't trust him or anyone else right now. Maybe she never would again.

She started to walk away. This time he simply placed a hand on her shoulder. "Don't walk away from me. You ought to know I won't force myself on you. I'd never do that to you or to any lady, and if I said too much to make you uncomfortable, I'm sorry."

Jewel stood perfectly still fighting back tears of frustration, not from what he had done, but for how she had reacted. He deserved better.

"I'm okay," she said softly. "I'm still just a bundle of nerves from everything that's happened. I really do trust you, or I wouldn't be here alone with you."

"Well, good, I'm glad that's settled." He changed the subject abruptly. "You snoop around a bit and I'm going out on the porch." He pulled out his cell phone. "I need to check in with my office. I do have an unfinished fort sitting out there in the Gulf of Mexico."

He left her standing alone beneath the portrait of Ula McDougle. Looking up, she felt an immediate connection with the woman on the wall. How many happy marriages had been cut short because of a war? Jewel empathized with her, and felt her sorrow at the loss of her husband.

Ula looked fragile in the portrait. The painter had captured the fine lines in her face, the delicate bone structure, and the aura of sophistication, but Jewel knew that to survive the ordeal of the war, she had to be a strong woman. Maybe she had been a fragile young Southern belle at the beginning of the war, but like everything else around her, she would have had to change. Obviously she lived long enough through the war and the hardships to raise a child, a continuation of the line of McDougle descendants.

Jewel continued to stare at the portrait until her eyes closed, shutting out the dim light that filtered through the floor-to-ceiling draperies. A heavy weight consumed her body. Her body became fluid. Her mind swirled with a sense of reaching out, communicating, touching the woman on the wall, but no words were communicated, no message passed on, just a feeling that something needed to be said or done. She felt it swirling around her, calling to her, but she was helpless to respond.

Her head rolled from side to side. Her eyelids clamped together, too heavy to control, but Jewel didn't let go entirely. She grasped a thin string, barely holding her consciousness together. She refused to fall completely under the spell that weighted her down and took her breath away.

The intense feeling of misery and heartbreak that gripped her now was the same sensation that terrorized her the night that Captain McDougle came to her.

She wanted to cry, to scream, to tear herself away from the sensation, but her body was immobile.

Ula McDougle was there with her.

"Jewel?"

Bryce's voice seeped through the heavy fog in her head. His hands held onto both of her arms.

"Jewel, it's me, Bryce. Wake up. It's okay." His words came in and out of the fog. "Lean against me. It's okay. Open your eyes."

She struggled into consciousness, opened her eyes and grabbed Bryce's arm.

"It's okay. You were swaying. I thought you might collapse."

She found her voice. "It happened again."

He pressed her against his. "I know. Just lean against me. Take your time."

Fresh air cleared her head as she focused on Bryce's face. "That horrible sadness came back to me just like in the fort. Total despair," she whispered.

Jewel rested against his chest, savoring the comfort and safety of his arms. "It was as if Ula was trying to tell me something. I felt her. I felt her sadness. Is that possible?"

Bryce shook his head. "I don't know for sure, but we know something's happening. It's too real to ignore. One of their spirits—or maybe both of them—is trying to communicate with you."

Frustration tore at her heart. "I want to believe it. I do. If she needs me to help her do something, I want to help, but what? What do they want? What can I do? I can't help them if I don't know what they want—or if I'm just losing my mind or dreaming all this."

Bryce humped. "You're not losing your mind, Jewel. Something real is happening to you."

"Spirits or whatever it is are not real."

Again he humped. "We'll see." He took a deep breath. "We'll figure this out. I think our next step should be to go back to the medium. The auction doesn't take place for three more weeks if there really is one. We have time to make a quick stop in New Orleans, then I need to go back to the fort before I lose my company."

Jewel nodded. "I have to get back to my campus. I can meet you back here in three weeks."

"That'll work, but I hate for you to leave." He smiled and touched her face. "I'm getting used to having you around."

A few days ago she was trying to escape the island. Now she was thrilled he enjoyed her company.

What a difference a few days made.

"Thanks for saying that. I kind of like being around you too."

Jewel looked back up at the portrait. "It's so sad. For all these years, Ula and Hilliard have just been a story of lovers caught up in a war. Now they're so much more than that to me. They were living and feeling beings, just like you and I are."

"Sometimes it's easy to forget that people who lived before us actually lived at all. You know. Went to school. Made a living. Fell in love. Hurt, cried, felt pain, but they all did. The more time I spend in the old forts, the more I've come to understand that."

Jewel sighed. "I almost feel as though we shouldn't leave her here all alone."

With his hands on his hips and his legs spread apart, Bryce looked from the portrait to Jewel and shook his head. "I'm not hauling that monstrous portrait out to the car and risk getting my butt thrown in jail. Trespassing is one thing, but breaking and entering along with theft is another. No, Mrs. McDougle has been up on that wall for a hundred and fifty years. A few more weeks won't make a difference."

"Now that you've put it that way, I guess you're right, but still it doesn't seem right."

"What's right is for us to crawl back through that window and leave before we have the local police crawling all over."

She laughed. "Can't you just see the headlines: Civil War ghost responsible for mansion break-in. Think the authorities would buy it?"

He took her hand. "Let's not find out. Come on."

Jewel followed him out the window, but once they got on the porch, she looked out at the river. "Can we walk down by the river?"

Bryce frowned. "I don't think that's such a good idea."

She touched his arm. "Please. I swear we'll be careful."

He kissed her lightly on the lips. "Okay, but don't get carried away."

"Promise. Come on."

Together they made their way through the tall grass of the lawn and around azalea and camellia bushes that had not been trimmed in years.

"We need our heads examined," Bryce said as he helped her across a large tree limb.

"Maybe, but you know you want to see the river up close as well as I do."

He groaned, but kept going. Before long, they were standing hand in hand just a few feet from the side of a natural levee that dropped down at least ten feet to the muddy water below.

"Wow, that's amazing," Jewel said as she watched the water swirl around a bend a short ways from them. "I can see why Hilliard called it River's Bend. According to what I saw when I did some research years ago, there are several bends and turns surrounding the western and the southern part of the property."

She looked toward the north where the bank seemed to get lower to the water and ran in a straighter line. "What's that?" She pointed to a dark indention about thirty yards away from them.

"I'm not sure but it could be a cave. I've read that a lot of these old plantations had natural caves along the river. They were used for everything from storage of crops waiting for the riverboats to pick them up to storing illegally gained property waiting for the right time to be sent up the river."

"Really? I've never heard of that."

"Oh yes. Not everyone fit the description of the noble

plantation owner. Lots of money was gotten from illegal activities back then just as it's done today."

"Well, I hope the McDougle family used their caves for their crops and not for anything else."

"I guess we'll never know."

"I don't guess you'd want to check the caves out, would you?"

Bryce chuckled. "Oh no. We're already trespassing. I don't want to have to call for help when one of us gets caught in one of those caves."

"Killjoy!" Jewel jokingly shoved him, but turned to head back to the car. She, too, understood the issue of safety.

She heard him take a big breath. "When we come back for the auction, we'll see if we can drive closer to one of the caves and do a little exploring. Might be interesting to check one out."

They walked across the lawn together. Jewel took one last look at the home and knew that her connection to this property was deeper than she ever imagined.

Jewel Ferguson had never given much thought to destiny, but standing on the lawn of River's Bend, she had the feeling this is where she was destined to be.

***

Lester threw down his cigarette and pulled in a deep breath. "That was close."

His friend who was hauling in the last box spit on the cave's packed down sand where he'd been walking. "They wouldn't have come down here."

"Yeah? Who says? That woman was staring in this direction. I have a feeling she'll be back."

The other guy shoved the last box against a back wall. "I know it's summer, but it's hot as hell down here."

Lester ignored him. "Get your stuff. Don't leave

anything out in the open. We only have to store this stuff for a couple of weeks. I have a buyer and we'll do the last transaction in time to clear all this out before the sale of this place."

"I can't believe the old woman is selling it. Where will we keep our stuff now?"

"I don't know, but I can't think right now. First things first. We'll sell this load. Clean up the place and never look back."

"Why does LeBreaux want to get rid of this land?"

"I guess he's scared some reporter will turn up his grandpa's past. I can't see where something his granddad and great-granddad did years ago could hurt his campaign, but he's running scared. So, I guess we'll say tallyho to our perfect little hole in the side of riverbank." He looked around. "Let's get out of here. I don't want to be caught with this stuff."

Chapter 8

Bryce drove around a crowded New Orleans block twice before finding a parking spot near enough to walk to Mr. Bourgois's house. Narrow one-and-two-story houses with their ornate wrought iron railings and wide front porches snuggled close to the crowded street. With almost no front yards, many of their second story balconies seemed to teeter over the pavement itself.

Mr. Bourgois's house was no different. The heavy gate opened into an almost non-existent front yard filled with overgrown flower gardens and shrubs. The three stone steps up to the porch, deeply grooved from years of wear, offered only a narrow footpath through an array of petunia-filled pots and concrete yard art. A small wood-carved sign hung near the leaded-glass door: Louis Bourgois, Clairvoyant and Medium.

The door flew open on the first ring. "Hello, again. I've been expecting you two. Come in. Come in." Mr. Bourgois stood with outstretched arms and welcomed Jewel and Bryce into his home.

Jewel smiled to herself. The yard, the house, the neighborhood—all fit the small, dark-complexioned man.

"Have a seat. I'll have my wife bring us a small toddy. Is that okay with you?" He directed his question to Jewel.

"That would be nice, thank you."

He led them into the formal parlor cluttered with every imaginable ceramic piece and ornate lamps. "Have a seat and let me call my Cerise."

Jewel sat stiffly on a satin taffeta couch with tiny legs and a curved high back and felt as tightly strung as Mr. Bourgois's old harp that stood jammed into a corner. What was she doing here and what would her colleagues in the science department say if they knew she'd turned her back on scientific theories that had come down to them through generations.

She wanted to spring up and run. As if Bryce knew what she was thinking, he sat next to her and placed his hand on her thigh. With a wink in her direction, she breathed easier and let her muscles relax.

"It's okay, Jewel. We'll listen to what he says again, and if you're not comfortable with his suggestions, we'll leave."

She nodded and smiled. "Thank you."

Mr. Bourgois stuck his head into the hallway, jabbered something in French, then came back into the room and plopped down in a wing-backed chair across from them. "Let's see now. According to your phone call, you got into the family estate and found a portrait of Captain McDougle's wife. Is that right?"

Bryce spoke up. "Yes, and as I told you on the phone, the portrait is a duplicate of Jewel except for her red hair. While we viewed the painting, Jewel had another experience similar to the two she had on the island."

Unable to contain his excitement, Mr. Bourgois ran a small, dark hand through his black hair and shifted several times in the chair. "I don't doubt it. There's a lot going on here."

A diminutive, gray-haired lady carrying a tray of refreshments entered the room and welcomed them with a nod.

"Just put the tray here, dear. This is the couple I told you about."

Fran McNabb

"I'm glad to meet you. I wasn't here when you visited my Louie earlier in the week." She smiled, graciously extended her hand to them, then quietly excused herself.

"Where were we?" Mr. Bourgois continued. "Oh yes, I was saying I'm not surprised by your physical reaction to the fort, the appearance of the ghost, and the portrait. It's not uncommon for something like this to happen when there's a connection that is so obvious."

"Obvious?" Jewel asked.

"Here, here, have a drink and a little tart. My wife makes excellent pastries." He reached over and took one for himself and waited for Jewel and Bryce to do the same.

Jewel wasn't hungry and didn't want to waste time eating and being social, but she took one to be polite. She took the drink eagerly. She was afraid she'd need it by the start of Mr. Bourgois's conversation.

Taking a bite into the flaky crust, she tasted a most scrumptious blackberry filling. "Ummm, this really is good. Thank you."

"Oh, Cerise makes the best little tarts in the French Quarter. We used to run a small bakery until her arthritis made her quit. She still bakes for me though." He took another bite and a big drink. "Now back to your story. Jewel, did you know that you have the same name as Captain McDougle's wife?"

"Not really. My name is Jewel and her name is Ula."

"Oh yes, I'm quite aware of that. Have you never looked up the origin of her name?"

"No. I studied Celtic literature and it's a common name. I know in the Celtic translation it generally refers to gems."

Before Jewel could say more, Mr. Bourgois spoke up. "You're right. Gems. Jewels."

Jewel's breath caught in her throat. "Jewel. Of course."

"Yes. The name Ula actually means 'Jewel of the

112

Sea.' You see, don't you, that I think we have here more than just a coincidence." His black eyes sparkled.

Bryce sat up straight. "Explain coincidence. You're not referring to reincarnation or something?"

"No, not exactly. I really don't believe in reincarnation, though I do believe a lost soul, a spirit, or a ghost as we commonly call them, can use a person still on earth as a vehicle to reach another soul. Use them for a purpose to allow their loved one to continue on their journey into the afterlife."

Bryce took Jewel's hand. "Use her for what?"

"Ula and Hilliard need to make a connection. Possibly this is the right time and the right person for Ula to use."

"Destiny?" asked Bryce. "Do you think Jewel's been destined to be this vehicle?"

Mr. Bourgois took a big bite of tart and washed it down with his drink. "Again, destiny is a concept that is not easy to explain or accept. I like to think about it as an opportunity that has come along in our century in the person of Jewel."

Jewel had been sitting quietly, listening to the two men talk about her as if she were a wire in a telephone system, but she was beginning to get the picture. She swallowed and found her voice. "You think Ula wants me to contact Hilliard for her?"

Mr. Bourgois tilted his head and shrugged his shoulder. "It's certainly been done before. I can pull out my books and show you incidents where people in your situation actually were used as conduits for the spirit of a dead loved one."

Bryce and Jewel looked at each other. Jewel swallowed and had the urge to run from the room. Bryce squeezed her hand, and she let the moment of panic pass.

"I don't know that I actually understand any of this, but if that's what you think is happening here, what should we do next?" she asked as she unconsciously leaned into

Bryce's body. He responded by putting his arm around her shoulders.

"Ever sat through a séance?" Mr. Bourgois asked.

Both shook their heads.

"It's not difficult to set up. I think it's our best bet. Possibly making contact with one of the spirits will give you an idea of the next step to follow."

A shiver shook Jewel's body uncontrollably. Bryce pulled her closer to him. "Today?" he asked.

"That's possible. If you have time, we could set it up now. Sometimes it takes several sessions to actually make contact. Sometimes we do it on the first try. Sometimes, it never happens, but it isn't because we didn't give it our best shot." His face wrinkled into a big smile revealing two shiny gold teeth.

Bryce turned to Jewel. "Are you game?"

Emotions collided within her chest. "I'm not sure, but I don't know what else to do." She looked at Mr. Bourgois. "Is it safe?"

"Oh, yes. The contact is usually made through the medium and we simply relay the information we learn. Sometimes, though, the sitters with the medium feel the presence in one way or another. I've seen all sorts of things happen. Since it's happened before with you, you might have another spell of some sort. But back to your question. I see no reason why you shouldn't be safe."

Jewel sat up straight on the couch. "I'm a little anxious. I want to find out what Ula wants to communicate to Hilliard or visa versa, if that's what's going on here, but, I have to tell you, I'm still not sure I believe in all this."

Mr. Bourgois squinted. "If you don't believe, my dear, nothing will happen. You must give me your full and undivided attention and consent or nothing will take place."

Bryce turned her around to face him. "You don't have to do anything you're not comfortable with, but it's like you said, we have no other recourse. Do you need a few minutes to pull your thoughts together and see if you can go along with this séance?"

Jewel could tell Mr. Bourgois and Bryce were a little put out by her lack of faith, but how could she put aside everything on which she'd believed in and based her entire career?

She turned her attention to Mr. Bourgois. "How will we know if we've done the right thing?"

Mr. Bourgois' face lit up, then he shrugged. "The apparition will simply disappear and not be seen again. That's what this is all about. Getting the spirit of the person to continue on his journey to what we call the Other Side or maybe doing something that will ease one of the spirits. We really don't know what's going on with your couple, but something has one of them irritated."

Both Bryce and Jewel nodded to themselves.

Jewel was afraid she was making a terrible mistake, but she couldn't turn her back on all that had happened to her since she'd entered the fort. She had to try.

"I'm ready," she said.

"Splendid. " Mr. Bourgois jumped up. "You two sit here and pour yourself another toddy from the bar if you'd like. I'll go get my wife. We need another sitter. She's good. She's done this so much with me, her presence and state of mind helps me make contact sometimes. Sometimes I wonder if she's not the clairvoyant and not me." Mr. Bourgois danced across the room and out the door.

Bryce took Jewel's hand again. "You sure you're okay with all this?"

"I think so. It's a little scary, but I don't see where we have any other choice. I can't just walk away, can I?"

"No, and I can't walk away either. That's why I searched for you. Feeling a presence that night with Marcus was all it took to make me find out what was happening. I have to agree with Mr. Bourgois. All of this couldn't have just been coincidental. I'm not into all this destiny stuff either, but I think it's what Captain McDougle and maybe his wife wants us to do."

Jewel groaned, reached over and tipped her glass up.

***

There's a time when you have to put your trust in someone else. Let that person guide you and even control you if that's what it takes, and Jewel decided tonight was one of those times—or at least she'd give it her best shot in trying.

After the experience with David, Jewel had sworn never to let herself lose control over her life again. Never to let anyone lead her away from her own will, but sitting down at Mr. Bourgois's table she knew she had to let herself go or nothing would happen. She'd read enough about a séance to understand that the mind had to be willing to cooperate with the medium for contact to be made with the other world, and hers was as willing as she guessed it could ever get.

Bryce squeezed her hand again and smiled at her. "You're going to do fine."

His whispered encouragement gave her a bit of courage, even though she was sure she was going to need a lot of that encouragement to get through this evening. Inhaling deeply, she closed her eyes and hoped for the best.

They followed Mr. Bourgois and his wife into a smaller room, and doing as she was told, she placed her hands palm down on the table with Bryce's spread on top of one of hers. Comforting, she thought to herself. Her other hand was covered by Mr. Bourgois's. Mrs. Bourgois sat between her husband and Bryce and held both of their hands.

After a quiet prayer, Mr. Bourgois asked Bryce, then Cerise if each was prepared to let him contact the spirit of Captain McDougle. When he faced her, Jewel nodded and squeezed her eyes tightly. "Yes," she whispered.

With soft music playing in the background, lights

dimmed to almost nonexistent and several candles lit around the room, for effect Jewel guessed, she relaxed. At first she tried to follow what Mr. Bourgois chanted. Listened to his words. Watched as his eyes closed and his head rolled from side to side.

Soon, though, without realizing it, her eyes closed also and her head bent forward. His indistinguishable mumbles came and went through a thick fog in her head.

Consciously she tried to lift herself above what was happening to her. The medium was supposed to go into a trance, not her. He communicated with the spirits. That was the plan, but as she fought for control, her consciousness began to slip away. For a fleeting second before succumbing to the pull, she was aware that she couldn't stop it and really didn't want to.

"Jewel, wake up." Soft words came to her. They were Bryce's words. His deep voice. His warm breath against her cheek. She wanted to hang on to the words that he spoke, but they came and went like the blinking of a neon sign. Sometimes bright. Sometimes flickering. "Mr. Bourgois said it was okay to wake up. You're with us now."

His hand cupped her neck, massaged it, comforted her with it. "Come on, Jewel. Wake up."

Ever so slowly she fought the weight that closed her lids. She blinked. Bryce leaned in front of her, his smile trying to disguise the worry in his eyes. She grabbed for him and he hugged her close.

"It's okay," he said with warm lips against her ear. "You're okay."

Never had she wanted so strongly for anyone to hold her. Bryce's warmth flowed into her. His strength energized her. She snuggled against his hard chest and clutched his shirt with both of her hands. Finally, her mind cleared. "What happened?" she asked.

Mr. Bourgois offered her a glass of wine. "Here. I'm sure you need this."

Pulling away from Bryce, she took the glass with a shaky hand. Sipped it at first, then took a big gulp.

"I have a feeling our little séance worked, even though I wasn't the one who achieved contact," Mr. Bourgois said. "Please tell us what you experienced."

Jewel dropped her gaze to the table. "I'm not sure I can."

She struggled to remember, to pull the images back into her brain, to see and feel what she had just been through, but to no avail. "I know I wasn't here. I was somewhere else, some other time, but I don't know where or when." Her brow tightened in frustration. "I feel it. I know I was somewhere other than here, but I can't remember."

"It's okay. Don't push yourself. It'll come back to you, but it might not come back tonight." Mr. Bourgois pulled out a large white handkerchief and wiped his face. "Sometimes the mind has a hard time dealing with matters like this," he said to Bryce and her, "especially if we don't have a total believer. You might remember something tomorrow or it might take a month, but it'll come back to you. I have a feeling that you were with Ula or Hilliard." His tiny dark eyes sparkled with delight. "I felt a presence, but I'm not sure whose. I think I must've felt them contacting you."

Jewel leaned into Bryce. "I can't think at all."

Mr. Bourgois touched her shoulder. "That's normal. Don't let it upset you. You'll be just fine." Then to Bryce he said. "Are you staying in the city tonight?"

"We don't have rooms yet, but I'm sure in the middle of the week, I can find us something."

"Good. If you think she needs to see me any time, even if it's in the middle of the night, don't hesitate to call."

Bryce lifted her head with his hand. "You feel like leaving now or do you need to lie down a little?"

"No, I'll be okay." She smiled at him then at Mr.

Bourgois. "Thank you for helping us. I hope I can remember something. I feel so strange not remembering, yet knowing that something happened."

Bryce paid Mr. Bourgois, then said his goodbyes.

The little man stood up, stretched his back and put his arm around his wife. "Take your time. It'll come back to you."

***

Jewel sat in the plush lounge chair in the hotel suite. It had taken inquiries at two hotels before Bryce found one with an available room. Conventions had the town booked up.

Bryce stood at the door paying for room service, making small talk with the young man in a stiff white uniform. In comparison, Bryce's loose T-shirt and shorts couldn't hide his beautiful body with which she was becoming more and more comfortable. He looked cool, relaxed and in total control.

That cool control both scared and enticed her, but that conflict of feelings was too much for her to think about at the moment. After taking a shower, she had donned the hotel's terry robe and snuggled into a huge overstuffed chair. Since leaving Mr. Bourgois's house, she tried to act normal, but her mind was still spinning at light speed.

She hadn't put up a fuss when Bryce told her there had only been one room available, a suite with a nice couch that he'd use. "That's fine," she remembered saying dumbly. How could she argue? She couldn't even sit up straight.

"Hope you're hungry," he said as he rolled the tray in front of her. "I wasn't sure what you wanted, so I think they brought one of everything on the menu."

Raising her head, she smiled at the tray piled high with covered dishes. "Thank you, Bryce. You're quite a host."

He bowed from the waist. "At your service, my dear."

She laughed at his antics, uncurling her legs and stretching. What she really felt like doing was crawling under the covers in the bed and sleeping for days.

The aroma of onion soup wafted up to her. "Umm," she said. "I think maybe I am hungry." She lifted the spoon and let the rich brown broth excite her taste buds. "This is really good."

Bryce took a bite. "You're right. I'm glad. I've never stayed here so I didn't know what the food was like."

"Well, by the looks of the room and the furnishings, nothing is done cheaply here. I feel as though I ought to offer to pay half of this."

"Don't be silly. I'm the one who dragged you out to an island then all over the Gulf Coast. This is my treat."

She didn't have the energy to argue.

They finished their meal with quiet conversation. After pushing the tray filled with dirty dishes into the hallway, he walked toward her. "I'm going out on the balcony. Want to come along?"

Jewel looked at the bed longingly, but got up and followed him out onto a small deck overlooking one of the back streets of New Orleans. High enough away from the dirt and noise and danger below, the two of them relaxed on comfortable outside furniture surrounded by live tropical plants. The air was heavy, but warm and pleasant. An occasional distant horn broke the silence.

Bryce stood up and leaned up against the railing. "This has been quite a day, hasn't it?"

"I'd say quite a few days."

"Yeah, I guess so." His steady gaze burned into her flesh.

Jewel shifted. "I don't get a lot of excitement in my academic world at the university. This has been, shall I say, unusual?"

"I'd agree, unusual even for me, and I have lots of excitement with my job. I think you've handled it well though."

"Oh, yeah," she commented, then laughed. "I nearly passed out four times already and I've been with you less than a week. I don't know if I'd classify that as handling a situation well."

"This isn't any ordinary situation, Jewel. I really don't know that you have much control over what's happening to you. I think our two lovers are playing havoc with your mind and body until you do whatever it is that they want you to do."

She pulled her robe tight across her chest. "If that's what it is, I wish I knew what they wanted because I'm tired of going wimpy on everyone."

At that Bryce laughed. "I wouldn't call it wimpy."

"I would. I'm not a fragile petunia, weeping and passing out. That's not like me."

He grinned. "I didn't think it was."

The crooked smile took her off guard. She blamed the sultry Southern night, not the fact that Bryce looked sexier than any man should having been through what they'd been through today.

"I'd better go in before I fall asleep out here."

"Humph. If I didn't know better, I'd say you think I'm boring company."

"No, no. I'm just exhausted." *Too exhausted to fight the urge to throw myself in your arms and ...* oh, gosh she needed sleep.

"I know you are," he said. "Come on. Let's get you to bed."

Putting his arm around her shoulder, he helped her back into the hotel room.

With her energy level slipping away by the minute, leaning into him was the most natural thing for her to do. The security of his arm around her and the warmth of his chest against her cheek were just too much to fight.

Natural wasn't such a bad thing.

***

Visions of horses and riders, guns and noise swirled around in Jewel's head. Claps of thunder overhead and the rumble of horses' hooves intermingled in an inseparable roar. She jerked her head from side to side on the sweat-dampened pillow.

For one moment, the claps of thunder shook the windows in the New Orleans hotel where Jewel lay in her bed, but the next clap scared the two matched grays and nearly toppled the carriage on which a Confederate officer and a woman sat. Confusion scattered any meaningful thoughts.

Then it happened. Jewel no longer lay in the bed watching the scene play out in her mind. Instead, she felt the cushioned seat of the carriage beneath her and the first cold drops of rain fall from the black clouds above. She was no longer Jewel Ferguson, science professor, but Ula McDougle, pregnant wife of Captain Hilliard McDougle.

Terror. Sheer terror tore at her heart as Ula watched her Confederate husband reach for his rifle. Panic seized her. She grabbed his arm. "No, they'll kill you," she screamed.

For a split second Hilliard's green eyes bore into hers. Love and sorrow poured into her heart. She wanted to beg him to stop. Drop the rifle. Surrender if necessary, but just live. More than anything, she wanted him to live. Think of our baby. The child needs a father. I need a husband. I need you. Her silent pleas stuck in her throat, threatened to cut the air to her brain as she looked from her husband to the wall of blue coats.

Captain McDougle lifted the rifle to his shoulder, but before he could pull the trigger, gunfire exploded in front of her. Blinding white light. Ear-shattering blasts.

She screamed and her screams blended with his, filling the evening air and becoming one with the thunder overhead.

As if in slow motion, her husband's body jolted back against the seat then rolled off the carriage seat and onto the dirt road below. Their two horses reared up, jarring the carriage and nearly throwing Ula off the seat as well.

Lying in her bed in the New Orleans hotel, Jewel struggled to scream, but nothing came out of her mouth. Her arms flailed from one side of the bed to the other, trying to get away from the scene that played out in her head.

A sea of blue surrounded her. Hands from a blue uniform grabbed for her, yanked her out of her carriage and onto his horse. Kicking and wrestling, she fought to get away.

Her husband lay unmoving in the middle of the road near the wagon, face-down. Blood oozed from the back of his shoulder where the bullet had ripped through his body and exited. He would be no help against the hot breath on the back of her neck and the sweaty hand on her breast.

In the mist of the confusion one clear thought stood out. The tiny baby in her womb didn't deserve this. He or she would never survive if she slipped out of the arms of the soldier and fell from the tall horse. She quit struggling and watched as one of the Union soldiers flipped her husband over, nodded, then helped another soldier lift him onto the back of a horse.

He was alive. That was all that mattered.

As the soldier galloped out of sight with Hilliard's limp body, Ula swore she would never rest until she found him again.

Jewel tried to scream, made muffled sounds then bolted upright in the bed. Sweat poured from her skin. Her breath came in jagged spurts.

She flipped on the bedside lamp.

Immediately Bryce was by her side, arms reaching for her. "What's wrong? You okay?"

Jewel threw her arms around Bryce. "I had a dream. There were Union soldiers. I was in a carriage with. . ." She stopped. "Bryce, it was Captain McDougle. I was with Captain McDougle. I was sitting by his side. I saw his eyes. I felt his love. They shot him."

Bryce's hands tightened on her shoulders. "Slow down, Jewel. Union soldiers? Did you see Union soldiers?"

She nodded. "Yes, they were all around me. They grabbed me and one of them pulled me onto his horse."

Bryce's stared into her eyes. "You were there with Ula and Hilliard?"

Jewel blinked and thought about what he'd asked. "Yes and no." Her voice was no more than a whisper. "I didn't see Ula." She looked up into Bryce's eyes. "I felt like I *was* Ula. I was there when they shot Captain McDougle."

Bryce lifted his hands from her arms and rubbed one across the back of his neck. "What else happened?"

Jewel sat up and held her knees close to her body. Frowning, she shook her head. "I don't know. I think I must have awakened then."

She sat silent, thinking hard about what she had just seen. "I was there." She looked at Bryce again, hoping he'd believe her.

He nodded and she exhaled a long breath. It was important that he believe her.

"How is that possible?" she asked.

Bryce fluffed a pillow behind his back and leaned against the headboard next to her. "Maybe that's what Mr. Bourgois meant by being contacted. Maybe Ula came to you to let you know what had transpired on the night her husband was shot."

"But I didn't see it all. At least I don't think I did. Ula was pulled onto a horse with a Union soldier and Hilliard was thrown on another horse, but that's when I woke up. Do you think that's when they killed her?"

"I don't know. Maybe. Probably not though. Where

were their children or their child? They had to have at least one and it survived. You're one of the descendants."

Jewel touched her stomach. "Ula was pregnant. She was worried about the baby." Then in an almost whisper, she said, "It was a beautiful carriage."

"What did you say?"

"The carriage. It was beautiful. It was rich."

"Well, by the looks of the house and all the property on the river, I don't doubt it. Captain McDougle must've had a lot of money before the war. He probably grew cotton. That was big money back then."

Jewel nodded again. "They had a good life before the war. I guess that was the last time Ula saw Hilliard. He was probably taken to the island as a prisoner. I guess she eventually made it back home."

"That's possible. We really don't know what happened to Ula. According to the letter in the archives, we know Captain McDougle didn't die on the road. He made it to the prison camp at the island where he tried to escape, probably to get to Ula. That's where they shot him, and if we let ourselves believe it, that's where his spirit is still roaming, probably still trying to get to her."

"I'm starting to believe it could be." Letting that thought settle, she whispered, "How sad. I saw his eyes. They were filled with so much love and so much sadness."

She inhaled deeply and tried to lean back, but Bryce extended his arm and pulled her to him. She stiffened, then looked up at him.

Everything in her body screamed for her to pull away. Send him back to his couch. Sink back into the safety of her covers. Safety is what she longed for, but the safety of the covers is not what she chose. Instead, Jewel relaxed against Bryce and let the security of his arms enfold her.

Bryce lowered his head. In the dim light of the hotel room, his eyes shone a slate gray. They were the last thing she saw as his lips touched hers ever so lightly, brushed them with a restraint that teased her. The faint smell of soap and aftershave lingered on his body and tantalized her. Inching closer to him, she returned his kiss. His jagged breath cooled her lips, but not her senses.

She expected him to kiss her harder. She wanted him to crush his lips against hers, but instead his lips moved slowly across her cheek and down her neck, leaving a trail of kisses that seared her skin. Tiny whimpers escaped from her throat as she tossed her head from side to side. Hopelessly, she succumbed to Bryce's manipulations.

Too many months had gone by since she had let herself go, not thinking of the consequences of giving in to someone else's wishes, but only enjoying the moment of being in someone's arms. She had avoided Bryce's attempts at getting close to her since she had arrived on the island, but tonight her guard was down and she wasn't going to fight it.

Bryce was a good man in every way she had come to know him, and there was no room to find fault now. Not now when his kisses were driving her over the edge.

Finally, he lifted his mouth away and pulled her head close to his chest and entangled his hand in her hair. "This is probably the time that I should say I'm going back to my couch. For you to go back to sleep. Get your rest." His breath came quick and deep.

Jewel searched for her voice and hoped that it was in contact with her brain when she answered.

It wasn't.

"No, stay by me." The words surprised her as much as they did Bryce. He didn't move, but the pounding of his heart against his chest told Jewel he wanted to stay.

Her stomach fluttered as his big hand moved from her hair down her back. His touch heated the skin beneath her thin gown. Bryce wore nothing above his waist and the hair on his chest tormented her as though no fabric separated them at all. She trembled against him, and he responded by ravaging her mouth with hard kisses.

When she thought she could bear it no longer, he said, "If I stay, I'm going to make love to you," his voice a raspy whisper.

Jewel had no voice at all. She nodded.

Bryce placed his hands on her shoulders and stared into her face. "I want to make love to you, but I don't want you to say that I've taken advantage of you. You've been through a lot, Jewel." He stopped to catch his breath. "Make sure."

Again she nodded, but this time her voice was solid and clear. "I want you to stay. I need you."

That was all it took. Bryce crushed his lips against hers and forced her lips apart. She lost herself in his kiss. She knew what she was doing and what he was doing to her, and she didn't want him to stop.

Bryce didn't disappoint her.

Her last thought before her world spun out of control centered on needing Bryce Cameron as she hadn't needed anything in a long, long time.

***

Muffled street sounds from far below their hotel window floated in and out of Jewel's consciousness. She lay on her stomach, naked, cool and relaxed. Bryce's soft breathing mixed with the sounds of the early morning, his warm breath tickling the back of her neck.

Awareness came to her slowly. For a moment it was hard to remember where she was, but not by whom she lay. There was no doubt in her foggy brain that it was Bryce whose heavy arm draped over her back and whose leg pressed against her thigh.

Her brain cleared to the realization of what she had done. She squeezed her eyes tightly remembering how she had needed and wanted Bryce and his lovemaking throughout the night. Since her ex, she had steeled herself against getting close to any man. How could she allow herself to be taken in so easily by Bryce after what David had done to her?

Her former fiancé had nearly ruined her life. What would have happened had she not found him with her secretary? Would she have lived in a make-believe world of love, or would she have come to her senses?

The prospects of where her life could have gone terrified her.

Now she had allowed herself to fall under the spell of a man so similar to David, yet so completely different. He was an enigma, a puzzle as hard to understand as the ghost of Captain McDougle.

Who was this man whose naked body lay next to her, his body reminding her of their night together? Just thinking about what they'd done together sent a wave of heat through her body. For hours after she'd awaken from her dream, they'd made love. Never had anyone ever been so caring and selfless with her. His caresses, his kisses, the driving force of his lovemaking, all kept her at the center of his attention.

Now his deep, long breaths told her he was in deep, restful sleep. How she wanted to lean into him and awaken the sexual drive that had driven her beyond her wildest dreams just hours ago.

But she kept her hands to herself.

If she were truthful with herself, she had to admit she really knew nothing about this man. The little time she had spent with him had shown him to be a caring man, but so was David in the beginning. Or so she thought.

She knew that Bryce had lost his wife, and she attributed that to his need for privacy. Still she had poured out her heart and soul to him about her ruined engagement, and he had refused to open up to her. Maybe there was more that he was not willing to share.

Now, she had become intimate with him. Gloriously intimate. A tiny smile curled her lips at the remembrance of their passionate night. Being in total control, yet caring and gentle, he had guided her into the most complete exhilaration she had ever experienced.

He moved and pulled her close to him. He inhaled deeply and then slowed his breathing as someone who is comfortably and content with the world.

She closed her eyes and hated herself for doing what she was going to have to do.

Chapter 9

Jewel stepped out of the marbled bathroom onto the plush carpet of their suite. With the lights still off, she assumed that Bryce had not gotten up. With only a towel wrapped around her body and one curled around her wet hair, she tiptoed to her suitcase and searched for something to wear.

"Good morning."

With her clothes from the suitcase clutched in front of her chest, she jumped back. Bryce sat in a chair by the window. With the drapes still drawn, only a shadowy silhouette told her where he was.

"Bryce, I had no idea you were up. I was trying to be quiet so I wouldn't wake you."

"Why? I wanted you to wake me. I was hoping to end a perfectly wonderful night by waking with you in my arms. I couldn't think of a better way to start my day." He opened the drapes slightly and a thin stream of sunshine striped a narrow strip of light down the center of the room.

Bryce wore his lounging pants, but nothing else. His bare chest jolted her with visions of what they'd done last night. She swallowed hard. "You were sleeping so soundly I hated to disturb you."

"Is that the only reason?" he asked in a flat voice.

She forced a smile and lied. "Sure. I didn't think you

were ready to get up." She looked down at her clothes. "I'll be right back."

Closing the bathroom door behind her, she collapsed against it and groaned. He knew why she had slipped out of the bed without waking him. He knew she was running, and there was nothing he could do to make her change her mind.

She dressed, then ran a quick comb through her wet hair, allowing her natural waves to dry on their own. Using a hairdryer only managed to add kinks and frizz to the unruliness, and having anything out of control at the moment was the last thing she needed.

Checking her image in the mirror, she put on a smiling face and hoped she could get through this confrontation without falling into his arms.

He had donned a shirt by the time she returned, but he still sat in the chair by the window. "Come over here." He reached out to her. "You need to explain what the problem is."

She chose the chair across from the small table. Her throat tightened. "No problem." She ignored his raised eyebrow that told her he knew better and continued. "I like an early shower."

Now her chest muscles constricted and her throat dried. She had never quite gotten the knack of lying. "Besides, I think I've decided to catch a plane back home from here since there's an airport so close."

He leaned back and stretched his legs. "I thought you had some free time this summer. I was going to suggest spending a little of that time on the island, enjoying the sun, relaxing a little before classes started up again?"

"No. I don't think I should. I have a couple of doctoral students who might need my help."

The muscles in his jaw twitched, but his voice remained calm. "I told you last night I wanted you to be sure before I made love to you. I told you..."

She cut him off. "I was sure. That's why I want to

leave. That's why I need to leave," she repeated.

"Hell, Jewel. That doesn't make any sense." Standing, he flung the curtains all the way open. Bright morning sun washed the room. "You wanted me to make love to you, but now you have to go because I did."

She swallowed and looked down at the beige carpet. "I'm not ready for this."

"Yes you are, but you're not ready to admit it."

"No," she jerked her head up. "This is happening too fast. I don't even know you."

He leaned close to her chair. "You know me. I'm the one who slept next to you last night. I'm the one who made passionate love to you all night long. I'm the one you held onto as you fell asleep."

"That's not what I mean. I know nothing about you." She looked up to him with pleading eyes. "I didn't even know who you were four or five days ago."

"But since then it's been twenty-four hours a day for those days. Most people don't see that much of another person in a month's time. And look what we've shared."

"Yes. I know. A ghost."

He didn't laugh as she expected. "More than that, and you know it."

He was right. There was nothing she could say to deny it. They had shared much, much more than a sighting.

He got up and walked around her to unzip his sports bag. "Why do you really want to leave? Don't you want to find out about Ula and her husband? I got the impression that you wanted to help them find an ending?"

"I do. I'm not running out on them. I need some room right now. A little breathing room to put some of this into perspective. So much has happened in these past few days, it's hard for me to think straight."

Bryce looked up from his suitcase and tilted his head. "I agree with that. You probably do need time to run all this through your head, including how you felt about me and responded to me last night." He yanked out a shirt and zipped the bag. "Because the way I see it, you loved every minute of it last night as much as I did."

Standing up, she glared at him. "That's not fair."

"Fair? Leaving before we can figure this thing out together is what I call unfair. My guess is you're scared just like I told you on the island. You're so damned scared you might fall for me that you won't even give me a chance."

He turned to walk away, then turned back around. "Maybe instead I should say you should give yourself a chance because from what I've seen, you're not doing that. It's easier for you to walk away."

"Maybe it is and if I choose to do that than it's my prerogative. I'm not ready to fall in that same trap again, not now, maybe not ever."

Bryce stood perfectly still, his jaw muscle twitching. "You just remember this. I'm not David."

She cut him off again. "No, you're not David, but by God, I don't know who you are. If you remember right, you've never told me a thing about yourself."

Bryce stared at her then marched into the bath and slammed the door behind him.

***

Traffic backed up bumper to bumper along Canal Street. The ramp to get on Interstate 10 was just ahead, but Byrce's SUV sat unmoving, leaving Bryce and Jewel confined and uncomfortable in the front seat. Bryce fumed inside each time he thought about her wanting to leave after their night of lovemaking. Since Nan had died, he was careful about his casual relationships and avoided serious involvement of any kind.

With Jewel it had been different from the very start. Something about her soothed him and challenged him all at the same time. He wasn't sure what it was, but he had let down his guard, allowing himself to open a tiny door in his emotional wall.

He wanted to talk to her during the night, really talk to her about himself and his life with Nan. He had never opened up to anyone since he had lost her, never told anyone about the deep hurt and horrible loneliness he fought day-in and day-out without her.

With Jewel he felt different. For the first time, he really wanted to share something personal and deep, but making love to her drained him both physically and emotionally. Completely fulfilled, but totally depleted, he had fallen asleep.

She would have gotten his complete story this morning, but having left him in the bed alone closed that door to his life. One of the things he had learned since Nan's death was that you didn't share yourself with every woman who came around. He didn't want to admit it, but maybe Jewel was like all the other women he'd met since her death.

He hoped he was wrong.

On the other side of the car, Jewel twisted her body and rubbed her hand through her hair. Bryce caught the motion from the corner of his eye. Her motions told him she was nervous or worried, but she still looked sexy. He was sure she had no idea what she was doing to his body.

She looked his way. "You think we'll get to the airport in time for all the preliminary checks?"

Thankful for something else to think about besides the burn that started to ignite deep within him, he kept his eyes on the road and answered. "Yeah. I think I see a break ahead of us. Must have been a wreck."

Both of them strained to see ahead. Jewel sat up straight and pointed to a crowd on the sidewalk. "Look over there. There're TV cameras set up. Wonder who it is."

Still stuck in traffic, they had time to watch as several men in suits came out the front door of what looked like a newly renovated building. Bryce finally saw the front of the building. "That's a new hotel that's opening. I read about it in the papers.

Seems like one of the Senators is speaking at the dedication."

The doors swung open and a group of men and women squeezed out together, but immediately gave way for one distinguished man to walk to the top step and wave to the crowd. Cameras flashed, newsmen swarmed as close as possible, and all eyes were on the man in the center of the crowd.

Jewel squinted. "I think that's Jason LeBreaux. I watched him on the news the other night. What a nice looking man."

Bryce leaned toward her side of the car for a better look, but instead of concentrating on the man working the crowd, his senses took in every fresh scent on Jewel's body. Clean, inviting, sensual.

Instantly, his body responded, shocking him back into reality. He sat up straight and tried to ignore the pressure in his lower body.

"I wish we could hear what he's saying," Jewel said as she lowered her window. "I'd love to meet him. From what I've read and heard, he's going to throw his hat into the Presidential race soon."

Trying to keep his mind off Jewel's body, he tuned into the man shaking hands only about a half block away from their vehicle. "That's what I've heard too. I don't know much about him. I think I saw where he spent some of his childhood just north of Baton Rouge, but lives somewhere up north now."

Jewel smiled at him. "If he wins, we can say we saw him in person."

Her smile crashed into his heart. How he wished that smile was for him.

He pulled his attention from her back to the sidewalk. Within minutes, the men behind LeBreaux closed in around him, moving him to the waiting limousine.

"Yeah," he said, "we can say we saw him for a total of two seconds."

"That's more than some people ever get to see a presidential candidate." Jewel looked back at him. "Kind of makes you want to follow his campaign now, doesn't it?"

Bryce agreed with a nod, but now with traffic moving, he concentrated on the road ahead.

"Maybe we'll get you to the airport on time after all." He faced her. "You're sure you don't want to visit the island again? You know I'd like for you to go back with me. The invitation still stands. Who knows, the captain might be waiting for you."

Her gaze darted from him to the road and back again. Nerves, he thought.

"I don't think he's going anywhere. He'll be there when I get back."

If you come back. Bryce wasn't so sure she'd return after she got home, but he wasn't one to plead. It would have to be her decision.

"You don't think I'll come back, do you?" she asked seriously.

A chuckle escaped. "What are you now, a mind reader?"

"Maybe. It wasn't hard to know what you were thinking." Inhaling deeply, she rested against the seat. "I do plan to come back. I want to finish this business with my ancestors, and I really do want to bid on the portrait of Ula. I'm not sure where I'm going to put it in my small apartment, but I have to have it."

He hid the disappointment she had not included him in her reasons for returning. "I'll help you get the portrait. Like I told you, I think it deserves to be in your family."

She lowered her head. "Thank you."

Traffic started moving again, and Bryce breathed easier. He didn't want to come on too strong. He was determined not to try to influence her return.

As soon as the bottleneck cleared, they made good time getting to the interstate, but to Bryce's disappointment, very little was said between them.

At the airport, Bryce walked her as far as he was allowed to go before being stopped by several security guards.

"Looks like you're on your own now," he said, realizing he hated to see her go.

"I guess." She stood by her bag, but didn't get into the line ahead of her.

"You have my cell phone number?"

She nodded.

"Call me if you want to get together again before I contact you. I'll keep in touch with the agents who are handling the auction of the house and will let you know if and when it will take place." He hesitated. "But if you want to come out to island before then, call me."

"Thank you, Bryce. You've been more than kind."

He shook his head. "Kind? You'd think after all we've been through together, I'd be more than 'kind' to you."

"You know what I mean."

"No, I don't." He knew he sounded annoyed, but he couldn't help it.

"This is all rather confusing, the ghost, my spells, the séance. You."

"Me, huh? I've been called a lot of things, but never 'confusing.' At least it's an improvement over 'kind.'"

Jewel smiled and caught him off guard. He looked away. "If you think about it, call me tonight when you get in. I'd like to know you made it okay."

"I'm a big girl. I think I can handle this little hop back to Houston, but I'll call if it makes you feel better." She looked down, then looked up. "Thank you for worrying about me. That's kind of nice."

He nodded, understanding her turmoil. "You'd better get in line."

She leaned as if she were going to kiss him, hesitated, then leaned into him again. No way would he let her leave without a kiss.

Taking her hand, he pulled her to him. She melted into his chest. *God, she felt good.* He held her close, felt her tremble, then let out a long breath.

She raised her face to his, and he kissed her with a longing he hadn't felt in years. When she pulled away, he saw sadness and confusion in her eyes. He wanted to tell her he wouldn't hurt her like David had. He wouldn't take her for granted or use her. But even as he thought those words, he knew there were never guarantees. How well he knew.

Even when love was genuine, things happened beyond a person's control that shattered dreams and lives.

He touched her lips with his finger. "I really want to see you again."

"You will."

She picked up her bag and took a step away. He, too, took a step back and then forced a smile.

With the line moving slowly, he turned to leave, but nearly changed his mind when Jewel sneaked a look his way. He smiled and waved, then cursed under his breath for letting her get to him.

At the car, he unlocked the door, but didn't get in. Instead he leaned against it, needing a couple of minutes to think before he got on the road. Jewel Ferguson was quite a lady, but damned if she knew what she wanted or how strong a person she was.

He wanted to take her by the shoulders and shake her into believing her one mistake with David didn't have to change her life. He smiled. That strong will of hers was going to take a lot of chiseling and if he had learned anything, it was to slow down and not force issues. Even the hard bricks of a fortress had to be handled with tender care.

If Jewel came around to see him for what he was, it would have to be in her own time. He could wait. He had a fort to refurbish and someone very special waiting for him.

Before getting into the car, he telephoned Nan's parents. Their peaceful acreage on the outskirts of Hattiesburg was just what he needed before getting back to the work.

"Mrs. Wilson?"

"Bryce? I was getting concerned. We haven't heard from you in a couple of days. Where are you, dear?"

"I'm at the New Orleans airport. Thought I'd take a little detour and come spend the night up there if that's okay."

"You know it is. I know someone who's going to very happy." In the background he heard her call. "Kevin? Come see who's on the phone?"

A shriek from the other end of the phone brought a smile to Bryce's face. His chest swelled.

"Daddy? Daddy? Is that you?"

"Yes, Son. I'll be there in about two hours."

Chapter 10

Jewel stood in the middle of her living room. Her shoulders drooped and her forehead wrinkled in a scowl. She couldn't ever remember feeling so alone in her life. The short flight home had been excruciating. As the plane lifted from the New Orleans airport, Jewel felt as though she had left part of herself back on the ground. A horribly gaping hole existed in her chest where just the night before exhilaration had overflowed.

Even after breaking up with David, her anger filled the gap of loneliness and kept depression at bay. His unfaithfulness had hurt deeply, but there was also a certain relief at saving herself from a lifetime of misery.

Now the apartment she so dearly loved seemed lifeless, empty and dull. Standing next to her suitcase, she wondered why in the world she had ever come home. Nothing but solitude and quiet welcomed her.

Maybe that's what she needed, she tried to convince herself. Time alone. Time to think without Bryce clouding her thoughts and sending every tiny iota in her body into an emotional tailspin every time he came close to her.

Her body trembled just thinking about their night together. Squeezing her eyes and throwing her head back, she sighed. *Don't go there, girl.*

Walking over to the double French doors that led to

her beloved balcony, she yanked opened the blinds. Her tiny balcony had become her island in the middle of the huge city of Houston. Her sanctuary.

Baskets of hanging petunias and pots filled with miniature roses sat amongst a stone gnome and several brightly painted concrete frogs. Remembering Mr. Bourgois's tiny front porch filled with similar flowers, she smiled, but then got serious. The visit with the medium and the participation in the séance still bothered her. Something had happened to her that she still couldn't recall.

Had Ula or Hilliard tried to communicate with her? Would she ever know? Was her mind so enamored to scientific research that it would never allow her to fully open up to the paranormal? She knew that was a distinct possibility. She loved the study of biology. How could she ignore everything she taught and studied to believe that something beyond this life was trying to contact her?

She definitely needed time alone to allow her mind to take in all that had happened to her, especially when it came to Bryce.

She leaned up against the doorframe and allowed the sound of her tiny fountain to fill her senses. She inhaled the fragrance of the roses, waiting for the normal state of relaxation to sweep over her.

Today, though, there was no refuge. No relaxation. Memories of another balcony washed over her instead. Her two prized foliage plants were as beautiful as the ones overlooking the streets of New Orleans, but standing there now, alone, they were unable to cheer her.

What they lacked was obvious. Bryce had ruined her simple pleasures. She loved her cozy quarters. She loved her plants. Before her visit to the island, her modest little apartment and quiet academic life on campus offered her everything she needed. Now?

Running scared is how Bryce described her. His remark had infuriated her then, infuriated her because he was probably right. But she had cause. Why shouldn't she be afraid to trust another man and why should she start with him?

Glancing at the suitcase, she exhaled deeply and stepped outside. Unpacking could wait. She grabbed the bright yellow watering container. As she filled it, the water sprayed across her arms, feeling surprisingly like the spray of the water along the beach of the island.

"Stop it," she said to herself and yanked the faucet shut.

Dropping the empty container after watering her plants, she marched into her apartment determined to find some sort of normality in her life again.

A warm bath and her comfortable bed would help her think straight in the morning. She'd use the same strategy she suggested to her doctoral students. Step away from your problem. Put it away, then come back and you'll be able to see it in a new light.

Bryce Cameron needed a lot of thought, but too many things boggled her mind at the moment. She'd see him in a new light in the morning when her mind was clear and fresh.

She'd have to deal with the possibility of a stranded ghost another time. Right now what she needed was a warm bath and her familiar bed.

***

A gentle breeze blowing across the Mississippi River ruffled Ula McDougle's hair and cooled the fresh tears flowing down her cheeks. Hilliard, her husband, was in the house packing, getting ready to leave her and the land that he so loved to join a cause that she didn't understand and a war that frightened her beyond thought.

She couldn't bear it. She and Hilliard were still so new at married life. How could he think about leaving now when they were trying so desperately to have a family? She rubbed her hand across her flat stomach. A tiny seed could be growing there even now. How she had dreamed of giving him a son to carry on the family name. A son with red hair and a strong body that would make him proud. A son to hunt with and pass down the estate that he cherished.

Hilliard said he'd probably not be far from their small town of St. Marks and their plantation estate, River's Bend. Being an officer he'd be able to drop in ever so often, but she knew how things would really be. He could ride away today and never return. How could she live if something happened to him?

From deep within her chest, a deep sob shook her body. She laid her head on the railing of the shoo-fly overlooking the grounds of the plantation and the bend in their river. The circular wooden structure with its impressive set of stairs was built around one of their massive oak trees giving them a cool, private place to enjoy each other's company.

It was their spot, he had told her, their spot to be alone with their love and with their dreams. With the cooling winds blowing in across the river, they could plan their future here and recant the joys of their days.

But today she'd found her way to the river's edge to be alone, away from the man she so dearly loved.

"Ula? Ula? Where are you?" Hilliard's deep voice reached her from across the yard. Standing on the wide back porch of the house he'd built for her as their wedding present, the now Confederate Captain McDougle presented her with a vision she'd hold in her heart forever.

His tall stance and perfect physique with his head of bright red hair had attracted her from the first time she had laid eyes on him. Never had she had a moment's doubt about marrying him. Never in her wildest dreams could she imagine being so totally happy. And now?

At first Ula thought about not answering. He had asked her not to cry, and here she was acting like a child.

She wiped away the tears. "I'm here, Hilliard. In the shoo-fly." She answered because she couldn't stand being away from him even for a minute.

***

"I'm here, Hilliard." Those words reverberated in Jewel's head. "I'm here, Hilliard." Jewel rolled her head from side to side on the pillow in her bed in her apartment. "I'm here, Hilliard," she heard herself say in the solitude of her darkened bedroom.

Awareness came to Jewel just enough to know she was in Twenty-First Century Houston, in her apartment and in her bed. She was Jewel Ferguson, a university professor—not Ula McDougle—but again the words escaped her lips. "I'm here, Hilliard."

Thoughts swirled around her head fighting with one another for their dominance. She struggled for consciousness, to awake fully to her own world, but the sorrow of Ula McDougle called her back into the past. She had no recourse.

***

"I'm here, Hilliard." This time Ula waved to her husband from the shoo-fly and forced a smile for him.

Returning the wave, he stepped briskly down the stairs. Excitement about going off to war made his steps light. All the men up and down the river were charged about fighting for their land and for the "honor of the South" as they called it.

She didn't understand it, but, then again, she wasn't a man. To her, honor meant taking care of your family. Staying with them. Protecting them, but that's not how they saw it. Pride and honor governed everything that her handsome husband did and this endeavor would be no different.

He would make her proud, she was sure. She just hoped he wouldn't make her a widow.

"I wondered where you had taken off to, Mrs. McDougle." Hilliard reached for her hand as he plopped his body next to her on the bench that surrounded the shoo-fly.

"I needed some fresh air," she lied.

"Oh, I see." He pulled her close to his body and kissed her on the cheek. "You know what I think?" he asked lightly. "I think you couldn't stand to see me pack."

Ula sniffled. "Is that so hard to believe? I can't stand the thought of your leaving me."

"Come here." As if she could get any closer to him, he squeezed her tightly. "We've talked about this. You know I have to go."

"I know no such thing." Ula knew she was pouting, but she didn't care. "Mr. Merriweather isn't going."

Hilliard groaned. "He's crippled, Ula. What could he do in a war? You've got to be sensible about all of this."

"But you've got this huge plantation to run."

"So do all the other planters around here. We're all in the same boat." He held her away from his large body with his hands on her shoulders. "I told you I'll be back as often as I can. I've been told that my troops will be near here for a while. I'll come home to see you every chance I get. In fact, we'll plan to take a little trip to New Orleans on my first leave to pick up that portrait you sat for."

Hilliard took a handkerchief from his pants pocket and wiped away a tear, a handkerchief she'd delicately embroidered with his initials to carry into battle.

"Everything will be just fine," he said, then smiled. "You wait and see. This war can't last long, not with the enthusiasm in the air. I'll be home for good before you know it."

Holding her head against his broad chest, she inhaled the scent of mint from his morning shave. She closed her eyes and refused to cry again, at least not in front of him.

"*Look over there.*" *Hilliard pointed across the river.* "*That's our family of egrets. They've doubled in number since we started watching them raise their family. When you see them, think of me. Remember our sign?*"

She sat up and smiled coyly, "Of course I do." With her palms facing her body, she hooked her thumbs together and wiggled her fingers. Like birds in flight, their sign since their courting day said they'd be together again. How many times had Hilliard sat on his big steed, then clasped his hands together before leaving her?

He had always returned, but today she couldn't be so sure.

"*You just remember that. I'm not going away forever. I'll return to you just as those egrets come back to the same nests every year. I need you, Ula. I'll come back.*"

He pulled her close and kissed her hard on the mouth. "*I love you,*" *he said afterwards.* "*I'd never leave you.*"

***

The quiet of the night in Jewel's bedroom was broken by her soft voice. "I love you too, Hilliard. You're my life."

Jewel twisted in the bed, pulled her pillow close to her body, and fought to push away the heavy sadness that pressed down on her chest. "I love you too," she whispered again.

For the moment, the sadness lifted and she breathed easier. Her mind floated back into the blessed oblivion of dreamless sleep. Her body relaxed.

Deep, restful sleep didn't last long though. Her eyelids twitched. Her breath came in short gulps, and her arms swung out in front of her body. She was still in her bed, but her mind was someplace else once more.

***

"Hilliard, wait." Ula lifted her light blue muslin day dress and stepped over limbs covering the grounds of River's Bend. Set-ins of imported lace snagged against branches ripping and tearing. "I can't keep up."

"I'm sorry. We need to hurry. I have to be ready to leave shortly." Hilliard took her hand and nearly pulled her along a nonexistent trail. "Now remember where you are. Keep your bearings by the river. All of this may be burned out one day, who knows?"

"Hilliard McDougle, don't you dare say such a thing. Who in the world would care about this insignificant piece of land in the whole scheme of things? It's not like we're in the middle of a thriving city like New Orleans. The Yankee army won't bother with River's Bend. Why should they?"

"Well, you just never know. I've heard too much and seen too much over the last six months that I've been involved with this war to ignore what might happen." He stopped. "Now look where you are. The second bend of the river is to your immediate right. That hill we tried to buy from the Austin's is over there just south of it."

"I know where we are," she said as she straightened her dress and pulled a torn piece back into its place. Too much had happened in the six months that Hilliard had been away for her to want to do this today. Just having Hilliard home, lying next to her, holding her for the short time that they'd be together was all she wanted, not tromping through brambles and briars.

Her early pregnancy tired her. The extra work around the estate was already taking its toll on her, and the last thing she wanted to do today was to tramp through the woods with her husband. She needed him by her in the bed, to feel his strength and energy to sustain her when he would ride away again in a few days.

God, how she loved him.

"Okay. Just be sure because I have many of our valuables buried here. The Yankees might get what's left at

the house, but there're some things that need saving no matter what."

Ula tried to focus on what he was saying. "I'm listening. Show me where you and the help buried my beautiful silver and jewelry. I'm surprised you didn't take my wedding ring just as you took my gold heart."

Involuntarily, she touched the empty spot on her neck where the gold chain and heart had hung since Hilliard presented it to her.

"I wouldn't have made you remove your wedding ring, but the rest of the stuff you can live without for a while. When we get back from New Orleans with the portrait, we'll bury it also. Wouldn't you rather have it buried for a short time than to have it stolen if those Yanks come here?"

"I guess, but the portrait might be ruined—and the heart," she hesitated, "I wore that heart all the time. You gave it to me. I'd feel as if you were with me if I had it on."

"I'm always with you, Ula. You don't need a necklace to remind you of that." He placed his hand on her heart. "I'm always right there. Forever. As far as the necklace is concerned though, I want you to have it always, not have some Yank's girlfriend up in New York wearing it after this war is over." He spit the words out angrily. "No, it's safer where it is, right here buried on River's Bend."

Ula twisted her mouth, then looked around. "And where exactly would that be?"

Hilliard nodded and pointed. "Right there."

Ula looked where he pointed. "Where? I don't see a thing."

"Good. That's the way I wanted it. It's right there under that big oak tree. Lucas did a wonderful job of hiding it with the leaves."

He grabbed her shoulders and looked her in the eye. "Promise me you won't tell anyone where this is until I get home after the war, or if," he stumbled for words.

"Don't even say it." Ula turned. Hysteria nipped at her heart. "Don't you dare say if you should not come home. I won't hear of it." She touched her stomach. "We won't hear of it."

Hilliard pulled her close to him. "I'll always be with you no matter what."

Chapter 11

Long, wooden black rails marked the beginning of the Wilson property. Two small pastures ran along the fence line with two quarter horses grazing alongside of Kevin's pony in the one. In the second pasture, two huge Jersey cows that had long ago become family pets stood in the shade of an oak tree.

The quiet pastoral scene made Bryce swallow hard. Coming here was bittersweet. Being with his son Kevin made him deliriously happy. Seeing him with his grandparents instead of with Nan, though, tore at his heart and always opened new wounds. Time had lessened the pain, but even time could never fully erase it.

Turning into the unpaved drive dredged up memories he'd painstakingly stored away. For so long everything that happened to him pulled up memories of Nan. Now it was only moments like this one that hurt him deeply.

The rows of camellia bushes had grown since the first time he drove up here as a young man to meet Nan for a date. He had been so nervous. So unlike himself he remembered. There was something special about the girl he was picking up, and he didn't want to ruin it with her parents.

Mr. Wilson stood stoically against the fireplace and didn't make it easy for him. Never cracking a smile, the man asked him a few questions and told him in no short terms that his daughter had to be in before midnight. Bryce never thought to argue.

Bryce smiled remembering that he had gotten her home forty minutes early, just to be sure.

Mrs. Wilson was totally different. From the very moment he entered the house, her pleasant disposition and smile made him feel as if he were part of the family. She spoke sweetly, offered him cookies and welcomed him back into their home when he'd left with Nan. He felt as if he'd known Mrs. Wilson all of his life.

Who knew that years later he would be welcomed back here, not as a guest but as the father of the son they were raising.

It hadn't been easy leaving his son with them. For months after the funeral he tried to juggle his job and take care of the toddler alone. It wasn't fair to either of them. When Bryce drove through these gates one day with the boy, Mr. and Mrs. Wilson met him and never asked a question, only watched as he cried and promised the boy he'd always be there for him.

Now this had become his new home. Putting in a small mobile home behind the main house gave him and Kevin some private time and let Bryce feel as though he wasn't a guest during the stolen moments he had with his son. It wasn't the perfect arrangement, but it was working.

He pulled the car into the driveway of the modest ranch style, but before he turned off the ignition, the back door of the house flew open, and Kevin bound out of the door. "Daddy, Daddy." With arms flying, the boy ran up to the car to meet his father.

Bryce jumped out of the car and grabbed Kevin, spinning him around and hugging him all at the same time. It had only been a little over a week since he spent the weekend up here, but it felt like ages to Bryce.

"How're doing, Big Boy?"

"Daddy, Daddy, come see. We got baby cats."

"Baby cats? When did that happen?"

"Yesterday. Come see. They're in the barn." Kevin wiggled to get out of Bryce's arms.

Mrs. Wilson made it to the car out of breath. "I swear. The boy gets faster every day."

Bryce reached over with his free hand and pulled her to him, giving her a quick peck on the cheek. "Hi, Mom. Looks like you're keeping up with him pretty good if you ask me?"

"I don't know. These old legs don't seem to move like they used to." She laughed. "But I'm not complaining. Doc Rice said I'm in better shape now than I've been in years and I know who I can give credit to for that."

"He won't let you stay still long, that's for sure."

Kevin shimmied down Bryce's leg and grabbed his hand. "Come on, Daddy. Come see the babies."

"Y'all go ahead," Mrs. Wilson said. "I've got a pot on the stove. Come on over for lunch when you feel like it."

Bryce winked at her. "Thanks. You can bet I won't be late. Haven't had a home-cooked meal since I was up here last."

Bryce spoke as Kevin pulled him toward the barn. As soon as he stepped into its dim light, the sweet smell of freshly baled hay bombarded his brain with memories of Nan. He smiled, remembering a lazy afternoon when Nan's parents had gone into town. After making love in the clean hay of an empty stall, he and Nan lay snuggled together. They chewed on pieces of hay, talked about their future together, and wondered if they could've conceived a baby.

Maybe they had conceived Kevin that afternoon because Nan found out she was pregnant the next month.

"Come on, Daddy. Come see."

Kevin's excitement brought Bryce back to the present. He followed his son to the stall next to where he and Nan had called their love nest. Six tiny, hairless kittens squirmed on or near their mother's belly. Instinctively, they searched for milk as the mother cat kept them safe.

That's how he felt lying next to Nan that day. He remembered telling her he'd never let anything happen to her. He'd be her protector. She smiled up at him and said she knew he would.

As Kevin flopped on the floor and pulled his hand to sit next to him, Bryce swallowed. He'd lied to Nan that day. He wasn't her protector and she died without him being able to help.

"They eatin'," Kevin said, unaware of his father's momentary belt of sadness. "They can't see their Mommy but they know it's her. Granny said so. Granny said that all they do is drink milk and sleep. Pretty neat, huh?"

"I'll say." Bryce pushed away his journey into the past and knelt down by his son. He spoke softly to the mother cat lying perfectly still. Her perked ears and sharp eyes told him not to touch her kittens. He obeyed.

"They're cute, all right." Bryce didn't want to talk about cats. He wanted to smother his boy with hugs and kisses, but he had learned long ago that Kevin wasn't the cuddly type. "Are you going to help take care of them?"

"Uh huh," he nodded and grabbed one of the stall railings and pulled himself up. "My job's gonna be to feed them when they get big enough to eat real food. Granny said I can have one and name it and everything, but I have to give the others away."

Kevin's bright blue eyes sparkled as he spoke with every inch of his body in motion. Arms swinging. Hands digging into his pockets and then out. Shoulders shrugging. Feet shuffling.

Bryce smiled at the little man who stood before him, a combination of himself and Nan. He was a miracle who never ceased to amaze Bryce. He had Nan's eyes and her giddy disposition, but he would be tall with dark hair like himself.

Kevin had grown so much and had learned so much from Nan's parents. Living out away from the city on several acres gave him a world to explore and learn about that Bryce knew he could never give him, not now with the way his job was keeping him on the road. But one day he hoped for better.

He pulled the boy close to him. "I've missed you, son."

Kevin allowed him to hug him for a second, but only for a second. Shortly Kevin pulled away and stooped down by the kittens once more, shrugging off Byrce's embrace. There was too much to do to waste time hugging. Bryce would have to wait until after Kevin's bath tonight to get his full attention and some return hugs. Those moments would make the ride up here today all worthwhile.

Bryce straightened up and found his voice. "Come on. Granny will throw the food out to the dogs if we make her wait."

"No, she won't. She always makes me eat. She won't give it to the dogs." His serious expression made Bryce laugh.

"Well, I don't know about you, but I'm not taking any chances. Let's race."

Before Bryce could turn around and get his footing, Kevin had darted out the barn door.

Bryce shook his head and followed.

These were the moments that kept Bryce going from week to week. He didn't want to miss a second of it.

***

Jewel opened her eyes, but didn't move. The clock to her left said 6:07. With the morning sun still just a hint outside her window, she knew it was much too early for her to get up on a day off. Normally she would have turned over and gone right back to sleep, but this morning something bothered her.

Something had happened to her last night. Something strange and unnatural. She felt it, but couldn't put a finger on it. She knew she'd had a dream but wasn't able to recall the details, just as she'd felt after the séance. Not remembering a dream had happened lots of times to her, but this one bothered her. She knew it hadn't been a normal dream.

Afraid to lose thoughts that swirled in her head, she lay unmoving, trying desperately to let them materialize. Her silky gown was twisted around her waist. Her sheets knotted and pulled away from their neat tucks. Something wasn't right—something that wouldn't come to her.

Closing her eyes, she concentrated on visualizing her dreams, anything from last night, but to no avail.

Finally after untwisting her gown and untangling the sheets from her body, she gave up trying to jar her memory and swung her feet to the floor.

Still in her gown after her morning routine, Jewel settled on her balcony with her cup of coffee. Wrapping her hands around the warm cup, she relished the aroma before taking her first sip. It was good coffee, but not as wonderful as the coffee she'd shared with Bryce in the New Orleans French Quarter. She closed her eyes and let the aroma of her remembered coffee au lait soothe her.

It was hard to get Bryce out of her head. The whole experience with him had awakened in her a spark that reminded her she had only been going through the motions of living since her breakup with David. That realization stung. Is that what she'd been doing? It's what Bryce had said, just as he'd said she was running away from living again.

She slammed her cup down a little too hard sloshing her coffee.

I didn't run. I just needed time.

In her heart though, she knew what he'd said could be true, but maybe "running" was the wrong way of describing her. She liked to think she was simply taking things slowly. Was it wrong to be a little skittish?

Inhaling, she relaxed against one of her balcony chairs. Her little apartment on the outskirts of the crowded city was just where she needed to be, here away from him where she could think.

Two large marsh birds flew into the trees across the complex lawn. Living near the coastline gave her a great opportunity to observe birds that normally wouldn't be in big cities. Many of the birds had taken up residence in a small lake surrounded by a tree-filled park, giving her a great place on her balcony to enjoy their beauty.

For a moment, she did just that. They circled the tree, lifted on the currents of wind, then settled amongst the thick limbs, hidden from her sight. Jewel lifted her coffee cup for another sip, but stopped in midair. With held breath and rigid muscles, she froze.

The birds' innocent scene jolted a fleeting memory deep within her subconscious. The same feeling she had experienced when she awoke returned to her, touched her, teased her, then left. She squeezed her eyes tightly trying to capture whatever it was that taunted her. Inhaling deeply, she gripped her cup and concentrated.

Then it hit her. The birds. Hilliard and Ula standing on the shoo-fly watching the birds across the river. It was her dream. She had been there with them last night.

Carefully, with trembling hands, she placed her cup down.

I was there. I was Ula— again.

Her body began to shake. It wasn't possible to live as someone else, even in her dreams she told herself.

But even as she tried to convince herself that it was only a dream she'd experienced, she knew it had to be more than that. She gasped for breath. Was it possible that Ula had shown her another part of her life as if she, Jewel Ferguson, had experienced it herself?

From the lofty position on her balcony she recaptured the feeling of being in the shoo-fly above the Mississippi River. If she closed her eyes, she could feel the wind cooling her skin where Ula's tears flowed. Jewel's heart broke for the young woman who had to watch her young husband go to war. She touched her own stomach and wondered when Ula had a baby and if she had been pregnant on the day that Hilliard left.

The weight of sadness descended upon Jewel. Uncontrollable tears burst from her eyes and sobs wracked her body. Nestling her head in her arms, she cried until she felt purged. Theirs was a love so deep that one hundred and fifty years later they were still trying to reach each other.

Their love was just as present and real to her today as it was on the banks of the Mississippi River so long ago. Her sobs were for them, two lovers who never had a chance, but who had never given up.

How could she not do something to help? But then again, how could she? If they had actually shown themselves to her, what was she was supposed to do? What else had Ula told her in her dream?

Jewel let the tears flow freely. It felt good to weep, but she knew her weakness wasn't helping them. Wiping the last of the tears away, she straightened up. "Okay, Ula, you're going to have to do more than this." Jewel spoke out loud. "Unless I'm losing my mind—and I guess that's a possibility— I know who you are, but I don't know what you want me to do. I need some help here, girlfriend."

She waited, but, of course, she knew nothing would happen. Sipping her now barely warm coffee, she watched as several other birds flew over the clump of trees. A warmth settled over her. She felt sure something about the birds would help her find a way to help the couple, but at the moment she didn't have enough information. What was Ula trying to tell her and what did the presence of the birds mean?

Frustration made her want to scream. The answers were out there somewhere for her, but she knew she couldn't do it alone, and certainly not from here.

Leaving Bryce was supposed to give her time to unravel the tangled web of thoughts that clogged her brain since she had stepped off the helicopter on the island. Now, though, her own problems would have to be put on a shelf for a little longer, but was she ready to open her eyes to the possibility of what all this meant?

Mr. Bourgois had told her that nothing would happen if she didn't believe. Could she allow herself to believe the possibility that this couple from the past was using her for their purposes? It was a concept so foreign to her that it made her head spin thinking about it.

Her entire adult life had been spent studying fact and separating fact from speculation. Now, she had a feeling she'd have to allow a little speculation into her world because if what she was feeling was possible, Ula and Hilliard McDougle needed her. She had no idea what they wanted her to do, but she wasn't going to turn her back on the young wife.

In her heart she knew a love that rare couldn't be ignored.

Chapter 12

The ringing of the cell phone irritated Bryce. Marcus was probably standing on his head needing him to return to the fort. Bryce had been communicating with him for the last few days over the phone, but now he had only a few more minutes with his son and he didn't want it ruined.

"That's your phone, Daddy."

"I know." Bryce looked at the phone lying on the table, but then turned back to Kevin without taking time to see who was calling. "I'll get the message when I get in the car."

Kevin shrugged. Bryce wondered if the boy knew how important these few minutes with him meant and how hard it was to tell him goodbye.

They sat on the floor together, cross-legged, watching cartoons. Empty cereal bowls and a box of sugar coated super hero cereal sat next to them. Kevin was engrossed with the television.

Bryce was engrossed with his son.

This was always the hard part for Bryce. Telling his son good-bye and driving away without him next to him ripped his soul apart. Each time he left, Bryce assured himself that it would be easier the next time. It never was.

The older the boy got, the more Bryce wanted to spend time with him. He was missing out on the best part of his growing up and he hated himself for it. The scene never changed for him. Driving away, he always made the choice to find a new job or at least to use his engineering degree in a capacity that would keep him closer to the boy. Luckily he had gotten this latest fort reconstruction job that put him close to him, but who knew where the next one would be.

Being realistic, though, he knew that one job would lead to the next and he'd have to make do with the little time he carved out for the two of them. Without a woman in his life, he'd have to allow the boy's grandparents to help.

Bryce's thoughts touched on Jewel. Being with her those few days had made a deep impression on him. He wondered what kind of impression his son would make on her. How would she react to his having a son?

Remembering how she'd left their bed just a night ago, Bryce snickered. *As if she'd give me the chance to tell her about my life!* The woman wasn't ready to let anyone into her life right now.

With a sigh of resignation, Bryce picked up the bowls and the cereal, cleaned the kitchen and went to the bedroom to dress.

"You leaving, Daddy?" Kevin had followed him into the bedroom and jumped onto the bed.

Bryce pulled on his shirt, then sat down next to Kevin. "Yeah, I have to go back to work, but I'll try to get back here within the week. I have to check on things at the island."

"Can I go with you to the island?"

The words stabbed him in the chest. He swallowed hard. "No, not this time, but I promise, before this job is over, I'll take you and Granny and Grandpa out there."

"Can I swim?"

"Sure you can. We'll get you out there before the water cools off. It's a really pretty island. Just like the last one. You'll love it."

"Can I fish, too?"

160

"Yep. We'll have to go shopping soon and buy you your very own fishing pole."

"Okay." Kevin stood on the bed, jumped a couple of times then hugged Bryce's neck.

Holding on to the boy for a few minutes, Bryce felt a surge of love and the all too familiar lump in his throat. "Come on and help me carry my bags." Finally, Bryce let him go.

Kevin jumped down and grabbed the shaving kit. "Race you," he shouted, but Bryce grabbed him by the collar.

"Whoa. No fair. I have this big bag. Just walk next to me. We'll race the next time."

"The next time tomorrow?"

"Well, not tomorrow, but soon."

Looking up to him with Nan's big blue eyes, Kevin nodded in childish acceptance. "Okay. I'll take care of the baby cats 'til you get back."

"Good boy, and I'll take care to not stay away too long."

But any time was too long for Bryce.

He drove along the two-lane in deep thought, determined to get through another week without his son, but more determined than ever to push the loneliness aside.

Once again his thoughts turned to Jewel. For some reason, he never shared the boy with women he'd gone out with since he'd lost Nan, but with Jewel, he had wanted to tell her about Kevin. He had plans to talk with her their night in the hotel. That is, until she made her quick exit after their lovemaking. *That's always good for the ego!*

He laughed to himself. He knew the situation with Captain McDougle and the sale of River's Bend would give him the opportunity to see her again, but he'd have to wait and see how things went after that. Jewel could be just another woman filling a few minutes of the vast void in his life, but, then again, he had to admit he really wanted her to be something more.

Whether or not she wanted to be something more to him was doubtful.

After he turned onto the highway, Bryce remembered the telephone call, but waited until he got to a gas station. Damn, he said out loud. To his surprise, the voice wasn't that of Marcus but Jewel. Quickly, he returned her call. No one answered. Disappointed, but hopeful, he left a message.

Aggravated with himself for not listening to the message before leaving the Wilson's, he pulled back onto the highway and headed for the coast. If he didn't get back to the fort soon, he wouldn't have to worry about seeing his son. He'd be without a company and a job!

***

Jewel came out of a meeting with her supervisor on campus. Even though she didn't have a full load of classes during this summer session, she had duties that had to be fulfilled. She didn't mind.

Campus life had become her second nature and had helped her to stay sane after her breakup with David. It was her home away from home. She could never stay away long.

She pulled her cell phone out. Bryce's voice greeted her on her messages telling her he was sorry he had missed her call and that he was on his way back to the island. In a fleeting thought she wondered why he hadn't gone back to the job when he left her yesterday. Where had he spent his night? Had he spent it with someone else?

A tiny twist of jealousy knotted her chest, but she knew she'd never ask. It had been her decision to return to Houston. Anyway, it was none of her business where or with whom he had spent the night. Had he wanted her to know, he would have told her.

Still, remembering their night together, she wanted it to be her business.

She punched a couple numbers into the phone, then hit the off button before it rang. What would she say to him now that she had time to think? Did she want to return to the island or wait and meet him at the house if the auction took place? Would he even want to see her again?

More importantly, should she see him before she had a firm grip on herself?

Putting her phone away, she met up with two colleagues and headed for the coffee shop.

A new associate professor from the history department walked alongside of her. He was tall, good-looking and recently divorced and hadn't wasted any time trying to get Jewel to go out with him. She attended a campus lecture with him, but other than that she always found an excuse not to go.

"Anything exciting taking place now that you're a lady of leisure this summer?" A cute little dimple highlighted his face.

She shook her head. "No, not really." *Only an encounter with a ghost and a trip to the Civil War Period.* She smiled. "I did take a little jaunt to my family's old estate in St. Marks. I'd never been there, and I was fascinated with the area's beauty and the old architecture."

"St. Marks, huh? You didn't happen to run into any ghosts while you were there?"

Jewel nearly tripped over her feet when he asked. "What? What did you say?"

"Ghosts." His eyebrows lifted and he rolled his eyes from side to side in amusement. "You know. Those airy souls still stuck here on earth even though they're supposed to be dead."

"Why would you ask that?"

"Well, according to all kinds of accounts, there are ghosts that still haunt many of the old buildings over there, some from the Civil War, some later periods. There're even tours that take you around to see the houses and the haunts."

Fascinated, Jewel stared at the man. "I had no idea."

"Oh, yeah. It would make an interesting weekend if you'd like to go again. I'd love to take you. There're lots of bed and breakfasts, but, of course, if you've just been there, you know that already."

"No, not really. I stayed in New Orleans. I had gone with, uh, a friend." Jewel didn't want to tell him that she had been with Bryce or their visit to the medium, not because the colleague meant anything to her, but because she didn't feel as if she needed to share that piece of information with this man. Her body flushed at the remembrance of her night in New Orleans with Bryce.

Her escort didn't hesitate. "I've got a weekend free at the end of the month, if you'd like to plan a trip."

Jewel swallowed. "I'll keep that in mind for another time, but right now I'm not really interested in going back," she lied. She couldn't wait to get back to her house and her portrait.

Why had she called it "her house"? Even the portrait wasn't hers yet, and the house and property were so far out of reach for her that it was insane to think about it.

"Well, you let me know if you change your mind." He touched her arm. "You keep putting me off, but I'm not going to give up. I'm not a bad person, Jewel," he said with a twinkle in his eye that made Jewel laugh.

"I know that. I'll see you around and who knows? One day I might give you a call and ask *you* out."

At that he laughed. Jewel knew that he had been around enough to know a refusal when he heard one.

Jewel stopped at the library before going back to her apartment and picked up a couple books about spirits and supernatural sightings in the South. She might not be prepared to face Bryce, but she would be as prepared as possible when she encountered Captain McDougle again.

The afternoon found her on her balcony with a hot cup of tea and one of the books about ghosts. Surprised that so many people besides herself and Bryce had actually encountered ghosts, she lost herself in the pages.

When the phone rang, she jumped. "Hello."

"Hey. That was a strange hello. Sounded like I scared you. Were you sleeping?"

Bryce's voice brought her out of her daze. "Bryce? Oh, no, I wasn't sleeping. I'm sitting on my balcony reading and was so enthralled with these stories that I forgot this world existed."

"Must be a good book."

"I'm reading up on ghosts. Sightings that have taken place in these parts. Do you know how many there are?"

"No, but I have a feeling you're about to tell me there's been quite a few."

"Oh, yes. More than I could possibly have dreamed of. Captain McDougle isn't alone out there just as Mr. Bourgois said. He may even have some airy friends in the fort with him."

"That's encouraging to know," Bryce said with a lilt in his voice. "Uh, I got your message. Sorry I missed your call and then I missed you when I called."

"I was in a meeting and didn't have my phone on." She hesitated. How could she tell him she was afraid to return his call after she was the one who instigated the exchange? Instead she lied. "I haven't had time to return your call, then I got involved in this book and lost track of time."

Silence. Jewel squirmed. "I called you this morning to tell you about a dream I had last night." Again she hesitated.

He helped her out. "You dreamed of our couple?"

"I did, and Bryce, I think I was there again. I swear I was Ula all over again." Her heart beat rapidly just recounting her dream. "I felt like her. I was sad. I felt Hilliard hold me. It was all so strange."

Bryce didn't answer right away, obviously taking in what she had just said, then answered in a thoughtful, quiet voice. "What happened this time?"

"I saw Ula telling Hilliard goodbye. They were sitting in a shoo-fly overlooking the river. She was so sad I cried when I remembered the dream this morning."

"You saw the house?"

"I did, at least from the river side. Hilliard was getting ready to leave. He was really excited, but Ula was upset. She didn't want him to leave her. She wanted to have a baby." Just talking about the two brought a lump to Jewel's throat.

"What do you want to do now?" Bryce asked.

"I'm not sure." She knew it would come down to this. What did she want to do? She squirmed some more. She had no idea.

Finally, she remembered Bryce on the line so she continued. "I guess I could try to meet you if and when there is an auction. Other than that, I don't know. I could go back to the island to see if the captain appears again, but then, what would I do? I don't have a message for him. I'd probably just scream like I did before and scare him away."

"Well, I think screaming wasn't exactly unexpected."

She shuddered remembering the white hand that had reached out to her. "He didn't hang around long after that. Even if I had something to tell him, I didn't give it time enough to take place."

"I wouldn't be too hard on yourself, Jewel."

She heard him take a deep breath. Bryce was miles and miles away from her, but she felt as though he was on the balcony, not on an island in the Gulf of Mexico.

"If you'd like to come out here to the island just to relax, you know you're welcome," he said. "I don't have the helicopter down here right now, but we do have a boat that comes out to the island every day."

His invitation was tempting. "I don't know if that would be such a good idea right now."

"Well, it's your decision. Here's another thought.

Marcus and I have a condo that we're renting on the beach in Biloxi if you'd like to fly into Gulfport and go there. The condo's yours for the asking, with or without us there," he threw in.

"That sounds wonderful, but I'm not so sure that's the thing to do either. Maybe I need to catch up on some of my research. I do need to visit with the captain again, but not until I'm armed with more facts and insight into all this." She stopped. "No. No, I'd better not go right now."

"Spoken like a true scientist. Have it your way."

His voice and hasty reply reeked with irritation.

"I feel this is the best way to handle this." *And you.* "I need time to put all of these happening in perspective. Things like this don't happen to me every day."

"You're right. You take your time and do a little research. I guess we both need to understand all of this a little better."

Was he referring to her as well as the ghost? Jewel changed the subject. "Did Marcus forgive you for staying away so long?"

"He's making me pay. I've only been back one afternoon and I've already been needed, as the men put it, on every dirty job out here, but I guess that's okay. They've handled everything just fine. Marcus could do the job without me if he had to."

"I wouldn't sell yourself short. Tell him I said hello, and Bryce?"

"Yes?"

"Give me some time."

"You got it."

Throughout the entire conversation, one of her hands had been gripping the book against her chest. After pressing the off button on the phone, she gently lowered the book and relaxed. Bryce had a way of twisting her in knots and tangling her smooth plans.

All of his kindness came crashing down on her. It

would be easier if he were self-centered and selfish, but he wasn't. Her suspicious nature, thanks to David, kept waiting for his true self to emerge. David's did. Why shouldn't his?

She grunted out loud, then opened her book of ghosts. Captain McDougle and Ula were more interesting than any of these other ghosts. She smiled at the thought of the couple. Maybe she'd write her own chapter one day.

***

To keep her mind occupied with something other than ghosts and a man in a fort, Jewel spent days in the library poring over research material for a new course she'd teach in the fall, but after a while, even that bored her. The same information could be found on the Internet, but the books produced a connection with the past that sitting at a computer lacked. For hours she lost herself amongst the wonderfully musty books in that section. Her arms ached from stretching up to the high shelves and carrying the thick volumes back to her table, but she wouldn't have traded those hours for anything else.

Walking down the history aisle, she saw a volume about Celtic folklore, a subject that neither lent itself to her science classes nor to her own research on plantations, but the past had a way of settling her and making her problems in the present seem manageable.

Convincing herself that she had time to deviate from her science class, she pulled the history book from the shelf and sat in a quiet corner alone. Flipping through the pages, she settled down and skimmed over tales of warriors and battles, maidens and monsters. By the end of the afternoon when she knew she had to leave the history section and return to the science section, she came across a tale of a treasure dug up and given to a lady fair.

Something undetectable stirred within her. Sitting at a

ococve*Forever, My Love*

huge mahogany table situated between tall shelves of books, Jewel raised her eyes from the pages and scanned the rows and rows of tawdry maroon covers. Her pleasant Celtic experience had come to an end and she wasn't sure why.

She squeezed her eyes. What was it that was within her reach, but stayed a breath away?

Once more she considered the words she had just read. Over and over she scanned the lines for something to unlock the mystery. Something was there amidst those lines that wouldn't let her move on.

Lifting her eyes away and stretching her neck, she tried to relax, but the muscles in her neck only tightened more. Again she looked at the words on the page, blurred from eyestrain, but this time something stood out. She froze. Over and over she read about a treasure, a treasure that had been buried for safe keeping from marauding bandits.

Then she remembered her dream. Hilliard had buried his treasured possessions hidden from the Union army. She saw Ula holding up her day dress as Hilliard led her through the thick undergrowth. She heard his repeated directions about the bend in the river and the Austin property.

She ran her hands across the page. It was a tale not from the Civil War nor from her own lifetime, but it had served its purpose. "Oh, Ula, I remember." Quickly, she looked around and smiled at a student not far her who frowned at her from over her glasses. Jewel's heart pounded. Ula had shown her where Hilliard had buried their family valuables.

After slamming the book shut, she returned it to its home on the shelf, then quickly gathered her belonging. With shaky hands, she snapped her notebook closed, fumbled with her pen, and straightened note cards that lay scattered around the table.

169

Her mind reeled with the images. A bend in the river. A huge oak tree. It was all there in front of her as clear as if she were standing at River's Bend.

Grabbing her cell phone, she hurried out the door and sat on one of the massive concrete steps. Dropping her load, she hit the green button on her cell phone.

"Oh, come on. Come on."

At the appropriate signal, she punched in Bryce's number. "Please have your phone on. Please. Please." She needed to hear Bryce's voice at this moment more than she had needed anything in a long time.

"You're there," she said when he answered the phone. "Thank goodness." She breathed a sigh of relief.

"Jewel? Is that you? Is something wrong?"

"No, no, nothing's wrong." Her ragged voice betrayed her, but she didn't care. "In fact, I guess, everything's really right. I remembered. I remembered the rest of the dream."

Chapter 13

"Would you stop pacing?" Bryce held his hand over the mouthpiece of the phone, whispered, and then smiled.

With arms crossed tightly in front of her body, Jewel walked back and forth in their quaint room in a local St. Mark's bed and breakfast. When she turned to face Bryce, she dropped her hands to her sides then pulled them up again.

"I can't. My insides feel like a ball of earthworms."

Bryce placed his hand over the mouthpiece again. "Thank you for such a nice description."

His smile weakened her knees, so she turned and searched for the TV controls to keep from throwing herself into his arms. It was hard for her to be around the man without feeling jittery and sweaty. Add his magnetism to the strange situation in which she found herself, her nerves didn't have a chance.

As soon as she'd revealed her dream to Bryce, he began making plans. Freeing up a crew of his men from one job, he arranged to have them and their equipment to meet him at the estate of River's Bend. He contacted both the Smyths in New York and a representative from the historical society. He never hesitated or doubted her for a second, but for her it was different.

From the beginning she was afraid she had created a

chaotic situation and would lead the men on a wild goose chase to dig for treasures that didn't exist. She knew Ula had contacted her—or at least she hoped she had. She worked to convince herself that her visions had to be real. Anything that powerful couldn't be imagined, she told herself, but the magnitude of what she was asking everyone to believe scared her.

Everything was in place for the big dig. Everything but Jewel's nerves.

Her perfectly ordered world of science labs and classrooms was about to be thrown into chaos. Never had she spent such a confusing couple weeks in her life, and now she felt as though it was about to come crashing down on her.

What if she had dreamed the events, really dreamed them without the help of Ula? When she'd called Bryce the morning after her dream, she had been so sure, but now that she was in St. Marks waiting for the dig to happen, her doubts took over. With all of her heart, she wanted the dreams to be true. How else could she help the two McDougle spirits—if indeed she hadn't conjured up their entire situation?

The closer it got to the time that everyone would gather at the estate, the more terrified she became. If nothing was discovered, she could handle being laughed at, but this endeavor now involved work crews that were costing Bryce's company money, professionals from the historical society who had their hopes high, and Smyth family members from New York who were traveling down to Louisiana to witness the dig on their property.

She groaned and plopped down on one end of a couch.

The rooms in the St. Marks bed and breakfast had two bedrooms and a cozy sitting area. Making sure she was still within hearing range of Bryce, Jewel flipped through the stations, keeping the volume low enough not to disturb Bryce.

She admired Bryce's dedication to this project. It had taken almost a week to receive needed consent forms for the excavation to take place and to get everything organized.

Bryce had not stopped there. For days he had been on the phone with one attorney and then another trying to determine ownership of whatever they hoped to dig up. His confidence in what she said surprised her, his voice never wavering as he talked with each individual firm. He was steadfast and determined.

Bryce shifted and looked at her, his gaze adding to her already nervous state. Finally he looked out the window as he listened to yet another clerk in a government office. Still, Jewel couldn't sit without twitching and shifting. Her stomach really did feel like a ball of earthworms.

After watching a short news clip about Jason LeBreaux and some of the others who were vying for a party nomination for the presidency, she flicked off the TV and walked over to Bryce and listened to his conversation.

"What is she saying?" she mouthed.

A big smile broke across Bryce's face. "Thank you, ma'am, I'll get back with you in a day or two. If you have other information, you have my cell phone."

He hung up. "Didn't your mother teach you manners?" he asked with another controlled grin trying to break. His face showed the beginnings of a five-o'clock shadow, dark and sexy.

Ignoring the urge to touch his cheek, she eased into a chair across from him.

"I've got manners. I'm just lacking in patience right now. What did the clerk say?"

"Not much more than we assumed before we called. Anything dug up is essentially the property of the estate owners. If it is historically significant, sometimes it can be transferred to museums in their names. If you can prove it belongs in your family, there's a chance the courts will favor you."

Fran McNabb

"Courts?"

"Well, it might not get that far. I think the Smyths would hand over personal family belongings to you since you're the one who has discovered them, assuming of course, that something is actually buried where you say it is."

That was the first time that Bryce had voiced a question. She hesitated, but had to ask. "Do you doubt I saw what I say I saw in my dreams?"

"Not at all. What I doubt is that it's still where Ula showed you where to look. After all of these years, who knows what has taken place out there? Floods could've uncovered the treasurers for anyone to pick up. Whatever he buried could've deteriorated, and, who knows, the Yankees might've dug around the property until they found something. I'm sure it was obvious to them the Southerners on the plantations they raided weren't going to simply hand over their valuables."

Jewel breathed easier. At this point she needed his confidence. "You're right, but for the sake of Ula and Hilliard, your crew, you and me, I hope something is there. I'd hate for your company to be wasting all this time, money and manpower on a phantom treasure. Maybe whatever we dig up will show us what to do next to help out our two lovers. We still don't know what they want us to do."

Saying the actual words made the belief in the spirits real, but did she actual believe in them? She wanted to believe, felt as though she'd been contacted, but still a tiny part of her brain refused to acknowledge the existence of these spirits.

"You're right," he said. He walked to the window and sat in a straight-backed chair.

The room, with its heavy brocade drapes and oversized furniture faintly smelling of lemon wax, surrounded them with uneasy quiet. They both sat deep in thought, him rigid in his chair, tapping his pen on the writing desk, Jewel slouched across the wing-back, nervously shaking her foot.

She was a jumble of nerves, ready to get on with what had to be done. Having to wait another day was tortuous.

He dropped his pen on the desk. "I saw a pizza place on the block. Feel like taking a little walk?"

She almost jumped out of her chair. "Sounds great."

He laughed. "You sure you don't want to think about it?"

"Are you making fun of me?" But before he could answer, she laughed at herself. She *had* answered pretty fast.

He walked over to her and pulled her close. "No, I'm not making fun of you. I'm, uh, just admiring your quick decision making."

"Sure you are."

Having his arms around her felt good. Way too good. Jewel's body went on alert. Leaning into him sent her already overloaded heart into double time. She pulled away gently. "Give me a minute."

The tiny bath offered her a moment's reprieve. She stared into the mirror and wondered how she'd ever survive the night being in the same room with him. It was the only room in the place, he had said, just like before.

She had agreed. Just like before.

Stupid. Stupid. Stupid. She berated herself because she knew she could never fight his advances. She probably didn't want to, but she had to pretend to herself that she could.

Rebound. Since David, Bryce was the first man she'd even looked at. On the rebound is what her closest friend on the faculty had called it when she mentioned Bryce to her. All the signs were there, but Jewel didn't think so. Bryce wasn't someone to take lightly, and she wasn't looking to replace David with anyone.

But the more she was around Bryce, the more she wondered why she had waited so long to get back into the dating scene.

***

Two slices of pizza and two cold draft beers later, Jewel sat back in her chair, her mind at ease and her belly feeling content. "I feel so much better. Thanks."

"I knew you would," he said, in between bites. He was on his fourth slice and she watched in amazement, wondering how many he could put away.

"You like to eat, don't you?"

He grinned. "Sure do, and I've noticed that you don't do so bad yourself."

Jewel held her palms up. "Okay, truce. No more wise-cracks about eating."

"Truce," he said then took his last bite.

"I think we should have gotten two rooms." Jewel surprised herself by voicing her thoughts out of nowhere.

He wasn't fazed. "We do have two rooms. Two bedrooms."

"Yeah, well. We had a bed and a couch the last time we spent the night together and that didn't work."

"I thought it worked very well."

"You know what I mean."

"I know exactly what you mean." He reached over and took her hand. "Look. You can lock your door if you want. I swear I'll stay in my room unless you call me. I don't want to, mind you, but I will."

"How can you be so calm about all this?"

"All this? You mean calm about the ghost and the visions, or calm about what's happening with us?"

"There's nothing happening with us." She wondered if she was trying to convince herself or him.

"If you say so." He raised his hand to get the attention

of the waitress. "I disagree. I think there's a lot happening between us. You just don't want to admit it."

The waitress, young, busty and oozing hormones, leaned closer than necessary to Bryce. "Here's your check, sir. I hope you and your wife had a nice meal."

"Thank you. We did."

At that, she grinned at Jewel, then turned away.

"Wife?"

"Hey, she's the one who made the assumption." He stood up. "Come on. I want to turn in early. Big day tomorrow."

Jewel let herself be scooped under his arm and led out the door. Her belly was much too full and her mind too jumbled to protest his help.

At the room when he gave her a brotherly peck on the forehead and left her standing at her bedroom door, her body protested. He hadn't even tried to kiss her goodnight.

At his own door, he turned, winked at her and smiled. "See you in the morning."

Totally confused at what her mind screamed and what her body needed, she closed her own door, sighed and mouthed the words she'd said earlier: "There's nothing happening between us."

Then she chuckled and said out loud. "At least not tonight with the doors closed."

***

Bryce pulled his SUV to a stop in front of the familiar gate of River's Bend. Jewel sat patiently on her side of the car and watched him remove the chains.

Driving along the river road with its one quick view of the house had given Jewel the same thrill as the first time she saw the estate. Her heart raced. Her skin tingled.

Sitting alone in the quiet of the SUV, her mind wandered and her eyelids became heavy. The leather seats of the SUV became the soft velvet of a carriage bench. She sat behind two matched grays holding a parasol over her shoulders protecting her delicate skin from the morning sun. The scent of roses wafted through the air. Soon, her jeans and cotton shirt became a tightly laced gown of baby blue linen. Her sports shoes, high-topped leathers with tiny buttons all the way up over the ankle.

The smells of the newly tilled fields filled her nostrils and shrieks of children playing touched her ears.

"Jewel?" Bryce touched her arm. "You with me?"

Jewel took a deep breath then slowly opened her eyes. Bryce leaned across the seat. Both hands cupped her face. At first she stared at him, then her gaze darted out the window, but no children played around them. She was still at River's Bend, but instead of tilled fields, overgrown grass and weeds stood as high as the fence line in some places.

Surprise and hints of sadness settled around her heart.

She nodded. "Yes. At least I think I am."

For a second more, Bryce leaned into her, then he straightened up and switched gears. As he pulled up to the front steps, he finally spoke, interrupting her deep thought. "Were you with them again?"

Jewel started to tremble. "I was, and I'm totally confused with all of this." She reached out and grabbed his arms. "It's as if I don't have any control over myself when this happens."

Bryce pulled her close and held her head tightly against his chest. "Do you really want to go through with this dig?" He held her away from him and looked directly into her eyes. "We can postpone this. We could call Mr. Bourgois and have him come up here if you think it would make you feel better. He said he would do anything to help you get through this ordeal."

"I don't know." Her mind was spinning out of control. "I'm nervous about all of this, but I do want to do it. All these people will be here shortly. I can't back out. It has to be done so we might as well not put it off. If I had to come back another time, I don't think it would get any easier."

His hand massaged her back and his voice was soft. "Those men work for my company. It's not a problem to cancel or at least postpone."

Jewel shook her head. "No. Let's get it over with. Just promise me you'll stay be me."

He touched her cheek. "You don't have to ask. You'd have to pry me away from you."

His face was inches from hers. His breath warm upon her skin.

Desire charged through her body, taking her breath, surprising her. She leaned into him. When his mouth came down on hers, she fell into his embrace and returned his kiss with a deep primal need. His kiss, violent and hard, awakened in her the longing she so carefully and meticulously had stored away. She opened her lips, but yearned to open her whole body to him. She strained against him, cursing the console that was in the way.

Finally, he pulled away from her. Breathing heavily, he held her inches away from him. "Where were you last night when my bed was cold and empty?"

"Don't talk. Just kiss me."

"No."

Surprised and hurt, Jewel jerked back. "No?"

"I don't need to give those men coming down the driveway any more fodder to feed their jokes."

Jewel didn't need any more encouragement to get on her side of the car. Frantically, she straightened her clothes, then flipped down the mirror to check her lipstick.

From the corner of her eye, she saw Bryce adjusting his pants. She smiled.

"That's not funny," he said, then opened the door and stepped out.

A truck pulled up alongside of their vehicle, but Jewel

didn't get out. Instead, she let Bryce face his men alone. Closing her eyes, she took a long, deep breath and tried to calm herself, but it was hard remembering the look on his face as he had straightened his pants. Her entire body now throbbed from Bryce's kiss. Her skin still smoldered from his touch.

Your fault, Jewel. You're the one who wanted separate bedrooms last night.

Stupid was what she had called herself yesterday from staying in the same suite with him. Stupid is what she called herself now for staying alone last night.

Taking a deep breath, she stepped out of the car and hoped the fire that still burned deep within her didn't show. Several of the men talking with Bryce looked familiar, and she assumed she'd met them at the fort.

Bryce guided her close to his side. It was all she could do to not turn into him and finish what they had just started. Instead she listened politely as he introduced each man.

"Hi and thanks for coming." Jewel found her voice and it sounded quite normal. She was pleased. "How's the island making it without Bryce out there?"

One of the men spoke up. "Oh, we're managing just fine. Marcus grumbles and gripes when Bryce isn't with us, but he does it just because he misses him. I swear the two of them are a real pair."

"I noticed." She turned her attention to each of the other men, greeting them individually, shaking each of their hands with as much enthusiasm as she could muster.

No one needed to know how leery she was about the events that were about to take place. These men were here expecting results. She hoped they wouldn't go home disappointed.

Before the introductions were complete, another car pulled through the gate.

Bryce stepped away from the truck. "Looks like the Smyths are here."

A black SUV rolled down the driveway and stopped

next to the group. Bryce went to the driver's side and shook hands with a portly middle-aged man who pulled himself out of the car. After appropriate introductions, Bryce and Mr. Smyth walked around and opened the door for an elderly woman.

"This is my mother, Mrs. Norton Smyth. She insisted on seeing the old home one more time."

"How do you do, Mrs. Smyth?" Bryce extended his hand.

Mrs. Smyth, a fragile, white-haired lady reached out and clasped her hands around his. "It's nice to meet you, young man. I couldn't stay up in New York with all this excitement going on down here. Oh, my. This is all so glorious."

Mrs. Smyth twisted around on the seat and allowed Bryce and her son to help her out of the car. Taking a cane from her son, she faced Jewel. "You must be Miss Ferguson."

"Yes, ma'am. I'm glad you were able to join us. I hope the trip wasn't too hard on you."

"Oh, no. Those airlines cater to old people like me. I'm treated like a queen, pushed around in wheelchairs, and tucked into my seat like I'm about to break in two." Even in her excited state at visiting her old home, the perfectly formed words oozed out of her mouth with inbred gentility and a hint of Southern drawl.

Jewel smiled. "Thank you for allowing us to be here today and to dig on your property. There could be so much history buried here. We're eager to begin." No need to tell the lady just how nervous she was.

By that time, another truck drove through the gate bearing the crest of the South Louisiana Historical Society on the side of the door.

"That will be Roland Jones, the last of the gathering," Bryce said as he reached into the car for a camera. "Looks like we can begin our search."

Mr. Smyth spoke up. "I've convinced Mother to wait in the house until we find the right spot. There's no need for her to be trudging around the woods in this humidity and heat."

Mrs. Smyth straightened up. "I think I've changed my mind. As much as I want to see the inside of the house again, it will have to wait. I don't want to miss any of this. I want to go. I know this property better than any of you. I'll even allow you to push me in the wheelchair as far as the trails go."

"Mother. We talked about this," Mr. Smyth said with exasperation in his voice.

It only took a stern look from Mrs. Smyth for her son to recant, turn and pull a wheelchair out of the back of the SUV.

Mrs. Smyth rolled her eyes at Jewel. "He treats me as if I'm two steps away from the grave."

Jewel took her hand. "Be happy he's there for you. I think it's very special." She winked back at the older lady.

With a twinkle in her eye, Mrs. Smyth winked back. "I know, but if I don't complain and gripe, he'll think something really is wrong and commit me to one of those awful places they call homes."

"Come on, Mother. If you insist on going with us, get in, but you know I don't approve."

"Oh phooey. I don't need anyone's approval."

Bryce helped her into the chair, but Jewel took the handles. "I'll push. You two follow the crew. We'll catch up."

Since Jewel had told Bryce as much information she remembered from the dream, he led his men toward the river, each carrying an array of tools.

A path from years past could be seen through the overgrown shrubs and thick grass. Even with the property being vacant for so long, it wasn't hard to follow the trail. Jewel pushed Mrs. Smyth easily.

"Over there. That's where the shoo-fly was." Mrs. Smyth pointed to a high spot on the river's bank as they emerged from the trees. "I did a little research while we lived here. It seems that's where Captain McDougle built it for his new wife. There's no telling how many times it had been rebuilt since the fifties when my husband had the remnants removed. Rot and humidity had ruined what was left of it, and we never got around to rebuilding it." Her gaze trailed along the bank. "Such a shame."

Jewel stopped abruptly remembering the structure so vivid in her dream. Just to make sure she wasn't imagining part of her dream, she had to ask, "Are you talking about the round structure that extended out over the banks of the river under the tree?"

"Yes, of course."

Jewel nodded. "I've seen pictures of them. They were quite impressive."

Staring at the spot, she could almost see its wide white stairs and benches built along the railings and even though there was no breeze today, she could feel the breeze from the river on her face.

She had been there with Hilliard, but she saw no reason to make that announcement to the group. How could she announce she knew where the shoo-fly had stood? How could she tell them she'd sat in it? She's the one who'd be committed to a "home"!

Bryce stepped up to her and touched her arm. He, too, said nothing about her visit there, but the concern in his face told Jewel he understood what she was feeling.

Nodding her thank you to him, she found her voice. "If that's where the shoo-fly stood, that's where we need to start." Jewel pushed the wheelchair a little faster as Bryce walked ahead. "From there we'll need to turn left and head inland a bit, but follow the course of the river until we get to the second bend." She leaned down and spoke to Mrs. Smyth. "Are you familiar with the bend across from the Austin property?"

Mrs. Smyth thought a moment before answering. "I think you must be talking about a place the children called Big Bend. In spite of all my warning, they tied a long rope and would jump into the river from it. There's a little curve that is much shallower with no current flowing through. That could be where you're talking about."

"If it's down from the shoo-fly, it just might be. It's as good a place as any to begin."

Mrs. Smyth kept talking. "I do seem to remember my father talking about the Austin family when I was a little girl. I think the last of the family died before I was grown, but I'm almost sure it was the name he used. The family had financial problems around the forties and subdivided some of the acreage."

With eyes sparkling and hands tucked on her lap, Mrs. Smyth began to reminisce about the days when she and her husband raised their boys here, the crops they grew and the hired help that became almost like family.

One anecdote ran into the next and before Jewel knew it, she had pushed the lady's wheelchair past the spot of the original shoo-fly.

Bryce stood waiting at the beginning of another overgrown trail that paralleled the river. "I thought you might need some help with the chair. It's pretty overgrown here."

Jewel's heart immediately jumped in her chest. Standing amongst the thick foliage, Bryce flashed the smile she had become so accustomed to and extended a helping hand to her.

"You doing okay, Mrs. Smyth?" he asked.

"Oh, yes. You're a dear for helping."

Bryce winked at Jewel and covered her hands with his on the wheelchair handles. "I'll take it from here."

Jewel nodded, but before stepping away from the chair, she turned her hands over and squeezed his. "Thanks."

With eyes dark with desire, Bryce looked as though he would lean down and kiss her, but instead he straightened up and pushed the chair away.

"You'd better get in front of us and start remembering your directions."

Jewel stepped away. "My, aren't we bossy?" she said, but grinned back at him.

She walked alone listening to the quiet jabber of Mrs. Smyth and Bryce at her back and concentrating on every tree and every shrub she passed. The farther into the property she walked, the more her body and mind began to react. A feeling of *deja vu* came over her though she knew she had never before been here at this particular part of the property except, of course, in her dream.

She stopped.

Bryce pushed Mrs. Smyth alongside of her, then reached out and touched her arm. "Take your time. There's no one here going to rush you."

Again Jewel just nodded.

Several of the crew members met them on the path. "We're back to river again. The path turns right into it."

"Then you've gone too far."

All the men looked at Jewel.

"If you've gone all the way back to the river," she explained, "we've passed the tree. It's a huge oak tree directly across from the Austin property." Jewel looked in Mrs. Smyth's direction for help.

Mrs. Smyth squinted and looked from one point to the next. "Well, it seems we're in the right place somewhere in here. There's the bend, and over there was the Austins' place."

Jewel quickly scanned the area. How would she know which tree it was? So many years had passed since Hilliard had buried his family's valuables. So many storms and other natural disasters. What if the tree no longer existed?

Her throat tightened.

As if he knew her thoughts, Bryce wrapped his arm around her and whispered in her ear. "Don't feel pressured. Maybe I'd better send all these people over to the river to rest and we'll walk around alone. Would that help?"

His words helped relieve her shattered nerves. "Yes. Let's try that."

Quietly, Bryce relayed the message to his men and to Mr. Smyth who was now tending to his mother. When they were alone, Bryce turned Jewel toward him. "Are you okay?"

"I don't know, Bryce. A few minutes ago, I felt as if I'd been here before. Now, I feel nothing. Maybe I've led all of you. . ."

He cut her off. "Don't even say that again. We're here, and we'll try to find something. If we don't, it's not your fault. We'll just give it our best shot." He pulled her to his body. "I know you don't want to hear this, but you feel so good. I think I'll send all these people up to the house and have you all to myself."

A tiny laugh escaped Jewel's lips. "Don't you dare. We'll never find anything then."

He groaned. "Talk like that, young lady, certainly isn't the way to cool a man down."

His lips passed over her forehead lightly. "We're going to be okay out here. I have a feeling it'll all work out."

Her chest tightened and a tinge across her forehead signaled an on-coming headache. "I just wish I could share your optimism."

"I've got enough faith in you for the both of us." He took her hand. "Come on. Let's walk."

Together they circled each oak tree, touching it, examining it, hoping to jar a vibe of remembrance for Jewel.

Nothing.

Fleeting moments of possible recognition touched

Jewel as she roamed through the woods. Stopping, she waited and concentrated, praying for something to click. Still nothing.

Sweat formed around Jewel's waistband. The morning's high humidity and mugginess were blame for some of it, but she was sure her nerves played a role in it as well. She was about to give up when the crack of a limb sent a charge throughout her entire body. Bryce had his arm around her. Her body trembled. Both of them froze.

Neither spoke. Together they waited, clinging to each other for the impossible to happen. Jewel closed her eyes and smiled.

"This is it."

Fran McNabb

Chapter 14

Bryce handed Jewel a thermos of water. "Here, this'll make you feel better."

She sipped the cool water. "I'm fine. Really."

"I know you're fine, but the water will make you feel better." His lopsided grin produced tiny wrinkles around his eyes. Working in the elements had toughened his skin, giving it a ruggedness that Jewel liked.

Sitting down on the soft grass next to her, he stretched out his legs then took a drink from the thermos. "That's the third tree they've dug under."

"Oh, don't remind me. I feel bad enough already."

"I wasn't being negative. I told you no one expects miracles from you. You're doing the best you can." He smiled. "The McDougles should've been more specific if they wanted you to find their treasure. Maybe this tree they're digging by now is the biggie."

In spite of the fact that her insides were twisted, his comments dragged up a smile. "I hope so. I want the guys to find something today. They're working so hard."

Bryce reached out and took her hand. "We will."

Through the tangled brush and thick tree trunks, she watched his men digging where she'd pointed out. One with a shovel carefully inserted the point, loosened and removed a small amount of dirt. The others on their hands

188

and knees used smaller spades to carefully remove smaller clumps of dirt. They spoke in whispers as if the site where they dug was sacred.

Closing her eyes, she prayed they'd find something. Had her mind played tricks on her with all the visions?

Frustrated, she slumped against the tree. "I'm feeling jittery again. I was so confident a few minutes ago. It was as though Ula had stomped on my toe with her pointed little button-ups and told me to have the men dig there." She scrunched her face. "I don't know what I felt. Maybe it was gas."

Byrce draped his arm around her shoulders, letting her cuddle against him. "It'll be fine. If something's buried anywhere around here, my men will find it. They know what they're doing."

"I wish I could be as confident."

His kiss on her forehead comforted her.

"Stop worrying." With that kiss, Bryce withdrew his arm, leaving her feeling cold and alone. "Looks like I'm being called. I'll be right back."

She tried to relax, but it was impossible. Squeezing her eyes, she tried to recall the feeling that had swept over her a short time ago. It had to have been a sign from Ula, but try as she would, nothing happened again.

Where are you, Ula? I need you? Don't let me down.

She rubbed her head. Nothing.

She watched Bryce moving from one workman to the next, giving instructions, laughing quietly, helping where he could. His easy manner and assurance generated smiles from most of the men. It was easy to see they respected him with the kind of respect that is earned, not demanded.

His jeans, wet from kneeling alongside the men at each tree, clung to his body in all the right places showing off his muscular thighs.

Jewel turned her head. Having Bryce send her blood pressure zooming wasn't exactly what she needed at the moment. She looked toward the canopy of twisted tree limbs above her and watched fluffy white clouds float across the sky.

Soon she struggled to keep her eyelids open. Something from deep within her pulled her away from the image of Bryce and his crew of men. She heard snippets of quiet chatter around her and gradually slipped once more into a world where she had never been though knew well by now.

Her mind emptied. Her body felt weightless as she was spirited away.

***

Ula McDougle lay quietly in one of the upstairs bedrooms of River's Bend or what was left of it. Furniture from other rooms in the estate, piled high against the walls, had momentarily been saved from the disrespect of the Union soldiers who now roamed freely in her home.

Bending down, she kissed the tiny head nestled against her breast. Only a thin fuzz of hair tickled her lips, but she smiled at its touch. Already the tiny boy's hair showed signs of red, just like his father's. Tears threatened to overflow, but she bit her lip and willed them not to come. There was no time for tears.

How long had it been since word had come about her husband? Months? She wondered if he even knew he had a son. Messages had been sent out to the island where she heard he'd been taken, but for months now, no one had been able to make contact with the Confederate prisoners.

Was her Hilliard even alive? Had his wounds healed or had he succumbed to some terrible fever as did so many of the wounded?

Fear, helplessness, and a horrible feeling of sadness weighed her down. She bit her bottom lip, refusing to visualize the agony her beloved husband might have endured.

If only she could also shut out the scene that played out in front of her daily.

Soldiers burned her furniture for campfires at night. Furniture that Hilliard had brought over from Europe or painstakingly carried in his wagon from New Orleans now became nothing more than piles of ashes.

Curses, crude jokes, whispers, and insulting words reached her ears each time she ventured out into her home to find food for herself and her house girl Mattie. Several of the younger Union soldiers were civil to her and helped her find the food she needed. Had it not been for them, she, Mattie, and her baby would have perished long ago.

It was all a bad dream. How had her perfect world been turned upside down so quickly? How did River's Bend, once her cradle for peace and love, turn into her prison? The bad dream had turned into a nightmare that wouldn't go away.

The tiny head moved. Milk ran down the side of the baby's mouth and Ula lovingly wiped it away.

"Oh, Hilliard, will you ever see your son?"

A pounding on the door startled her. She pulled the baby's head tightly to her breasts. "Who is it?"

"Open the door, Mrs. McDougle. I have a message for you from Lieutenant Brackdon."

Ula slid off the big bed, tucking the baby against a pillow. Quickly she pulled her bodice together, then draped a shawl over herself.

She moved several chairs away from the door and peeked through the crack. A soldier stuck out his hand. "These are orders from the lieutenant for you and your son and the girl to vacate these quarters. You've got to be gone by tomorrow night or they'll have you physically removed."

Ula stared down at the handwritten note, but couldn't make out a single word. Her head spun. "Excuse me? Did you say I have to leave this room?"

He nodded. "This room and this house. You can take anything you can carry, but the horses and the carriage are now possessions of the Union army."

Ula blinked in confusion. "My house? You want me to leave my home?"

"Ma'am, I'm just delivering a message. You have to get your things together and get out. This is no longer your house. We have wounded troops coming in soon. We're going to need all the space we can grab, including this room."

"Where will I go?"

The solder's eyes showed concern. "I wish I could tell you, but you'll have to figure that out for yourself."

With those words he turned to go, but looked back at her. "I really am sorry, but this has to be done."

Ula grabbed the door facing. Her whole body trembled. How could she pick up her baby and go? The nearest town was miles from here, and as far as she knew Union soldiers had taken over it as well. Hilliard had cousins on the other side of the small community if they were still alive, but getting there with their few possessions would be almost impossible without a horse.

"Miss Ula, did the man say we have to leave?"

Ula turned to see Mattie, the house girl, coming out of the small adjacent bedroom that had once been decorated for her new baby. Born in the same year, Mattie and she had become close friends and companions. Mattie had even followed her here to River's Bend from her own home in northern Louisiana when Ula married. Now the two had no one but each other, and for the sake of her friend, Ula would hide the fear that tore at her breast.

Ula reached out and hugged her. "We have to go."

Mattie stepped back, her big black eyes welling up with tears. "But where? Where will we go?"

"We'll find a place. There are people along the river who'll take us in. Right now we have to get out of here as the soldier said." Jewel fought back tears. This wasn't the time for weakness. "It's not safe here at River's Bend anymore."

"But this is our home."

Ula pulled the girl to her. "Not any more, Mattie. We'll have to find another home until this war is over."

The two women held onto each other searching for strength. Ula felt Mattie tremble as she cried quietly into her shoulder. It felt good to have the comfort of another human being, but she longed for her husband's strong arms and strength. She missed him so much, it hurt.

Mattie stepped back and wiped her eyes. "Miss Ula, no one is here to help us. We can't move. We can't carry all our stuff and our baby too."

"We can and we will, Mattie. These soldiers aren't giving us any options. You start getting things together. Only those things we really need. And the family Bible. We can do this. We have to." She looked over at the small bundle on the bed. "We have to do this for Hilliard's son."

***

Groaning, Jewel rolled her head against the rough bark on the tree. "Yes, for Hilliard's son." The words woke her. Again, she repeated the words, this time in a whisper. "For Hilliard's son."

Her eyes flew open. Bryce and three of his men stood twenty feet or so away from her, whispering. Another group of workers rested on a break. She was here on River's Bend with Bryce, but she had once again soared into the past with Ula McDougle.

Once again she had dreamed or visited or imagined herself with Ula. No, she corrected her thoughts. Not with. As Ula. *I was Ula. I held that little baby.* She touched her breast. *I nursed him.*

The uncontrollable weight of sadness had not left her. It was with her now just as it had been in her dream. She wondered if Ula McDougle, now as a spirit, still suffered the tragic heartbreak from losing the things she had loved so many years ago.

Was it possible for a feeling to live on in the spirit? Was it this feeling that kept the two spirits of the lovers alive searching for something to put them at rest?

Bryce left his men and collapsed beside her on the ground. Looking strained, he stretched his back, but managed to produce the smile that Jewel had come to love. "Did you take a little nap? You looked as if you were asleep a few minutes ago. I didn't want to disturb you."

Jewel nodded.

Rubbing the palm of his hand against his neck, he squinted at her. "Is something wrong? You look worried." He patted her leg. "I told you everything will work out."

"I know. Nothing's wrong. Not really." She looked into Bryce's eyes. "Just another visit with Ula."

Bryce got serious. Sitting up straight, he reached for her hand. "You sure you're okay?"

Jewel nodded. "Yes, but my heart is breaking for what Ula went through. Every time I see her or Hilliard, I can't stand the feeling that comes over me." She looked at the ground. "It's awful. Almost unbearable."

"Where were you this time?" His voice was soft with concern.

"In the house," she answered as softly, "locked in one of the upstairs bedrooms while the Union army occupied her house. She had a baby, Bryce. A tiny little boy. Hilliard's son." Jewel touched her breasts again. "He was nursing."

Her words trailed off. Bryce pulled her close to his chest. "That little baby would've been one of your ancestors. He's the bloodline that survived."

Jewel sat up and smiled. "Yes, he would be, wouldn't he? I don't recall his name right now. Once I even researched the lineage, wrote down all the names in the family, but I can't recall the boy's name." She exhaled. "That's so sad."

"Doesn't matter," Bryce said. "You don't need to know his name to know he survived and fathered children of his own."

Jewel smiled. "Yes, he did, didn't he, or I wouldn't be who I am today."

"Does that make you feel better?" he asked with a twinkle in his eye.

She nodded. "He was going to have red hair. I kissed the thin fuzz on his head."

Bryce touched her hair and brushed it back over her ear. "Hair just like yours. Yours and Hilliard's."

"I'm still amazed and totally confused about all of this. How can any of this actually be? I sure hope I'm not just dreaming it all. That's what everyone in my science department would say is happening."

"Naah. I'm convinced that too much has happened to be coincidence. Your visions or visits, or whatever you want to call them, have to be real. No, I have to believe you're making some sort of contact." He started to get up once more. "I have faith in what you're seeing."

"Bryce, what if we don't dig up something today?"

"I don't know." He kissed her on the nose. "We'll think of something, I'm sure. Ula led us here. She's not going to let us go home empty-handed."

He left her sitting on the ground.

The afternoon waned. Jewel retreated to the house to check on Mrs. Smyth. Her son had insisted his mother wait inside when the day's heat became too much. Mrs. Smyth roamed through the big estate reminiscing to anyone who'd listen about the years she'd raised her children here. Jewel followed her around and listened quietly, wondering what it would be like to live in a place so magnificent and one so rich in history.

When the pair reached the front parlor, they stopped in front of the portrait of Ula.

Mrs. Smyth's hands flew to her breasts. "Oh, my. That portrait hung there the entire time we lived here, but I never paid much attention to it." She looked directly at Jewel. "You are identical to that young lady."

"I am," Jewel said softly. Seeing the mirror image of herself on the wall again sent another wave of shock through her body, but she inhaled deeply and continued. "I knew she was an ancestor, but I had no idea I could look so much like her after all these years."

"The hair is different, of course."

Unconsciously, Jewel touched her hair. "It's Hilliard's color, her husband. I look like her, but I have Hilliard's mass of red hair. Quirky, isn't it?"

Mrs. Smyth shook her head from side to side. "I've never seen anything so uncanny."

The front door flew open. "Miss Ferguson? Mr. Cameron wants you back down by the river."

Jewel looked from the young man to Mrs. Smyth.

"Go," she said. "Go. My son will come get me"

Jewel nodded, then left Mrs. Smyth standing in front of the portrait. She raced out of the house, took the stairs two at a time, then ran across the lawn.

The group of men now huddled around yet another tree with two more small mounds of dirt nearby. Bryce raised his head and smiled as Jewel ran toward them.

He reached out to her. "See, I told you she wouldn't let us go home empty-handed."

At his feet lay several wooden barrels with years of mud and rotting vegetation stuck on their sides. Two leather pouches also lay unopened.

"We didn't want to open anything until you and the Smyths were present."

"I passed Mr. Smyth running toward the house. I assumed he's on his way to get his mother." Jewel's heart pounded and her head spun. It was here right at her feet, the things that Hilliard had hidden away from the Union army.

Tears welled in her eyes. Her dreams had been real after all.

Bryce placed a hand on her shoulder. "You still okay?"

It was hard to contain the emotion in her chest. "I'll say. You can't imagine how happy I am that you dug something up. Even if it's nothing but worthless trinkets, I wanted something to be here."

"I had faith in you."

"You mean in Ula, don't you?"

He tipped his head to the side. "Whoever. I simply had faith in what you were saying."

"I'm glad you did," Jewel whispered. "For a while, I had my doubts."

She looked up.

Mr. Smyth rolled his mother's wheelchair up to where everyone stood. "Oh, this is just marvelous," she said with her hand to her chest. "Can you imagine? These things were buried here for all the years we lived here, played here, ran over them with our mowers and tractors. Oh my, I'm amazed."

Jewel squatted next to her chair. "Then these things and Ula and Hilliard are part of your lives too, aren't they?"

Bryce spoke up. "If everyone's here, shall we open them?"

Roland Jones, from the historical society, stepped forward. "If you don't mind, I'd like to help. We don't want anything destroyed. Better yet, I'd really like to take these things back to the lab and open them there."

Several men and Mrs. Smyth spoke out at the same time. "Oh no. Please. Let's try here."

Mr. Jones shook his head. "I'm not sure that's the best way to do this. We could easily ruin a valuable part of history if we're not careful."

Again, everyone spoke up at once, each pleading his case.

"Well, I'm not in favor of this." Disgusted, he looked at Bryce. "It's on your shoulders if anything gets ruined."

"I'll accept that responsibility. I've worked with enough historical pieces to know when they're untouchable.

197

My men won't do anything that'll jeopardize what's here. I want to save this stuff as much or more than you do."

He stooped next to Roland and together they gently brushed away the debris that clung to the sides of one of the barrels. The wooden sides showed deep signs of deterioration, but three iron strips, rusted but still sturdy, held the wood together.

Bryce began the tedious job of prying open the container while his men spread several large tarps around the work site. Bryce worked carefully with a small pry, circling the top of the barrel time and again until the wooden pegs loosened and the top slid off effortlessly.

Taking a deep breath, Jewel knelt next to him as he carefully pulled out bundles of damp fabric, the remains of crude cotton sacks and remnants of shiny brocades.

Bryce handed one bundle to Jewel. "I think you should open the first one."

Jewel didn't hesitate. She placed her hand on the bundle. Closing her eyes, she felt the years melt away as she touched the rich brocade. Somehow she knew that this had been a piece of one of Ula's dresses, a ball dress worn before she had married Hilliard. For a moment she allowed herself to hear the mellow sounds of a small orchestra to which Ula and Hilliard had danced. Cigar smoke and the smell of candles engulfed her.

A warm hand on her shoulder brought her back. "Everyone's waiting," Bryce whispered near her ear.

She opened her eyes and nodded. With fumbling fingers, she began to unwrap the delicate fabric. Some of the outer layer fell apart as she unwrapped. Afraid to harm what was inside the wrappings, Jewel clinched her teeth, held her breath, and frantically looked up at Bryce.

"Take your time," Bryce said. "Mr. Jones won't let you harm anything. He'll stop you before you do."

The sweat on Bryce's forehead told her that even though he was reassuring her, he had his doubts.

Carefully, she continued to unwrap the fragile bundle. Bit by bit, she worked her way toward the center. There, she found a drier fabric of bright red floral that opened up to expose several pieces of heavy silverware, intricately carved, but tarnished from years of neglect.

A quiet hush fell on those that gathered around. Jewel ran a finger along the edge of one piece of silverware. It and all of the pieces in the bundles were from another time and another life. Today for the first time, they were being introduced to another world, touched by another generation, and admired through eyes that saw more than just utilitarian pieces.

A tear formed in the corner of Jewel's eye. She swallowed hard. "Hilliard must've cherished these pieces. He knew their value and wanted to save them." She looked up to find Bryce staring at her.

"And he did," he said. "They're beautiful even after all the years buried in this land."

"His land," she whispered.

"Imagine these beautiful pieces lay beneath our feet for all those years," Mrs. Smyth whispered. "The enormity of it all is beyond words."

Jewel looked up to the lady in the wheelchair and nodded. "We all agree with that. There's no way I can explain how I feel right now."

Bryce reached over and covered her hand with his. Mrs. Smyth's son placed his hand on his mother's shoulder, and for a few moments no one said anything.

Finally Bryce and Roland began to unwrap the rest of the bundles in the barrels. A complete set of silverware, three trays, and a variety of small serving dishes, all in silver were unwrapped and laid out carefully on the tarps.

The other barrel produced delicate china with a motif of peacocks and white flowers, all exquisitely decorated in what appeared to be gold. All but two pieces had survived their underground stay in perfect condition.

For several hours, the men worked until the last of the barrels were emptied. Only the two leather pouches remained.

Bryce rubbed his hand over one of them. "I think these are papers, but I'd like to open them here." He nodded to Roland. "If it looks like they're too deteriorated, we'll move to your lab."

Roland grimaced and shook his head. "You know how I feel about it, but I've got a feeling it doesn't matter. You're going to open them anyway."

Bryce carefully worked to unlatch a rusted buckle on the first pouch. Jewel watched in amazement as his big fingers gently manipulated the damp leather. His motions were smooth and painstakingly slow, as if he were making love to a woman, but not any woman, to her. Jewel's body trembled in remembrance.

"There." Bryce looked up. "It's opened." He moved aside. "Roland, I think you need to take it from here."

Roland got down on his knees and pulled on a clean set of sheer gloves. With motions as careful as Bryce had used, he began to meticulously remove bits and pieces of paper soaked from years of rain. Each piece was examined and laid aside, but it was easy to see that all the writing was illegible.

Jewel sighed. Bryce pulled her to him. "Don't give up. The middle layers might be better just as the fabrics were."

For long, tedious moments, Roland painstakingly pulled out piece after piece of wet paper, and just as Bryce had guessed, the writing became more and more legible with each drier piece. Finally, several intact pieces lay before them.

Bryce knelt down beside Roland and together tried to read the first document. The handwriting was partly legible, but long passages were so blurred that only scattered words here and there could be read.

"Look, Jewel, this one has to do with the sale of

cotton. It's a delivery to the West County Cotton Mill in Mississippi. Seven thousand pounds were delivered on October 13, 1861."

"Seven thousand pounds," Jewel repeated. "I had no idea this plantation could have produced so much."

"Rich land," Mr. Smyth added.

Jewel wanted to add that it was rich land that Hilliard's family never benefited from after the war, but she kept that thought to herself. Mr. Smyth's ancestors had paid the exorbitant taxes during the period of reconstruction and had legally taken over the plantation. This man and woman who stood by her now had reaped the benefits of that action, but actually had nothing to do with how it had come to be in their family so many years ago.

Still, it saddened Jewel to know that Ula had to survive with nothing. Another family had taken over her beautiful home while she and her son tried to survive. That is, if she actually managed to live through the war.

Roland and Bryce continued to pull out documents until they got to the very bottom of the pouch. There, covered in a layer of mud, were twelve gold coins. Bryce rolled one around in the palm of his hand.

"I wonder why Ula never returned to try to get these things." He spoke as if he were thinking out loud. "You'd think that somewhere after the war there would've been a time that she could've gotten here and dug this stuff up."

Jewel touched the coin. "Maybe she wasn't alive at the end of the war."

Bryce nodded. "That's altogether possible."

Roland stood up and spoke directly to Jewel. "Now that we've found these things, would you explain to me how you knew they would be here?"

Bryce and Jewel looked at each other, then at Roland. Bryce spoke up. "Jewel went to a medium and, well, she had a vision."

"A vision?"

"Let's just say she was led here."

Mrs. Smyth, who had been sitting quietly in her wheelchair, spoke up. "Miss Ferguson, can you trace your lineage to Mr. McDougle?"

"Yes, ma'am. I have the Bible that belonged to Hilliard's family. I guess it was one of the few things Ula carried with her when she left the estate. My grandmother gave it to me before she died."

"Is there any way I could see this Bible?"

"Yes, I think I could have someone to go into my apartment in Houston to find it. We could have it shipped overnight if you think it's important."

"Oh, it's important, all right."

Mr. Smyth stepped near his mother. "Mother, what are you thinking?"

"Why, this plantation was snatched right out from under the McDougle family. Something must be done about that."

"Now, Mother, that was over a hundred years ago. Our family bought this property legally, just as most of the new property owners did after the war. I'm sure if you checked the sales records from that time, there were very few original families who were able to keep their property. It was a war. Those things happen."

"That's right." Mrs. Smyth sat up straight in her wheelchair and creased her brow. "The original families had nothing left after the war, not even their homes when they were made to pay taxes so high no one down here could afford them."

Jewel spoke up. "Mrs. Smyth, I'm not trying to take your property. As your son said, those events happened many generations ago. I only hoped I could convince your family to let me have some of the things that were dug up here."

Bryce put his arm around Jewel. "And to buy the portrait of Ula that hangs in the parlor."

Mrs. Smyth looked at her son. "We have to talk. Let's go into the house."

Mr. Smyth rolled his eyes and placed his hands on the wheelchair. "I don't think there's a lot to talk about."

"Well, I do. Push."

As the two of them left the area, Bryce knelt down by the hoard of treasures from Hilliard and Ula's life. This is all so unbelievable."

Roland, who was working with the buckle on the second leather pouch, stopped. "It's incredible. These things need to be in the local museum."

Bryce placed a hand on his arm. "We'll certainly talk about that. Right now we have two families who have links to these things. It will be up to them as to what should be kept and what should be put on public display. We don't even know for sure who actually has claim."

"Well, I can tell you," Roland said with a serious face, "that the laws will favor the Smyth family. It'll be up to them and the goodness of their hearts to share any of this with Miss Ferguson's family or with the public."

"I'm aware of the law," Bryce answered. "But had it not been for Jewel, no one would have known this stuff existed."

Roland pulled out a handkerchief from his pocket and wiped his forehead. "I'm simply telling you what the law will point to. Let's see how much pull Mrs. Smyth has with her son. I think she's on Jewel's side."

Bryce laughed. "Yeah, I think she is, and from the looks of things, I think she pretty much runs that family."

For the next agonizing half hour or so, Jewel paced around the tarps spread out on the ground and watched as Roland and Bryce pulled out more papers from the next pouch. Just as in the first pouch, the papers were in different degrees of deterioration and legibility. In the center, though, a document was pulled out that made Bryce smile.

"Look, Jewel. Hilliard had the foresight to include the

papers that proved he owned the land." He spread out two sheets of papers, handwritten in beautiful long cursive strokes that named Matthew McDougle as the owner of fifteen hundred acres of land on the Mississippi River.

Jewel spoke up. "I remember that name. Matthew was Hilliard's father. I guess he gave the land to Hilliard when he married."

"The family Bible can prove the family lineage."

Roland spoke up. "Look." He held up a tarnished gold chain with a heart-shaped pendant. "This was at the bottom of the pouch."

Jewel's head spun. "Oh, God, that's Ula's."

The pendant in Roland's hand still caught a tiny shimmer of light in spite of the years in the damp ground.

Jewel reached out and touched the piece of jewelry. "Hilliard gave it to Ula before their wedding day. She wore it all the time."

Roland crossed his arms in front of his chest. "And you know this because?"

"Because she just does." Bryce spoke up before Jewel had time to answer. "Family stories and all."

Jewel smiled her thank you to Bryce, but went on to elaborate. "Ula and Hilliard were quite the characters in our family stories. Their love lived on in my family for all these generations." No need to mention that no one had ever mentioned a golden heart on a chain. "Anyway, that's the necklace she's wearing in the portrait in the front parlor."

Roland acquiesced. "Oh, sorry. I wasn't doubting you. I haven't been inside yet."

"You need to go in. The house and the portrait have held up beautifully." Bryce took the necklace, examined it closely then handed it to one of his men. "Take this to Mrs. Smyth. Tell her we'll be there shortly." Bryce touched Jewel's arm. "Let's head toward the house. I'm interested in what the Smyths are saying."

As the two of them strolled arm in arm through the

now worn path, Jewel placed her head on Bryce's shoulder. "This is all so confusing. Strange. Eerie."

Before they reached the open front lawn, Bryce stopped and turned her into his arms. Without another word, he lowered his head and kissed her on the mouth.

Jewel's breath caught in her throat. The surprise of the kiss. The strength of his arms around her. The masculine smell that enveloped her. All produced an instant flame in the pit of her stomach that only one thing could put out.

She returned his kiss with unrestrained emotion. Pressed her body against him to help squelch the flame and held onto him with a force that surprised her.

Bryce gently pulled away. "Wow. I wasn't expecting that."

Jewel placed her head on his chest and inhaled. "Neither was I."

"You think we could send all these people home?"

Looking up, a smile crossed her face.

He pecked her on the nose. "No such luck. I'm afraid we're stuck with them."

Bryce pulled her to him and she melted in his arms. "Thank you for being here with me. I don't know that I could've gone through this emotional ride into Ula's past without you."

His hand brushed the hair back away from her forehead. "My pleasure, young lady. Believe me. My pleasure." At that he kissed her once more, then stepped away.

"Come on. Let's see how Mrs. Smyth is handling her son. Or should I say how he's trying to handle his mother. I feel sorry for the guy. I don't think he has a lot to say in this matter or in many others."

"Well, let's hope she has her way. I really do think she won't let him leave my family out completely."

"Let's hope. Come on. Let's go see how Sonny's doing."

Chapter 15

Jewel heard the door slam before she saw Mr. Smyth stomp out onto the front porch. By the time she and Bryce reached the front of the house, he had disappeared around the side of the house.

"Well, I guess he didn't want to talk with us," Jewel said as she took the first step.

Bryce grinned. "From the looks of it, he and his mother aren't thinking in the same direction." He raised his eyebrows. "That could be good for you."

Excitement raced through Jewel's already heated veins. "Let's go find her."

Mrs. Smyth sat in a straight-backed chair in the parlor holding the gold necklace and staring at the portrait of Jewel. She looked around when Jewel and Bryce entered.

"Please come in," she said, then turned her attention back to the wall. "You know, I knew there was something special about this portrait. For all those years it hung here, I just couldn't take it down. Several times I wanted to sell it. The frame is worth a fortune, I'm sure, but I didn't have it in me to do it. Couldn't figure it out. Do you think that young lady staked out her place on the wall and refused to let it go?"

"Could be," Bryce answered. "Mrs. Smyth, is there any way we can convince you and your son to allow Jewel and her family claim on some of the pieces that were dug up today?"

Mrs. Smyth turned around to face them. "Before we discuss ownership of anything, I'd like to talk with Jewel privately."

Jewel and Bryce exchanged a nervous glance. Deep inside, she wanted and needed him with her, but the time had come for her to open up to Mrs. Smyth, alone. She prayed she'd have the courage to tell someone else about the visions.

"Sure." Bryce touched her arm. "I'll be on the porch if you want me."

When the door closed behind Bryce, Mrs. Smyth went straight to the point. "Tell me exactly how you knew there were family items buried on my land and where to dig."

Jewel pulled up a chair, sat down and inhaled deeply, wondering just how much to tell this lady. "Well, it's a rather strange story. I'm afraid you'll laugh me out of the parish when I tell you."

"Jewel, I'm an old woman. Nothing surprises me anymore."

Jewel blew out a deep breath and fortified herself with the knowledge that, just a few steps away from her, Bryce was waiting to come to her rescue. "Okay, you asked for it."

She began her story with her dreams and episodes and then the phone call from Bryce. "It never occurred to me not to go out to the island. It was as if I had been waiting for that call all of my life. I just knew I had to go." She hesitated.

"Let me help you. Mr. Cameron called you because he found something from Mr. McDougle, right?"

Amazed that the lady was so perceptive, Jewel nodded. "Yes, he did, and when I got to the island, I had another episode, similar to what I'd already been experiencing, but much stronger. We were sure there was a connection between what was happening to me and the fact that Captain McDougle had died as a prisoner on the island." She wanted to interject that she'd encountered the spirit of the captain, but she held that tidbit of information back.

"I see. So how did you make your way here?"

Feeling as though Mrs. Smith believed her story, Jewel relaxed and took a deep breath before beginning again. "I knew this plantation existed. The love stories of Ula and Hilliard have been part of my family history, but I don't think anyone actually visited the plantation in recent history. We lost it during Reconstruction."

Mrs. Smyth grunted. "Go on. Continue. Tell me how you found your way here."

Jewel hesitated. "We visited a medium," she finally said. The idea of the séance and medium had been hard for both Bryce and her to accept, but Mrs. Smyth showed no surprise even when she told her about the visions.

"I guess you could call the visions dreams." She cleared her throat. "Very vivid dreams. During the visions, I found myself here at River's Bend in the eighteen hundreds. Not only was I here, but I experienced the things that Ula experienced."

Again, she stopped momentarily to examine Mrs. Smyth's reaction. Nothing unusual, so she went on. "I felt the sadness she felt when Hilliard was getting ready to leave for the war. I saw when Hilliard was shot and when he buried the family valuables here."

Jewel's heart raced in her chest just talking about it, but her voice was a soft whisper. "It's almost as if I was the person of Ula McDougle." She looked at Mrs. Smyth. "I know it's hard to believe, but that's how I knew where to dig."

Jewel watched as the elderly lady looked around the parlor. "There were times when I felt her presence here. I never saw her, but I knew. There was a presence in this room by this portrait. As I said earlier, that young lady staked out her territory and was determined to hang onto it."

"So you believe me?"

"Oh, my darling. Yes, I believe you. There could be no other explanation as to how you knew about the things we dug up."

"I have a feeling your son won't be so receptive to the idea."

"Oh, phooey on him. He's a wonderful son, but he's like all the other young men around today. They have no feelings for the past."

"I have to disagree with you," Jewel said. "Not all men are like that. Bryce has a great respect for the things of other ages. His life is devoted to restoring old forts and homes from the past. You ought to listen to him talk about them. He loves them."

"Then you need to latch onto him because anyone who can appreciate where we came from is someone who will appreciate what he has today." The little lady's eyes twinkled. "You love him, don't you?"

Jewel was taken aback. Love? How could she love someone who was such a new acquaintance? "I've just met him."

"That's not what I asked. I want to know if you love him. I can see it in your eyes. And it's there in his too." She nodded slowly as if she'd made a profound statement.

"Well, uh, I recently broke off an engagement, and I'm not really ready to think about being in another relationship again."

Mrs. Smyth laughed. "Ready? Young lady, no one is ever ready to fall in love. It's not as if you can plan something like that. It just happens. Timing has nothing to do with love."

Jewel couldn't stop the smile that spread across her face and creased the corners of her eyes. She looked down at the floor, embarrassed that a complete stranger had so easily read her, but inwardly ecstatic that the other lady had put into words what she was scared to admit.

Mrs. Smyth reached out and touched her hand. "Does he know?"

Jewel shook her head.

"Well, then, you need to work on that. The young man is too good to let get away."

"Thank you for your thoughts. I'll see what I can do."

Mrs. Smyth smacked her hands on the side of the chair. "Now, let's talk about who owns what here. You said that you can have the Bible delivered, right? I'll expect that to be sent to my home in New York. Mr. Bryce has my address."

"Certainly." Jewel couldn't control her excitement. "As I said before, I'm not trying to take what rightfully belongs to your families. You have children that I'm sure are dying to get their hands on some of these beautiful pieces in this house and the property as well."

Mrs. Smyth shook her head and rolled her eyes. "These young people know nothing except money. They're not interested in anything but their bank accounts that will grow from its sale."

"Do you mean that they don't want these antiques?"

"Nope. My daughters-in-law all refuse to have antiques in their modern homes. Said they're stuffy."

Jewel's hands went up to her throat. "That's unbelievable."

"The portrait is yours."

"Well, let's talk price. We can have it appraised if you'd like. I'm going to have to do some fancy financing if the price is beyond my means, but Bryce said he'd lend me the money if you'll sell it to me."

"No, no. The portrait is yours. I want nothing for it. The picture is you and no one else should ever have it but you and your family." She looked down at the necklace. "I think this should also be yours. Everything else will have to be evaluated and appraised. We can discuss those items later."

Jewel swallowed hard. Tears welled in her eyes. "I can't believe you're being so generous. This is beyond my wildest dreams to get these two items." She reached over and kissed Mrs. Smyth on the cheek. "Thank you so much."

"You're quite welcome. Now, go find your young man and tell him how you feel about him."

Jewel smiled again. "I'll go find him, but I have to ease into that second suggestion."

"Love is a wonderfully amazing experience. Mr. Smyth and I were in love for over fifty-five years right up to the day he died. Don't let that feeling pass you by." With twinkling eyes, she lifted her head to Jewel. "Without it, life is meaningless."

Jewel reached down and touched the hand that Mrs. Smyth extended to her, but she could say nothing. With a squeeze, Jewel turned and left the room.

She found Bryce on the edge of the porch, sitting with his legs over the side. When he turned to see her, he ended a conversation on the phone, then held out his hand and helped her sit alongside of him.

"Everything went well, didn't it?"

"How did you know?"

"Could be the smile."

She nodded, then told him about the portrait and the necklace.

"Now that's a lady who understands the meaning of the past and the value of keeping it alive today. How does she think her son will react?"

"She's not worried about her son. She said her family only cares about how much money they'll get from the sale of all this." She shook her head. "How sad. Some developer will probably buy this gorgeous land and cut it up into an exclusive subdivision for people who will spend a couple hours a day here. Ooh, it just infuriates me that all this will be gone."

"Now, don't jump the gun. We don't know who'll buy it. There may be someone out there who wants to see this plantation restored to its glory. Who knows?"

"You think that's possible?"

He laughed. "Possible, but not probable. There's a fortune to be made by subdividing this property, but maybe the house and a small piece of land can be preserved. We'll keep our fingers crossed."

Jewel sighed. "Fortune. I guess fortunes are like beauty. It's all in the eyes of the beholder. I see this place as a fortune as it is."

"It's a fortune, all right. It's a jewel to be treasured."

***

With the feel of the chain and heart around her neck, Jewel sat on her side of the car in deep thought. Before she and Bryce headed out of St. Marks, they stopped at a local jeweler and waited patiently while he brought life back into a necklace that had been buried for over a hundred and fifty years.

Unconsciously, her hand touched the gold heart. Warmth spread through her knowing that Ula McDougle had worn the same piece around her tiny neck. It was a physical connection to Jewel's past and to the couple whose love was eternal.

Bryce glanced in her direction. "It looks nice on you."

She smiled. "It would look nice on anyone. It's so beautiful. I can't believe Mrs. Smyth gave it to me."

"And why shouldn't she? Who else would deserve to wear it?"

"Thank you for saying so."

Bryce shrugged. "It's the truth."

"She and her son were not on very good terms when they drove away today. I'd hate to have been sitting next to them in the plane going home."

"We were lucky to have her on our side. Had she not come down here, I'm afraid you wouldn't have had a chance of getting anything."

Jewel thought about her good fortune. Everything had happened so quickly she could hardly take it in. The visions, the house, the treasure, even Bryce——none of this had existed to her just a few weeks ago. Now her life revolved around what was going to happen at River's Bend and what the dream episodes meant.

Were the spirits of her ancestors trying to tell her to do something more or had they accomplished their wishes by digging up the treasures? If they wanted more from her, how would she ever find out how to help them? She and Bryce had decided to return to the island. It was a long shot, but maybe, being in the place where the captain had been killed, she'd be contacted once more.

Bryce looked from side to side of the main street. "As soon as I find us a gas station, we'll be back on the interstate. Are you sure you don't want to stop at our medium's house? Mr. Bourgois doesn't live far from the interstate. It wouldn't be any trouble."

"No, I'm scared he'll tell me something I don't want to hear. Right now, I'm confident we're doing the right thing. I don't want to stop."

"Your choice." He nodded in the direction of a gas station. "I'll pull in there. Want something to drink?"

Jewel nodded. "Sure. I'll get out with you."

The gas station's quaint storefront had room for three rockers, each occupied by old men. "I like this place," she said as she slid off the seat. "Matches the mood I'm in."

Bryce turned to the gas pump. Jewel walked into the store, bought some snacks and drinks, then stepped under the overhang by the old men.

"Howdy." One of the old men tipped his hat in her direction.

"Why, hello. My friend and I have been admiring your town. Have you lived here long?"

"Oh yeah," one of the other guys answered. "I'm Harold, and this here is George. He's older than dirt and hasn't ever stepped foot out of this town."

"Aw pshaw. You don't know nothing. I went to New Orleans just last year with my granddaughter. Hated the place. Why should I leave here?"

Jewel laughed. "Well, New Orleans can be quite intimidating. We were there recently. It has its charm, but it has its big city problems too." She looked around. "Not like this town at all. This is lovely."

All the old men smiled at their town's compliment, but the man at in the far rocker spoke softly now. "I remember when the last paddle boat passed here with its horn a blowing. I was a kid, but I remember it like yesterday."

The man's old eyes came alive with the remembrance. He sat quietly for a moment and Jewel didn't interrupt.

George didn't seem to notice. "You and your man on one of our tours?"

"No. We drove up to one of the old plantations I can trace back to one of my ancestors in the Civil War. It's such a shame. The place is for sale and will probably be torn down." Jewel's heart constricted, just saying the words.

"You talking about the LeBreaux plantation?"

Jewel shook her head. "No. We went up to the Smyth's property. It used to be called River's Bend."

"Yeah, that's what I said. The LeBreaux plantation."

Harold knocked George with a bony hand. "The young lady don't know all that marrying business and what all went on out there. Leave her be."

Jewel zeroed in on Harold. His thin gray hair peeked out from under a green tractor cap. "You're right. I don't know about the LeBreaux family." Her mind raced. "I met the present owner, a Mrs. Smyth from New York. She didn't say anything about anyone from the LeBreaux family?"

"She wouldn't. Been some bad blood in that family for years. She ignores the young whippersnapper whose picture is plastered all over the news." He leaned over and spit into an old coffee can sitting by the rocker. Jewel assumed he was chewing tobacco.

She juggled the snacks in her hands. "You don't mean the same LeBreaux who's thinking about running for the presidency?"

Harold sat up straight and wiped his mouth across his sleeve. "Yep. One in the same."

She motioned to Bryce coming out of the store, then

turned back to the men. "Would you mind telling us some more about the ownership of that property?" She nodded to Bryce who walked up next to her. "This is Bryce Cameron. He spends his life restoring old structures."

"How'd do?" Bryce extended a hand to each in turn.

"These men know the property well, and they say Jason LeBreaux is part of that family."

Bryce straightened. "Go on."

George spoke up. "That Mrs. Smyth you met from New York. That's LeBreaux's grandmother. His mama was a Smyth before she married that LeBreaux fellow."

Bryce scratched his head. "Why in the world would he want to get rid of a piece of property like River's Bend? You'd think he'd restore the place. I mean, can't you see all those politicians sitting around the big porch talking politics?"

"Just like in the old days," the third old man said, "except it wasn't politics they were talking about." He ran his thumbs along the straps of his overalls.

Jewel looked at the man. "And what is it they'd be talking about?"

George now started rocking faster. "Ain't no politics that's for sure. The concern way back then was who the sheriff was and how much they'd have to pay him to turn his head."

Now Harold's chair rocked as fast as George's. "Harold's telling the truth."

Jewel swallowed. "You mean the family was involved in something illegal?"

As if on cue, both rocking chairs stopped. "Maybe, but you didn't hear it from us."

"Nuff said," mumbled the third man. "These good people don't need to hear all that rubbish."

George speared him with squinty eyes. "Ain't no rubbish and you know it."

"Well, rubbish or not, it don't matter no more. The

family is selling the place, and all that ugly history will be forgotten. Now we'll probably have ugly little houses jammed up and down that river."

When it looked as though the men wouldn't offer any more information, Bryce and Jewel thanked the men, then headed up the interstate. They'd gone at least a mile before Jewel spoke up. "What're you thinking?

"I'm thinking this all seems a little odd."

"Yeah, about as odd as my episodes have been."

Over and over they tossed around the information the three men had given them, but now that they had it, they weren't sure what to do with it.

"I don't know," Bryce said. "I wonder how many people know LeBreaux is part of this family. You'd think he'd use that as a selling point for the people here in Louisiana. The way I understand it, his party's not as strong as it could be around these parts."

"You'd think. I wish we had time to do a little research."

"Yeah, I do too, but I have to get out to the island. I have a feeling this isn't the last time we'll hear about LeBreaux and his connections with the property."

She nodded. "I wonder if the sale of the property has one of the McDougles upset?"

Bryce lifted an eyebrow. "That's a thought."

"You think they know?"

Now Bryce smiled. "After spending lonely nights in some of the forts I've worked on, I don't doubt anything."

Jewel laughed. "You're not telling me you've seen ghosts in other structures too?"

"Not really, but I've had feelings—impressions—that I wasn't alone."

Inhaling deeply, Jewel rested her head against the back of the seat. "Yeah, I know what you mean. Believe me, I know."

The atmosphere in the car was charged with unspoken

tension. From the corner of her eye, she watched Bryce at the wheel, and it was all she could do not to reach out and touch him. She wasn't sure how or when it had happened, but, in such a short time he had become an important part of her life. She wanted Bryce to be with her during her involvement with the plantation, and if she were honest with herself, she wanted him to be around after the auction.

Mrs. Smyth had been observant. Just as the lady had said, Jewel couldn't deny she had feelings for Bryce. Allowing herself to admit it was an accomplishment on her part, one that took some of the weight off her shoulders, but one that still scared her.

Letting someone into her life again was more than she had anticipated when she began this journey a couple weeks ago. Now that she was heading back to the coast, she wondered where it would lead.

She closed her eyes and let Bryce navigate the crowded interstate. He always seemed so cool and so confident. He made everything look so easy. She wished that navigation of the heart was as easy.

***

Jewel opened her eyes to a wide expanse of open road.

Bryce smiled at her. "Hey, welcome back. I thought I'd have to start a conversation with the truckers on the CB. I was getting a little bored."

"I'm sorry. I didn't mean to fall asleep on you." She looked around. "Where are we?"

"We're about halfway there. Interstate 59 is not far."

He hesitated as if he were about to say something else. Jewel waited for him to continue. "Is that supposed to mean something to me?" she asked.

He laughed. "No, I don't imagine it would, though, uh, it means a great deal to me."

She waited. "Because?" she asked when he didn't

continue. "You've got my curiosity up now. You can't leave me hanging."

"It leads north to the Hattiesburg area."

Again Jewel waited. "And?"

"And, well, I go up there sometimes."

Remembering how David never let her into his thoughts, Jewel shifted around and faced him. "Look, you don't have to tell me anything personal you don't want me to know, but you're the one who started this conversation."

She watched him swallow. "I go up there as often as I can, usually twice a month or more depending where my current job is located. Nan's parents have a nice place up there. Lots of land. It's very peaceful."

Jewel's heart stopped. It had never occurred to her that he was still so close to his wife's family, but then why wouldn't he be? Her parents were his connection to her. She envied them for sharing that kind of love. "You still miss Nan, don't you?"

A small smile creased his face. "Of course I do. She was my life. I miss her unbearably sometimes, but that's normal, I guess." He glanced her way. "That's not why I go up there though."

Jewel straightened up, waiting for an explanation.

"Uh," he hesitated again. Jewel could see that what he was trying to say wasn't easy for him.

"I have a little boy."

Jewel blinked and let the words settle. "You have a son?"

Bryce nodded.

Vice grips couldn't have crushed her heart any harder than his announcement. She swallowed her hurt. Her words came out in a whisper. "Why didn't you tell me?"

"Please don't take it personal."

"Personal? I think a son is very personal. I thought we had shared enough in these few weeks that you'd let me in on something so meaningful in your life." She turned and stared out the window. "But I guess not."

Bryce reached over and touched her leg. "Don't be angry with me. It's not that I didn't want to tell you. I want to shout it to the world that I have this beautiful child, this small image of my wife still with me today, but it's difficult."

"How difficult can it be to tell someone you have a son?"

"It's very difficult." His voice was stern, leaving no room for misunderstanding on her part. He was still having a hard time dealing with what had been dealt him. Bryce might've made love to her and gave her the impression he enjoyed her company, but she could tell he still loved Nan and hadn't come to terms with her death.

Again the vice grips tightened around her heart.

He cleared his throat. "I still have this uncontrollable feeling that my son really isn't there at all. That one day I'll go up there, and he won't be there. I can't explain it. I just know it's very hard for me to share him with the world."

In spite of the shock of realizing she'd almost given her heart to someone who was not ready to return that love, she reached out and touched his arm. "I understand how you must feel, but I'm not the world, Bryce. I'm Jewel. I thought I was a little more personal than the general population." She couldn't keep the hurt from her voice.

"I'm sorry. I truly am. I wanted to tell you." He glanced her way. "I planned to tell you the morning after we made love, but you were so quick to leave our bed I figured we had made a mistake. That maybe I had misread your cues and talking about my private life wasn't what you wanted to do."

The remembrance of her actions on the morning after sent a little wave of guilt up Jewel's spine. "I guess I did leave rather suddenly." She lowered her voice. "I got scared."

"Humph. That wasn't hard to figure out." He turned

slightly to be able to look at her. "But I wasn't sure what scared you."

Jewel kept her eyes on the blurred centerline of the interstate. "Me. You. What we had done. I don't know. Everything."

Bryce shook his head. "I don't understand you at all. Before I made love to you, I told you then I didn't take making love lightly. It had been a long, long time for me. It meant something to me."

"That's what scared me." The words poured out before she could stop them.

"Now you're really not making any sense."

"It does to me. I shouldn't have let you get to me. It's too soon. I didn't want to get involved with anyone."

"Jewel, listen to yourself. David hurt you, but it's time to get over him and move on."

Jewel snickered. "Listen who's talking. You can't even tell me about your son. Have you moved on?"

Bryce snapped his head in her direction. "That's completely different. Nan didn't cheat on me. She died. There's a difference."

Jewel's face flushed. "I'm sorry. You're right, of course. You and Nan shared something every couple searches for, and yes, that would take time to get over. I guess I'm hurt you didn't trust me enough to tell me about your son."

"For that I'm sorry, but I told you I was going to tell you about my son, but you skipped out on me."

Silence.

Bryce passed the few cars on the interstate, driving a little faster than he normally did as he passed the turnoff to I59. Jewel sat quietly on her side of the car trying to think of something to say to ease the tension. He was right. She had run out on him after he'd made love to her because what they had shared hadn't been just sex. It had been making love, and to her there was a tremendous difference.

It was the difference that scared her. Terrified her.

Now, she had hurt him by comparing what David did to her and what he and Nan had. How stupid could she be?

"I'm sorry," she said.

"You just said that." His voice was flat.

"I know, but I truly am. I shouldn't have made such an inconsiderate comparison. That was cruel."

She saw him glance in her direction, but he said nothing.

"You're not like David."

"No, I'm not."

She shifted uncomfortably. "Can we start over? Pretend we never had this conversation? I'd rather us be as we were this afternoon at River's Bend."

"That's fine with me," Bryce answered her, but she wasn't so sure he meant it. She had touched a sensitive nerve in him, and there was no way to take back what she had said.

He glanced in her direction. "I compared you to someone too, you know."

Jewel shook her head.

"That day you flew to the island in your helicopter, I instantly threw you in the same category as the woman who ran into Nan's car."

Jewel blinked. "Why? Why would you do that?"

"Something about you reminded me of her. She was beautiful like you, classy and rich, and it didn't matter that she'd killed my wife after she'd had too many glasses of wine. She got off."

His voice dropped. His chest heaved. Jewel watched but said nothing.

"When you stepped off that helicopter, there was something I couldn't put my finger on, something brought back those feelings of resentment I've felt for all these years."

"I don't understand," she said when he seemed to want to say more.

"I can't explain it, and I can't help what I felt. You reminded me of that woman."

The hurt she'd felt earlier about not knowing about his son didn't compare to how she felt now. She wanted to tell him she understood, but she couldn't.

"I'm sorry if I made you feel that way, but I can't help the way I look. Thank you for thinking I'm beautiful— though I doubt many people would agree with you—and I can't help the fact that my aunt's husband had a lot of money and shared her good fortune with me. I'm sorry for what you felt, but I can't and won't apologize for how I look."

He didn't say any more.

She watched as he concentrated on the road. For several long minutes neither said anything.

"What changed your mind or *have* you changed your mind about me?" she finally asked.

From the side, Jewel could see his lips curl a tiny bit. "You. You changed it. You're nothing like that woman."

His words helped but they didn't take away the horrible realization of what must've gone through his mind while they were on the island together. "Thank you for saying so."

"You could never be like her."

She thought about his son. For so long she had dreamed of having a son or a daughter with David. Thank goodness that hadn't happened. "What's his name?"

"You mean my son?"

She nodded.

"Kevin. His name's Kevin. He's three and a half, and he's the most wonderful little boy in the world. He wasn't even a year old when Nan died. My parents are on the west coast so her parents have helped me raise him ever since. They're more like his parents than I am, but with my job there's no other way right now."

She placed a hand on his arm. "He knows you're his dad."

"Yeah. But it's not the same as being with him every night. I try to talk with him every day no matter where I am, but it's not the same as being there with him."

"That's got to be hard."

"It is, but it's gotten so much nicer since he can actually hold on a conversation with me. You ought to hear him talk."

It wasn't hard to see the pride and the love that Bryce had for his son. His eyes sparkled, just talking about him.

"I'd like to meet him."

Bryce glanced at her. "I'd like for you to meet him."

"How would he react to seeing you with a woman?"

"I don't think it would make a difference. He's so young. He doesn't remember Nan. That's the sad part. She was a wonderful mother, and he'll never know."

"He'll know."

"I hope so. I owe it to her to keep her memory alive for him, but I'm afraid she will always be just a name."

"He'll know he was loved and that's what matters."

His answer was soft. "And love is all that matters, isn't it?"

Chapter 16

When I-10 intersected Highway 49, Bryce took a sharp turn on the off-ramp and headed north.

Jewel straightened up in her seat and looked around. "Now, I'm not from around here, but I do know we're going to have a hard time finding Ship Island if we head north."

Bryce kept his eye on the congested highway, but answered without looking. "You're right. I'm taking you to the Wilsons' place. I want you to meet Kevin."

"Now?"

"Now. This is another road that leads up there."

"But they're not expecting us. We can't just barge in on those people." Yes, she wanted to meet Kevin, but a sinking feeling eased its way down into her stomach. What if the boy didn't like her, and how would Nan's parents feel about her being with Bryce?

"They're family."

"But I'm not. You've got to warn them. I'm a complete stranger, an intruder. I can't just walk up and barge in on them."

"You're right." When he stopped for a traffic light, Bryce picked up the cell phone. He grinned as he hit the pre-set number. "I was planning to call them once I was sure you weren't going to make me stop the car to get out."

"Give me more credit than that. I consider it an honor to meet Kevin, especially since you kept him a secret for so long."

Bryce looked as if he would say something to her, but spoke into the phone instead. "Mrs. Wilson. . .

Jewel twisted in her seat uncomfortably and listened as he talked briefly with his in-laws. She wasn't sure about this up-coming visit. She'd always liked children, but children were so unpredictable. What if the boy hated her on sight? Even if she wanted to have a relationship with Bryce, she had a feeling he was the kind of man who would sacrifice his own happiness for his son.

Bryce pushed the button on the phone. "Now they're expecting us." He reached out and touched her leg with one hand. "I want you to meet Kevin, and this is as good a time as any."

"What about going to the island?"

"We can't get to the island until tomorrow morning anyway, so this will work out just fine. I'll get Marcus to hold one of the boats until about eight. It takes a little over an hour to get to the dock from the Wilsons' place. You can handle that, can't you?"

"Handle what?"

"Well, we'd have to get up really early to make the boat."

She crossed her arms and held back the giggle that threatened to escape. Did he think she stayed in bed until the noon hour? "I can get up early if I have to. I work, remember? Do you think all my classes are in the afternoon?"

"Okay, then it's not a problem. I'll get to see my son, and you'll get to meet the most important little fellow in my life."

Jewel could see only Bryce's profile, but she could tell it was hard for him to contain a smile. Just talking about his son lightened his mood. His excitement was contagious. All of a sudden, she couldn't wait to meet the little fellow. She'd find a way to make him like her.

Traffic thinned considerably as soon as they left the coast. Tall pine trees lined the road with a scattering of blooming magnolias peeking through the roadside thickness.

"This is pretty country, isn't it?" Her comment broke their comfortable quiet.

He nodded. "Where the Wilsons live, there's an occasional hill with lots of thick pines. There's even a stream that runs along their property line. Lots of wildlife. Really a great place to raise a boy."

Bryce got quiet. Jewel guessed he was thinking about not raising the boy himself, but she didn't make a comment about her thoughts. It had to be hard for him to leave Kevin each time he returned to work.

They turned off the highway and traveled along a winding road lined with a few houses with huge, azalea-filled yards and rolling pastures. For several miles theirs was the only car on the road. Bryce turned to look at her. "Don't look so scared. He's just a little boy. He'll love you."

"I hope so. Except for a few nieces and nephews, I haven't been around a lot of children."

He smiled. "Kids don't worry a lot about the things we adults do. They pretty much go about the business of playing, and if we adults happen to come into their little circle of fun, we're included if we're lucky enough. Kevin will let you know what to do."

"I hope so." She sat with her hands twisting in her lap, but Bryce's smile helped to ease her fears.

A short time later, when they pulled into the Wilsons' drive, Jewel knew she was probably worrying for no reason. "Is that him?"

Bryce tooted the horn and waved. "That's him."

A little boy kneeling by a row of flowers with his grandmother jumped up and waved as the car inched its way down the long driveway. The older woman grabbed his hand

and held him back. As soon as the car stopped Bryce threw his door open and ran toward Kevin. With high-pitched shrieks, Kevin dashed into the waiting arms of his father.

Holding the boy tightly, Bryce spun around to the excitement of Kevin, who whooped and hollered. Then Bryce got quiet, and Jewel could tell he was squeezing and kissing his son.

Before getting out of the car, Jewel swallowed the unexpected lump in her throat and wiped her eyes.

"Jewel, come meet this big man that I have here."

"I'm not a man. I'm a boy, Daddy," Kevin corrected and giggled.

"Oh, no," said Bryce through his smiles. "You've grown so big this past week I thought you were a man already."

"Daddy, you're silly!" He giggled again.

"Jewel, come meet my son."

Jewel walked around the car and extended her hand to Kevin, who looked at Bryce.

"It's okay, Kevin. This is Miss Ferguson."

Jewel touched his arm. "You can call me Jewel, if you'd like."

"Jewel?" the boy laughed and contorted his face. "That's a funny name."

She had to laugh with him. "It is different, isn't it?"

The boy began to squirm in Bryce's arms so Bryce lowered him to the ground.

"Come on. Let's show Jewel the baby cats." Kevin took off toward the barn. Bryce reached out and gave Mrs. Wilson a quick hug. "Mom, this is Jewel Ferguson."

A pleasant-looking lady with salt and peppered hair smiled her greeting and extended her hand. "It's so good of you to visit with us." She looked up to follow Kevin with her eyes. "We'd better visit in the barn, though."

"Good idea." Jewel shook her hand lightly, then walked alongside of her. "You have a lovely place here."

"Thank you. We dearly love it in the country, and it seems to fit Kevin as well."

"Oh, yeah," chimed in Bryce. "He's already got it in his head he needs a four-wheeler to follow his cousins around."

The boy stuck his head out the barn door. "Come on, Daddy. Come see how they growed."

Bryce stepped ahead of the two women.

"Go on," Jewel said. "We'll catch up."

Bryce extended his long legs and left the two women alone.

"I hope you didn't mind us popping in on you unannounced."

"Oh, no, Bryce is welcome up here anytime he wants to drop in. The poor man runs himself crazy on the interstate and the airports to get up here to spend time with his son. His time with him is precious, and I'd never think twice about discouraging it. The boy loves his father."

"And Bryce misses him. I hope it's not too uncomfortable for me to be here with him. We're working on a project together. We've just come from St. Marks, and we're heading back out to the island. He wanted me to meet Kevin."

The lady just smiled. The gray specked curls around her face softened the age lines, and the gentle smile told Jewel she was sincere. Immediately, Jewel felt at home.

"Bryce can bring anyone he'd like here. We want him to feel at home, and I think he finally does after all these years. After the initial, horrible first year we spent without Nan, we've all adjusted quite well, I think. Having Kevin has helped all of us cope."

Jewel nodded and followed Mrs. Wilson into the barn. There was nothing she could say to this lady who had lost her daughter. She didn't need a perfect stranger telling her how sorry she was for her loss.

The smell of hay and feed surrounded her. Bryce knelt

alongside his son with several kittens crawling over his legs. His hand was on Kevin who held a squirming kitten next to his chest.

"Come see. This is Chocolate. It's my kitten. Granny said I can have it and I can name it what I want."

Jewel knelt down by the boy. "He's beautiful and he does look like chocolate."

"Yeah. That's his sister. She's Cotton. We can't keep her though. We got to give her away. Grandpa said I can't have more than one."

Bryce rescued the kitten and returned him to the mother cat's nipple, then gently lifted the two from his lap and placed them next to Chocolate.

With unrestrained excitement, Kevin threw his arms around Bryce's neck and kissed him on the cheek. "I like you coming when I don't know you're coming. This is fun."

Bryce held his son's head close to his own, but said nothing. Jewel was sure that the lump in his throat was as big as the one in hers.

For the rest of the afternoon everyone took turns trying to keep up with Kevin. Bryce tossed him a ball, wrestled on the lawn with him, and sat with the kittens for a long time. Jewel let him have his time with his son and went into the house with Mrs. Wilson where they fixed homemade whipped potatoes and gravy and several bowls of steamy vegetables. Mr. Wilson brought home fried chicken from a near-by deli.

After Bryce cleaned dirt and grass off Kevin, everyone sat down at a long maple table. The dining room, decorated in a homey country style, brought back faded memories of a time she'd eaten with her real parents around a kitchen table in their modest home on the outskirts of Bedford, Kentucky. It was getting harder and harder to remember specifics about those few years she'd had with her parents before they were killed, but she'd always associate peaceful gatherings like this with

Fran McNabb

her family. They didn't have a lot of material things, but there was plenty of love. That part of her life would always be vivid.

Bryce got up to go to the kitchen for a serving spoon as Mr. Wilson passed her the platter of chicken. "So Bryce tells us you teach at a college in Houston."

"Yes, sir. I've been with the science department at the University of Houston for about five years. I really like it. I work with a lot of doctoral students right now and that's quite rewarding. It gives me time to do some research and to write on the side."

"That's interesting."

"So you're from that area?"

"No. I'm originally from a small town in Kentucky, but when my parents were killed, I moved in with one of my mother's sister and her family around the Boston area."

Mr. and Mrs. Wilson didn't say anything, but looked at each other. The mood around the table changed instantly.

Mr. Wilson put his glass of tea down. "So you lived in Boston?"

"Not exactly in Boston, but in one of the suburbs." She chuckled. "It was a cultural shock for a little girl from Kentucky. I had a lot of adjusting to do. Mother had two sisters, one lived right in the center of Boston. I'd spend a little time with he in the summers. As I got older I realized I'd be sent to Boston to give a break to the one I lived with. I guess I was a handful. I loved both of my aunts though. The one who lived in the city was fun to be around, always shopping and involved with different organizations. Between my mother's two sisters, I feel as though I had a nice rounded childhood."

With a serious face, Mrs. Wilson passed the bowl of potatoes to her husband as Bryce walked back into the room. "Yes, it does sound as though you were exposed to a lot of things."

"Well, some of those things are nice to have in your experience, but some of them are a waste of time. I like to think I'm a little of my aunts and a lot like my mother and dad."

"That's a nice way of thinking about who we are," Bryce threw in as he took his place next to his son. Nothing else was said about her past as Kevin started telling a story about the bull that Pa had to pull out of the mud around the pond.

After supper, Bryce and Jewel relaxed on a swing that hung from the limb of a gigantic oak tree. They watched Kevin run after a calf in the pasture. His grandfather ran near him, trying to slow him down, but the boy ran circles around him and the calf.

Jewel giggled. "He's a bundle of energy."

"He's great, isn't he?"

"He really is. I'm still mad at you, though, for not telling me about him before now. He's too wonderful not to share."

"But in my eyes, he's too good to share with just anybody."

Jewel glared at him.

He touched her hand and answered quickly. "I just had to make sure you weren't just anybody before I brought you here."

A tingle ran up her arm. "I'll accept that. Thank you for making the detour. I feel very special."

He winked at her. "You are."

"Daddy. Daddy, come help us."

"I'm being called. Let me go run off that pound of potatoes I just ate. Want to come? You didn't do so bad at the table yourself."

"Bryce Cameron! How dare you. . ." But Bryce had already jumped up from the swing and was heading for the pasture.

Jewel followed with a heart bursting with joy.

***

A yawn surprised Jewel, but it was useless to try to conceal her physical exhaustion from Bryce as they headed back down the highway early the following morning. Once more she covered her mouth, but she was sure Bryce was inwardly laughing at her.

The sun told her it was morning, but her body was having a hard time cooperating. She should have gotten enough sleep, but her body hadn't cooperated last night either. Everyone in the house had gone to bed by ten o'clock, but she had lain awake for hours in the cozy guest room.

Bryce and Kevin had stayed in the house with everyone until Kevin fell asleep on the floor in the middle of a game. Bryce lifted his limp body and carried him to their mobile home.

Earlier in the day, Kevin had taken her into the mobile home and led her through the narrow hallway into their room, decorated in a super hero theme.

"This is my bed. That's Daddy's," he pointed out proudly, then immediately started digging through a box of toys. "We get to stay in here when Daddy comes."

Jewel walked over to the small bed, much too small for Bryce's tall body. Sitting down, she ran her hand over the Spiderman spread, then spoke to Bryce. "You sleep here?"

"Yep. Wouldn't have it any other way. This is our spot when I'm up here. You don't mind sleeping up in the house without us, do you?"

"Of course not. You need time with your boy."

The guestroom in the house was perfect, but sleep refused to come to her. Earlier in the evening, she had made a call to her grandmother to have the family Bible shipped to Mrs. Smyth. It had been years since she had scanned the faded longhand that named members of her family, but she was sure she had her story straight.

What if she were wrong? What if the names didn't

actually jibe? Would Mrs. Smyth still give her the portrait and the necklace?

Long into the night she had tossed and turned. Her body and her mind imagined being with Bryce in the tiny bed near Kevin. Being with him for the last two days had set her on edge, reduced her to a bundle of sexually charged nerves, and left her feeling emotionally stimulated. How could she possibly sleep?

Then there was a nagging thought that wouldn't leave. What had she said at the dinner table that had changed the mood so abruptly? No matter how hard she tried to recall her exact words, nothing surfaced that could've made the Wilsons get so quiet.

The tall numbers on the digital clock continually changed in front of her until the morning sun peeked through the sides of the ruffled curtains.

Now trying to sit up straight on her side of the car, she ached for sleep.

"You okay?"

She looked at Bryce through scrunched eyelids. "Yes." It wasn't really a lie, but it was close.

Grinning, he looked back at the highway.

What would happen on the island tonight? Would she be able to control her growing desire for the man who sat next to her or would she succumb to his charms? Maybe she didn't want to fight him off any longer. Heat ignited in her lower body just remembering the night they had spent together.

Glaring sun blinded her as Bryce turned into the eastbound traffic of I10. She flipped the sun visor down, then dug around for her sunshades and stuck them on her face. She groaned.

"You can take a nap on the way out to the island. The boat's small, but it's pretty comfortable." Bryce's voice penetrated her morning haze.

"You're mocking me," she said under her breath without looking at him.

"I'm not mocking you," but his low laugh told her differently. "I'm just letting you know there's hope for you yet. If it's not windy and rough, the boat ride will put you to sleep."

"Thank you."

Telling herself it was to keep the sun out of her eyes, Jewel tilted her head back and closed her lids, but try as she might, there was no slipping off to sleep. Bryce's nearness and the anticipation of being in the fort with him again had her mind in tangles.

She wasn't sure what was the most nerve-wracking, spirits who held their territory or a man who held her heart in the palm of his hand.

You'd think a woman with two degrees behind her name would have enough sense to run the other way.

But she didn't.

Chapter 17

"It's about time you showed your face out here." Marcus stood on the pier and shouted to the boat as it pulled up to the docks on the island. "This partnership is getting to be a little lopsided."

Standing on the bow of the boat with a rope in his hand, Bryce shouted back to him. "Stop your complaining and grab the rope, would you?"

From her seat in the stern, Jewel laughed at the two men who both tried to feign anger. In reality she knew Marcus and Bryce were a team with one taking up the slack where the other left off. Even now, after Bryce's absence from the job, Marcus couldn't contain his excitement at seeing Bryce again.

Marcus whipped the first rope around a piling then ran to the back and grabbed the stern rope. He winked at Jewel. "Hey, Lady, welcome back to the island."

"Why, thank you, Marcus." She waited for a few minutes until the boat was secured, then she gathered her belongings and grabbed a piling to lift herself up. Bryce grabbed her arm and gave her a little help.

She turned and smiled at him.

Marcus stepped near her. "I'm glad to see you're here to brighten this place up again. Welcome."

"Thanks, but I don't think I can brighten the island

any more than it is. Mother Nature's surrounded us by all this beautiful water and white sand. I think this little spot is special the way it is."

A big smile spread across Marcus's face. "You're right. This is pretty great, isn't it?"

Bryce hopped up on the pier, scooted up behind Jewel and casually placed his hands on her waist. "Come on, you two. I have work to catch up on."

A shock wave spiraled up Jewel's spine at his unexpected touch. Hoping Bryce hadn't detected her reaction, she stepped away, but his wink told her he knew exactly how she felt. "Come to work sometimes," Marcus said, "and you wouldn't have work to catch up on."

Bryce threw his arms around his friend. "Oh, stop complaining. Tell me how you're doing?"

For a brief second, the two men hugged, and a wave of relief swept over Jewel for the moment's diversion from contact with Bryce.

"We're great," Marcus answered. "Wait 'til you see the progress. That south casemate is coming along. We were able to get into the wall without removing even one of the iron tongues."

Jewel looked over the top of her sunshades. "That sounds interesting."

Both men laughed. "We'll show you the area. It's where some of the smaller cannons were mounted," Bryce explained. "If you're interested, I'd be glad to explain it in detail. Frankly, I can't wait to see it. Come on."

All three of them grabbed a bag and headed down the pier. The mid-morning sun had already warmed the planks on the pier. With each step, Jewel felt the weight of the world slip away from her shoulders. For the moment even the remembrance of what lay inside the walls of the fort escaped her thoughts and allowed the pristine surroundings to invigorate and cleanse her.

But the feeling didn't last.

The planks near the fort, shaded by the high walls, instantly cooled not only her feet, but her feelings as well. Her chest tightened. Her breath deepened, and as she stepped into the sally port, a sense of helplessness wrapped around her until she had to place a hand on the wall for support.

Bryce and Marcus both grabbed her arms.

"It's happening again."

Bryce hadn't asked a question, but she nodded.

"Sit," he demanded.

"No, I'm okay." Inhaling deeply to clear her head, she dragged up a feeble smile for Bryce.

"You think Captain McDougle just welcomed you—again?"

"I hope so. Maybe if he's hanging around, he'll let me know what we're supposed to do. I have to find some resolution to this."

Marcus, who stood quietly next to her, lifted his eyebrow. "Well, that's a change of tone, if I ever heard one. If you really think his spirit is out here now, you and Bryce must've had yourselves quite an experience in New Orleans and in St. Marks. I want to know all about it."

Feeling stronger, Jewel eased away from both men, but Bryce stepped next to her and placed his arm around his shoulders. She didn't object.

"I don't know if his spirit is really out here," she said, "but I do know something affected me the first time I walked into this fort, and since I've had several episodes since then, I need to find resolution. It's a little embarrassing to keep falling into Bryce's arms."

The pressure of his hand on her shoulder increased a tiny bit. "I kind of liked it myself."

She smiled at his comforting squeeze and cute remark.

Marcus scratched his ear. "I can see your point, but I'm not so sure I want Captain McDougle to be out here. You two already have me looking over my shoulder every time I go into one of these dark rooms."

Jewel laughed weakly. "Thanks for the encouragement."

Bryce tugged at her elbow. "Come on and let's go see what my crew's done while we're been chasing ghost stories around the countryside." Then with a look that took Jewel's breath away. "That is, if you're up to it."

"Yes, and I promise to try to stay on my feet."

***

The last boat pulled away from the pier leaving Bryce and Jewel standing alone. For a long, silent minute, neither of them said a word as they watched the small speed hull quickly become nothing more than a small black dot.

"Want to take a walk?"

Jewel looked up. "Sure."

With bare feet, they jumped onto the sand beach. She smiled remembering her first day on the island when she was hesitant to allow the handsome corporation owner to help her. Now, if she hesitated at all, it was for another reason.

Now she knew him intimately and making contact with his body in any form distracted her and dragged up feelings that scared her.

"The sand feels great." Bryce stood inches ahead of her digging his feet in the sand, his hands on his hips, and his eyes scanning the end of the island. "Looks like there's a flock of something at the end." Turning, his blue-gray eyes devoured her. "Would you like to make it down there again?"

Jewel swallowed. "Of course. If you are."

"Sounds like a challenge to me," he said as he squinted, creating a small dimple in one of his cheeks.

"You're on."

Jewel didn't hesitate. Just as the first day she'd walked with him down this beach, she inhaled deeply, then darted past him. She headed for the western tip of the island, now drenched in the afternoon sun. From a short distance behind her, she heard his low chuckle. The grit of the sand announced as his steps in the soft shoreline and a splash told her he stepped into the edge of the water.

Within minutes, sweat dripped down Jewel's face and neck and down her back. Her breath became shallow and ragged, and a distinct pain stuck beneath her left rib. She placed a hand over it and pushed on.

Almost to the end of the island, she stopped. Panting, she bent down and placed both hands on her knees. She gasped for breath.

Bryce stopped beside her. "The challenge was to the end of the island."

Jewel looked up and groaned. "You win."

Bryce laughed. "You're no fun. You give up too easily."

"I guess I've sat behind too many desks and stood behind too many podiums to do this. I'm completely out of shape."

"Oh, no. Your shape's just right." He chuckled again and left her staring into the white sand and water that formed a small pool around her feet.

Jewel had never quit anything in her life, so gritting her teeth, she followed Bryce down the last leg of the beach where he finally stopped. When she reached him, it was all she could do to not reach out and touch his body. The sun highlighted his deep chocolate hair and glistened off of his skin, shiny now from the run.

Her heart pounded.

"Our egrets are still nesting." He squatted, then pointed.

"They're beautiful," she said under her breath.

At that moment, several large white birds took flight. Jewel grabbed her chest and gasped.

Bryce turned. "What's wrong?"

Words didn't come. Jewel stared at the birds as they swooped and dove into the clear water searching for an

Fran McNabb

afternoon meal, but what she saw wasn't birds on this island. Instead they became the birds flying over the Mississippi River as Hilliard told Ula goodbye. Her visit to the past at River's Bend flooded her memory with vivid images. Closing her eyes, she felt Hilliard wipe away the tears gathering in Ula's eyes.

Without thinking, Jewel brought both of her hands up to her breast, crossed her wrists and clasped her thumbs together. It had been Hilliard and Ula's sign. He would always be with her, he had said.

Bryce's touch brought her to the present. "What's wrong, Jewel?"

She shook her head. "I just remembered something. The birds. They were there when Hilliard and Ula said goodbye."

Bryce said nothing. Words weren't necessary for Jewel to know he understood. He placed an arm around her shoulder and pulled her to his side, then together they quietly watched the birds.

Jewel's hands stayed clasped at her chest as she watched the birds. Just as before, Ula's pain descended upon her. She squeezed her eyes to ward off the feeling, but it did no good. The sinking sensation from losing a loved one and the ultimate despondency remained.

The dread that Ula experienced at the thought of losing her husband to a cause she didn't understand would be a feeling Jewel would never forget. It was as real for her today on the beach with Bryce as it was for Ula so many years ago.

Finally, she found her voice and remembered her clasped hands. "Hilliard did this." Spreading her fingers and moving her hands slightly, she showed Bryce the sign. "He said he'd always be with Ula, and the birds would be her reminder of his love." Stopping, she grasped Ula's gold heart that lay against her skin.

Bryce pulled her to him even tighter. Laying her head against his warm, bare chest, now musky from the run, she

240

allowed herself to be enveloped in his strength. At the moment she needed to know she had his support.

"I feel so helpless. It's as though they're begging for me to help them, and I'm just fumbling around in the dark."

"Maybe that's your answer," he whispered in her ear.

She looked up with a questioning glance. "What do you mean?"

"This might sound a little farfetched, but if his spirit's here, maybe using that sign will help to communicate to him."

"Yes, of course, that's got to be it." Her heart pounded. "That's got to be why Ula showed it to me."

Bryce nodded, pulled her back to his chest, and pressed her head against his body. "There's only one way to find out and that will depend on the captain. Let's hope he's around tonight."

Instead of going farther around the bend of the island to see the birds closer, they turned and began to walk in the direction of the fort. Neither Bryce nor Jewel spoke much.

Silence walked with them, but it was an easy silence, quiet moments spent with someone who didn't need words to know the other's thoughts or feelings. Jewel felt that with Bryce, and instinctively she knew he understood her.

Unconsciously, she tucked her arm into his and leaned against him. How could her first impression of him have been so wrong? Where was the arrogance and selfishness she expected to find in someone in his position? What she found instead was gentleness and caring.

Her thoughts moved to David. She thought she had loved him, but she never realized until now she hadn't felt this way with him. Never felt she was understood the way this man beside her made her feel. Never felt he really cared what she thought or how she felt.

She prayed that Bryce was real. She hoped they had time enough together for her to decide how genuine he really was.

Jewel squeezed Bryce's arm. "Thank you."

He looked down. "For what?"

"I don't know. Just for being here with me and helping me get through this."

"That's a switch. I figured you'd eventually curse me for getting you involved in all this. Let's keep our fingers crossed that we get another sign."

A hint of fear tightened her chest. "You don't think there's any chance of danger if he shows himself again, do you?"

He shook his head. "I don't think so, but I'm no more experienced with this than you are."

She inhaled deeply and placed her head back on his arm.

Leaning down, he lowered his lips to her forehead. She relished the feeling of protection. She lifted her face and met his lips with her own. The kiss was soft and gentle, restrained. What she wanted him to do was to throw her down in the sand and make mad, passionate love to her, but his restraint tempered her own passion. Instead, they shared a perfectly innocent kiss.

Later, she told herself— later after the McDougles are taken care of—I can concentrate on my own feelings. Right now she knew she was vulnerable and ready to do almost anything, but she didn't want to regret her actions later.

Grateful for his momentary restraint, she straightened up, took his hand and squeezed it.

***

The kerosene lantern cast tall shadows on the wall. Jewel lay still in her single cot pushed up against the wall in the big room, not behind her protective screen as before. Bryce had positioned his cot about ten feet from hers, near enough for Jewel to feel his presence.

If the captain sent a sign, she'd need Bryce to help her get through the ordeal.

Bryce moved about, in and out of the room, checking to make sure things were secure for the night.

A smile threatened Jewel's countenance. Here she was hoping to get a sign from a spirit inside an isolated fort in the Gulf of Mexico, and the only thing she could think about was how luscious Bryce looked in his knit pull-ons and bare chest.

Shaking her head, she turned on her side, punched her pillow, and watched the shadows flicker up and down against the curvature of the ceiling.

"Think you have enough cover?" Bryce's voice broke her concentration.

"Yes, thank you. I'm really very comfortable."

"Scared?"

Haven't had time to think of spirits with you marching up and down in front of me in your sexy nothings.

"Just a little, I guess," she answered instead.

He walked closer to the bed. "I'm right here. I don't think I should sleep any closer to you. It might make the captain avoid us." He chuckled. "I can't believe I just said that."

"I know what you mean. I feel a little silly too, but as long as I know you're in hearing distance, I'll be fine."

"Wake me if you need some moral support. I'll try to stay awake, but I can't guarantee my body will cooperate. Marcus and the crew almost killed me today. They're still making me pay for being away so long."

With only inches separating them, Bryce towered over her low cot. She held her breath, hoping he'd lean down to kiss her. Every iota in her body tingled with guarded anticipation.

In the flickering light of the lantern, he stood still, motionless, and instinctively she knew that he would turn to go to his own bed, alone.

Surprising herself, she said. "I could use a little TLC right now. It just might boost my courage."

A smile spread across his face. He raised one eyebrow and looked around the room. "You don't think Captain McDougle is here with us, do you?"

"I don't know what to think. I can't believe I've let myself actually become involved in something so totally foreign to what I teach and what I believe in. A few weeks ago I would've laughed you out of my office had you come to my campus and confronted me with your story."

"Yeah, that's why I wanted you to come to the island. You had to be here to understand."

She nodded. "You're right."

He brushed the hair away from her forehead. "I'm glad you came."

"Me too."

Bryce grinned. "Move over." He lowered his body next to her and sat, or rather leaned, on a small empty spot. "Think this cot will hold me and you?"

"I thought we agreed not to be together in case we have a visitor."

His arms wrapped around her. "But we didn't say I couldn't lay by you for a few minutes for that moral support you mentioned."

Her heart leaped, scooting over for him. He pulled her to him and held her close. She relished the warmth and security of his body. "After finding things that McDougle buried at River's Bend, I know we haven't dreamed all this up," she said. "I just hope he'll show up tonight so we can put this behind us."

Jewel inhaled deeply. Tremors slithered down her body.

Bryce pulled her even closer and kissed her. "It'll be okay. If he comes, I'll be with you."

She pressed her body to his. "If I thought he'd show himself again with you next to me, I wouldn't let you leave me. I could be a little braver being near you."

He kissed her again. "I don't won't to leave you,

but…" He pulled away. "We have to try it this way."

She swallowed hard. "Fingers crossed I won't scream and scare him away if he shows."

Bryce turned off the lantern, but within minutes Jewel's eyes adjusted to the darkness. A small light from the moon peeking in through the tiny slits in the window covering allowed her to see him move around the room and finally climb into his cot.

The hours dragged. Jewel's body screamed for sleep, but her mind raced from one subject to the next. From Captain McDougle to Bryce. From Bryce's son Kevin to David. One moment she was in her classroom on her campus. The next she stood at River's Bend wearing a long, baby blue day gown with a large, floppy straw hat.

There would be no peace for her until Captain McDougle or Ula or somebody from the other side told her how to put an end to their visits. She glanced over at Bryce on the tiny cot. Every time she thought she might ease off to sleep, Bryce turned in his cot, straightened his blanket or got up to check on something in the room.

It was well after midnight when Jewel fell asleep, but that lasted only for a few minutes. The sounds of men sloshing through water broke through her web of sleep. Squeezing her eyes, she tried to ward off the sounds and the feeling of alarm that threatened to take away her breath.

Then she saw it. The caves by the river. A barge tied up along the small canal. Men hauling in boxes of cargo.

But something wasn't right. These men weren't dressed in the attire of the nineteenth century. They were men dressed in clothes from a not-so-distant past.

Jewel tossed her head from side to side trying to push away the images. She needed Hilliard to give her a message to let her know what she was supposed to do, not to dream about men from the Twenty-First Century, but she had no control over the scene playing out in her head.

The men hauled in container after container, stacked

them far into the bowels of the caves, then left the estate in old cars and trucks.

Then she saw other men, men getting out of modern SUV's and trucks, then sneaking around the caves, carrying in smaller containers, vanishing into the dark tunnels. The images went back and forth from one century to the next.

In the last moment before the visions vanished, a young man rushed out of the cave alone.

Jewel wanted to scream. Nothing made sense to her.

Hilliard, Ula, please. One of you, help me.

As soon as the words floated through Jewel's thoughts, she inhaled deeply and relaxed. Her mind emptied itself of the presence of the men in the caves. For the moment she was calm and felt herself drifting back into sleep.

But something wasn't right. She tried to open her eyes and call out for Bryce, but her body remained helpless. Her mind closed to everything as she slid once more into a place she could neither understand nor escape.

Captain Hilliard McDougle stood before her. She knew he was there before she saw him. The stench of wet wool seeped into her nostrils. Her eyes flew open against her will. Hilliard was no longer the handsome young man telling his young wife goodbye. Just as before, his uniform with a bloodied hole on the left shoulder hung on an emaciated frame, his hair, long and wild.

Jewel wanted to scream, but the sound didn't come. Instead, she watched as the man before her lifted a transparent hand to within inches of her face, then with long sinewy fingers touched the golden heart around her neck. Jewel let out a low moan.

With a lifeless hand resting on the gold heart, Hilliard stood motionless. His gaze moved from Jewel's face to the heart and stared with eyes that showed a spark of life.

Jewel spoke in a soft voice. "It's the heart you gave to Ula."

The hand rose from the heart and touched Jewel's face, resting weightlessly against her skin. No physical sensation of hot or cold, moist or dry, heavy or light, touched her, but she knew the hand was there. Hilliard's presence touched beyond the skin and into her soul. Slowly her fear began to vanish.

Hilliard stood before her, and she was Ula.

With calm hands, she touched her chest and clasped her thumbs together and made their sign. Hilliard stepped back as if to watch what she was doing. She made the sign again.

"I'll always be with you, Hilliard. You'll always be with me. Remember? When the birds fly over the river, I'll think of you, and we'll be together." Jewel's voice cracked and tears welled in her eyes. "We are together still. Now. Right here." She placed her hand on her chest covering her heart.

Captain Hilliard McDougle, Confederate officer and Prisoner of War, stood back away from the woman, and for a moment he was a young man again, clean-shaven and handsome.

Reaching out, Jewel grasped his hand, and the years fell away. She was Ula McDougle, overwhelmed with a love that flowed from her chest. "You'll always be with me, Hilliard. Always." Tears flowed down her cheeks.

She blinked and Hilliard vanished.

Jewel inhaled deeply again, wanting more than anything to call out to Bryce, but she couldn't call out his name. For a few moments Jewel was conscious of where she was and who she was. She was no longer Ula McDougle and the spirit of her husband was no longer with her, but as she was pulling herself out of the last remnants of her vision, a new feeling gripped her heart.

Hilliard was back, but he wasn't facing her. Instead she saw him at the entrance of one of the caves on River's Bend Plantation with his back to her. In front of him was another figure, a young man holding a shovel.

The ghost turned, looked directly into Jewel's eyes, then was gone.

Jewel groaned out loud. She had to get to Bryce. She tried to stand, but when two hands grabbed her from behind, she collapsed.

***

Bryce grabbed Jewel as her body slumped against him.

Ever so slowly, as the spirit hovered over Jewel, Bryce had carefully inched his way behind her. Not once had the vision paid any attention to him. Jewel had been the one he had come to see, but Bryce was certain the captain had not seen Jewel at all. Rather he had come face to face with his young wife, Ula.

There was no doubt in Bryce's mind that what he had witnessed was the coming together of two souls, two spirits from the past who had never given up on the love they had known.

As she had spoken with the ghost, Jewel's voice changed. Her deep, perfect diction of a college professor had changed into a girl-like Southern drawl. Would she remember what had taken place? Would she recall the love that obviously had been shared during the encounter? Willingly, she had let the ghost of Captain McDougle touch her.

Bryce ran his hand along her hair, now wet from perspiration. Gently, he brushed it away from her face and placed a kiss on her forehead before laying her on the cot. As he slid under the covers next to her, her body, limp and hot, curled into a ball next to him. He wrapped his arms and legs around her. Held her tight.

She spoke, her face close to his chest. "Bryce, did you see him?"

"I saw him, Jewel, but he's gone now. It's just you and me."

"I saw something else. In the caves. I saw things happening."

She tried to get up, but Bryce held her close. "We'll talk about it tomorrow. You need to rest. I'm here with you. Everything's okay."

A soft whimper, a few mumbled words, then a deep breath told Bryce that she was asleep. Burying his face in her hair, he closed his eyes, but sleep was nowhere near. He would have to come to grips with what he'd seen tonight, but a thousand thoughts flashed through his mind as they always did when he was around Jewel.

Thoughts of Nan were always there, but being with Jewel lifted those thoughts to another level, reminding him what true love was supposed to be. Nan would always be with him, just as he was sure Ula would always be with Hilliard. As he'd watched the exchange between Jewel and Hilliard, he felt a sense of peace he hadn't experienced since he'd buried Nan. It was as though Nan had been with him tonight, letting him know that she was okay.

Had he wanted peace for his wife so badly that he imagined this feeling? It wouldn't matter. Whether the feeling had been real or not, he clung to it and stored it away in his heart.

He closed his eyes and relished the feel of Jewel's warm body next to him. Yes, Nan would always be with him, but thinking of her no longer immobilized him. Jewel had done that for him.

He let his thought settle on Kevin. Once just thinking about his son filled him with guilt because he wasn't with him. After seeing Jewel and his son together, though, he knew there was still hope. He was certain one day he and his son would have a home together and one day be a family again even though the boy's real mother was gone.

Whether that included Jewel or not remained to be seen, but he was sure that his dreams for his son would be fulfilled.

Then the thoughts of Jewel drove out all others. The red-haired professor had sneaked into his private thoughts without him knowing it. How had he ever thought she was like that driver who used her wealth to get out of killing his wife? No, Jewel was sensual, yet loving. Exciting, yet gentle. Strong, but unaware of her own strength.

She was an enigma he wanted to understand. Watching her with his son warmed his heart. Watching her face the visions and episodes gave him great respect for her. He had known what it was to love with his entire being, and there was no mistaking that what he was feeling now was genuine and real.

The problem would be convincing Jewel that she could love again also.

Pulling her tighter to his body, he worked to sift through the thoughts that raged through his mind, but before that happened, the long hours and events of the day took its toll and he drifted off to sleep.

Chapter 18

Bryce awoke to wet lips on his neck and warm hands on his chest. It had to be a dream—a glorious dream—and Bryce didn't want to wake from it.

"Am I going to have to do this alone?" Jewel's soft voice registered in his foggy brain.

Bryce's eyes flew open. Jewel's face was inches from his. She smiled then bent her head down and continued trailing her kisses down his neck. Bryce inhaled and moaned as every part of him came alive.

Stopping the glorious manipulations with her mouth and hand was the last thing he wanted to do, but stopping them had to happen. Even half awake he knew that if he wanted to last in this little game she was playing, he had to turn off the magic for a moment.

He grabbed her by the shoulders and effortlessly flipped her on her back. "My turn," he said through ragged breaths.

With careful, slow motions he removed her knit shirt, then lowed his head to taste the sweetness of her velvet white skin.

Jewel moaned and pushed herself against him, her hand clamping his head against her chest. "Now, Bryce. Now. Make love to me."

"No." The word was barely audible as he buried his

face in the warm crevice of her neck. "Not now. You've kept me at bay too long to rush this."

"Bryce Cameron, you'll pay for this." The words were soft and breathy, sending Bryce's blood driving through his body.

Striving for control, he whispered, "I hope so."

Lifting himself up, he kissed her hard on the mouth, causing an all-consuming passion that took away years of sorrow.

Knowing the pleasure that awaited him, Bryce couldn't last much longer. He fought to steady himself, tried to pace himself, but in the end, he gave in.

Then their gazes met. Anticipation sliced through the thick air and obliterated all else in the room. No one else existed. Nothing else mattered but this union.

***

Jewel's body still tingled. Again and again before the morning sun opened the world to them, Bryce had made love to her. Each time was different, each time more wonderful than the one before.

He made her feel as she had never felt before. In the moments of quiet between their lovemaking, they talked about what they'd seen. She told him about glimpses of the caves, small glimpses into a past that confused her. They talked, but mostly they loved.

Now lying next to him with his dark hair mussed and falling onto his forehead, it was all she could do to keep her hands off of him.

A smile tickled her lips as she remembered how she couldn't keep her hands off of him last night either. Waking next to him after her encounter with Captain McDougle just hours before, she'd had to touch him. It had been the most natural thing in the world for her to start their night of love making, though she had never done anything like that before in her life. Awakening him with kisses left him no doubt that she wanted him to make love to her. Even with her ex-fiancé, she had never felt comfortable enough to instigate the lovemaking.

How sad that she had almost given her life away to that man. How frightening to think that she would never have known how it felt to be equal in a relationship.

"You're in awfully deep thought." Bryce lifted his hand and touched her face. "If you're thinking about getting up and running like you did before, forget it. There's not a boat here."

She smiled and nestled her head in the crevice of his neck. "No way. I can hardly think much less run."

Bryce closed his eyes. "That's a relief 'cause I just don't know if I have the energy to chase you down and make you come to your senses."

"My senses, huh?"

"Yeah. Sometimes it takes a little longer for some people to realize what's happening to them than for others." He reached over and pulled her even closer to him.

The scent of their love making still lingered on his body. Inhaling the muskiness, she felt her body beginning to react to him. He too must have noticed her heat and the rapid breaths because his lower body responded.

Jewel laughed. "I thought you didn't have any more energy?"

"I don't. Just some parts of the body can't seem to get enough of you."

Jewel relaxed against him. "So you think I don't know what's happening to me?"

"I'm not sure. One minute I think you're catching on to what's happening between us, and the next thing I know you're running away."

She eased away from him. "I'm not running away. I'm here."

"I know you are, and I'm thrilled, but I'm never sure if you'll be here when I turn my back."

He had touched a nerve. Jewel tried to pull farther away from him, but he held her close.

Her voice was flat. "Maybe I have reason to run."

"We've talked about that before. David gave you reason to run, but what he did to you isn't the norm. Not with me it isn't." He ran his hand along her arm. "This is real and natural, not that." He touched her face and held her cheek in the palm of his hand. "This is real. You and me, right here in this cot and what we shared last night."

After a long minute, she relaxed. "I know," she whispered and snuggled up against his chest.

"Do you? Are you open to the fact that you might just be falling for me?"

Keeping her face buried in curly mass of hair on his chest, she smiled. "My, aren't we being a little arrogant?"

"Maybe. Maybe just hopeful."

Jewel pulled away from him again, but this time sat up and pulled her knees up to her chin. "Hopeful? Really?"

"Do you find that hard to believe?"

Shrugging, she turned her head and let her gaze follow the arched contour of the brick wall. "No. Yes. Maybe. I think it's possible, and I believe it could happen, but I just don't know right now."

"There you go again." His voice reeked with irritation. "It's not like you and David just split up yesterday. He's been out of your life—what did tell me?—five or six months. Get over it, Jewel."

"Get over it? Had I married him, I would've ruined my life. You can't blame me for being a little careful. I can't go around just falling for the first man who sends me to the stars in bed, especially one who hasn't opened up to me about anything. I thought I knew David, but obviously I didn't." She looked him straight in the eye. "And I'm not sure I know you at all."

Bryce shook his head, then slid off the side of the bed, standing before her completely naked. It was hard for her not to look at him, he didn't seem to notice.

"I shared my son with you."

"Yes, but not at first. I still don't know anything about you and Nan."

He stared at her before answering, and when he did, he completely ignored her last statement.

"You said you saw stars. Do you think you would have seen stars if there wasn't something between us," he asked, dropping one eyebrow, never averting her gaze. "Good sex is, well, good sex, but you don't visit the heavens unless there's something else there with it."

Turning, he grabbed his sweat pants off the floor, pulled them on, then looked directly into her eyes. "And there *was* something there, Jewel, whether you want to admit it or not." At that, he walked away from her.

Jewel watched him disappear into the courtyard. She looked around the empty room. "Now, how did that happen?"

She picked up her own clothes, but before dressing, first went to the small basin of water and washed the best she could. As she stepped out of her room, Jewel saw Bryce examining a wooden structure in the courtyard that his crew had put together yesterday. She leaned against the wall and watched him before making her presence known.

He tested joints and butts, then ran his hands over the wood as if he were communicating with it. She smiled, remembering how those same hands had caressed her body just hours ago, definitely communicating with her.

Right now, watching him sent tingles up her spine.

She moved and he glanced in her direction.

Gathering her thoughts and her composure, she walked over by him. "Will they use that today?"

Bryce turned back to the structure. "Yeah. It's a brace that'll hold up that ceiling over there so that we can replace some of the bricks."

She walked nearer to the frame and touched the wood, still damp from the morning haze. "Why didn't they build it directly under it?"

"Most of the time we do that but this particular area is hard to get into. We all agreed it would be easier this way." He looked at her for the first time. His voice softened. "I didn't mean to get edgy in there. The night was too beautiful to end it in that way."

"I agree. It was very special, the most special night I've ever spent," she confessed.

He looked up from the frame. "Ever?"

She nodded.

"You mean that?"

"Yes I do. I don't think I've ever had a night quite like that one." Her cheeks burned from admitting it.

"I have, Jewel, and I can tell you that what we have doesn't come around often."

With her heart in her throat, Jewel wondered if that feeling would last forever or vanish like the happiness she'd planned with David.

He took her hand, turned it over a couple times, then looked up into her eyes. "I'm sorry you think I'm secretive." He inhaled deeply. "It's hard for me to talk about Nan."

Jewel placed a hand on his cheek. "I'm sure it is, but you say we might have something together, and yet you can't share her with me. If you can't talk about her to me, then I have to think you're still so much in love with her that you're not ready to let anyone else into your heart—and I guess I can understand that," she added quickly.

"I'll always have Nan in my heart. We had something special, very special, but I know I'm ready to move on. The heart can be as big as we need it to be. I can have my love for her and let someone else in as well."

He took her hand again. "Come sit and let's see if I can make you feel like I'm not trying to keep anything from you."

She followed him to the bench where she had poured out the ordeal she'd gone through with David. Still not believing she'd spilled her guts to a complete stranger that night, a warm flush of embarrassment inched up her neck. Now that she knew Bryce a little better, she felt as though he understood her a little, and now it was time for him to do some sharing.

Could he allow someone else in his heart with Nan?

***

"Nan and I met in our freshman year at the University of South Carolina. She was at a fraternity party with one of my friends and we hit it off right away."

He stopped and allowed visions of her warm smile and quiet laugh come to him as if he were sitting in the room with her now. He cleared his throat. "I think we sat in the kitchen with the house mother for the entire night talking and laughing. It was as if I had known her my entire life."

"That's wonderful when that connections happens, isn't it?"

"Yes it was." Nodding, he took a deep breath. "We were inseparable after that night. We went to all the sporting events, took in concerts. . ."

"You like concerts?" she asked. "I've never been able to convince any date to take me to a concert."

Bryce chuckled. "No. I don't like concerts, or I thought I didn't, but I had fallen so much in love with Nan that I would've done anything to be with her. So, I went to concerts and I surprised myself by actually enjoying some of them."

Jewel relaxed against the brick wall, her eyes twinkling from the soft light of the moon. "It does happen that way, doesn't it? Love makes a person open up to things that were foreign before."

"I guess you're right. She had me doing things I'd never considered before. She majored in elementary education and was perfect for those children. She taught second grade for a couple years until Kevin was born. It was tough making ends meet, but I wanted her to stay home."

Again he got quiet, letting the belt of pain in his chest ease. "I'm so glad she did because he was only about six months old when she died."

Jewel squeezed his hand and he held onto her.

"I want Kevin to remember her so bad, but I know it won't happen." A lump formed in his throat. He appreciated Jewel waiting for him to get control again. "I think watching Kevin grow up without Nan is the hardest part."

"I'm sure it is, but I know you miss her for what you and she shared. I can't imagine loosing someone you love so much."

He looked into Jewel's eyes. She was so sincere.

"Yes, I do miss what we shared together. I slept on the couch for months after she was gone. I couldn't force myself to crawl into an empty bed."

Jewel leaned over and put her arms around him and held him. "I'm so sorry. In a way you have a lot in common with Ula. She lost the one she loved and had to raise her son alone."

"I thought the same thing. When I saw Hilliard last night with you and he spoke to you as if he saw Ula, I felt a sense of peace I haven't felt since I lost Nan. I'm not sure what it all meant, but I'd like to think that my wife is at peace just as they are."

She pulled away just enough for him to see her eyes. "Was she alone in the car when the accident happened?"

Could he actually talk about her accident? Could he tell her how he'd felt that night? Was it possible for another human being to understand the fear and complete helplessness that consumed him while he waited for emergency personnel to rescue his family?

Jewel waited expectantly, but he knew if he chose not

to talk about it, she wouldn't understand. He had to make her believe that he wasn't keeping anything from her, so he swallowed the lump in his throat and continued.

"No, Kevin and I were with her," he said and surprised himself that he was actually going to open up. "I was driving. She was in the passenger seat and Kevin was in his car seat in the back. He dropped his patsy and started crying. Nan unbuckled her seatbelt and reached over the seat at the exact moment that woman's car ran a red light and hit us broadside."

He stopped, trying to catch his breath. His heart pounded in his chest remembering what he didn't want to remember. He squeezed his eyes. "Nan was thrown out the front window. Kevin and I managed to survive with only a couple of scratches, but not Nan. She lay on the side of the road, alone. I couldn't get to her." Tears burned his eyes.

His body tensed, remembering.

Jewel pulled him close to her and kissed him gently on the cheeks. "You don't have to say any more."

"I'm okay. I'm kind of surprised I'm telling you this. I've never talked to anyone about the accident."

She kissed him on the forehead and held him close.

He nodded and continued. "Nan had all kinds of internal injuries. She suffered for weeks before pneumonia set in and took her life."

He pushed away the urge to hit the brick wall with his fist then took a moment to calm himself. "Those weeks in the hospital were the worst weeks of my life. I felt totally helpless as I watched her slip away from me."

"I'd like to say I understand your pain, but I know no one can say that unless they've been there. Thank you for sharing with me. I know it was hard."

For a long time they sat close together, neither talking, as they waited for the sun to rise. When orange and pink streaks reflected on the metal plaque on the side of the cannon sitting on top of the fort, Bryce pulled her to him and squeezed hard.

"Life can be hell, Jewel, but sometimes, if you get yourself through the initial flames, there's always something that might cool the hurt."

He touched the tip of her nose and whispered, "You've helped to cool my pain."

Chapter 19

Later in the day Bryce helped Jewel out of the boat and into his truck they'd left at the harbor the day before. Within minutes he pulled out into the traffic on the beachfront road in search of the city library.

Jewel sat on her side of the truck trying to make sense of the all that had taken place. After Bryce had opened up to her about losing Nan, she understood more why he was so secretive with details of his life. After they'd left the bench to wash up before leaving the island, she watched him carefully. Inside his exterior, the man was a loving husband and father, a man hiding his pain.

She also understood a love like he and Nan had would be forever, just as Ula and Hilliard's love. Nan might be gone, but she was still a real presence for Bryce, one that she knew he wasn't ready to set aside.

That realization made her wonder how they could've had such a wonderful night together. She'd felt as if he was making love to her, not just having sex. She'd believed his words of endearments and let herself hope they might have a chance together.

Now she wasn't so sure.

Uncertainty seemed to be at every corner of her life right now—not something she embraced. She wasn't sure what to do next with Bryce or with all she'd found out about River's Bend.

Now that Captain McDougle had been encountered, she knew she couldn't walk away. The next step could only be to find the connection between the disturbed spirits, the plantation, and Jason LeBreaux.

She closed her eyes and prayed they'd find answers before the auction took place. She had a feeling her encounters wouldn't go away if she and Bryce didn't find the answer to whatever was disturbing the peace of the McDougle spirits.

"The library's just a block or two away from here," Bryce said as he maneuvered through heavy beach traffic.

His words pulled her attention to him. The morning sun shone into his window, highlighting tiny streaks of auburn in his black hair and emphasizing high cheekbones and gorgeous lips. A rush of hot desire flooded through her body remembering where his lips had touched her body last night.

He squinted behind his sunshades. "We shouldn't have any trouble using their computers."

She swallowed hard and brushed away the urge to lean into him. "You really think we can find information about LeBreaux's family?"

"Let's hope. I have a feeling if he's kept his connection to that estate a secret, he has a reason. There's got to be something he's hiding. Using the plantation to hide stolen goods like the old men suggested might be enough, but I'll bet there's more."

She nodded her agreement then pulled her gaze away from him. She couldn't go into the library with thoughts of Bryce's naked body on her mind. There was work to be done if she could keep her hands off of him.

With just a couple of turns off the beach, Bryce pulled into the parking lot of an impressive modern structure housing the city library.

Forcing her mind on the task at hand, Jewel jumped out of the truck and reached the front entrance before him. With one hand on the door handle, she turned. "Someone in public office like LeBreaux couldn't keep dark secrets hidden for long. There're too many hungry reporters out there."

"You're right. We might be wrong, but I've got a hunch." He led her through to the main desk then off to a side room filled with computers. They settled at two against the back wall and started their search.

For thirty minutes, Jewel and Bryce searched topic after topic on separate computers with no results. Bryce got up and stretched. "Maybe I *was* wrong."

Jewel didn't answer. Instead she squinted and concentrated on a story in a small newspaper that no longer existed. "No, wait. Come see this."

Bryce bent over, placing his hands on her shoulder. "You found something?"

"Maybe. Look. It's from the late seventies. It's a column by A. W. Fountaine, slamming the use of the river estates for illegal trading."

"What?"

"Here." She moved aside so he could see. "He doesn't mention any names, but he does name St. Marks and a couple other towns. It says 'the rich and elite old families along the river using their plantations for illegal trade are disgracing the memory of the old South.' He doesn't say anything specific."

"A. W. Fountaine. Wonder if he's still living?"

With a quick check of the directory, Jewel had a telephone number and an address.

Bryce reached over and kissed her on the cheek. "Good work. Let's get back to the car where we can use our telephones."

Bryce wasted no time in making the call. Jewel watched his face light up when someone answered the phone, but could almost guess what was being said when he asked for Mr. Fountaine. His expression told it all.

"When did he die?" He listened. "I see." He told the

person on the other end of the call   he was researching some property on the river and knew Mr. Fountaine had used some of them in his columns. "You don't still have your father's notes, do you?" He turned around and winked.

When he hung up, she touched his arm. "Good news?"

"Yes. She said she'd looked at them recently and knew where they were. There's not much on St. Marks, but she's going to fax them to us as soon as I give her a number. Let's go back inside the library."

Jewel's heart raced. "I knew we wouldn't run into a dead-end street. I had a feeling."

"And a dream."

"Yes, and a dream." She hesitated a moment, wondering if she had remembered everything that Hilliard had shown to her last night. She had a feeling there was more to her vision, but shaking her head, she followed Bryce back into the library. If Hilliard or Ula wanted her to know more, they'd make sure she remembered. They hadn't failed her yet.

They located a fax machine, and within minutes of calling Mr. Fountaine's daughter with the number, they received about a dozen pages, handwritten, but still legible.

Dividing them, they sat down in upholstered lounge chairs and picked over the reporter's notes from three decades ago.

Bryce sat up straight. "Just what I thought. Fountaine connects the Smyths with smuggling stolen property. He says 'They couldn't let a good thing die like the rest of the property owners along the river.'"

Jewel leaned over to get a better look. "Sounds like something that would've taken place a hundred years ago, not in our own time."

"You're exactly right. Before the turn of the century there's no telling how many plantations made a little extra profit hiding stolen property. Now we know for sure the Smyths were involved." Bryce harrumphed. "I can't believe this. Look, he even mentions 'young LeBreaux helping his grandpa Smyth until the mishap with the Mallett kid, then old Mr. Smyth ran him off the property.'"

Frowning, Jewel took the paper. "I wonder what that means."

"Who's the Mallett kid?"

They both looked at one another. "Back to the computer," they said in unison.

In less than an hour they exited the library for the second time that day, got in the truck, and drove away without saying anything. By the time they'd gotten the condo that Bryce and Marcus kept on the mainland, Jewel spoke up.

"Now what?"

Bryce shook his head. "This is getting more involved by the minute, but there's too much coincidence not to be connected. The Mallett kid goes missing. He's never found. He's reportedly with Jason on his last day hunting. Jason gets kicked off the plantation."

"Yeah. Too much coincidence."

"We know there were some shady dealings along the river. We can't stop now. I think we need to visit our three old men again at the gas station."

"My bags are packed. If we leave early tomorrow morning, we might be able to find them before the auction."

***

The next day Bryce looked down at his watch as they drove down the main street in St. Marks. There was time to stop at the gas station and still to explore the caves along River's Bend before dark.

He forced back a smile.

Except for the new information about LeBreaux that might throw a wrench into the auction, he'd been waiting for this day since the first time he and Jewel stepped on the property. Taking a quick glance in her direction, he wondered how she'd react to his surprise. Of course, his surprise might come in second to what they might find out from their guys at the station.

"I hope our old men are there."

Her shy smile told him how she felt. How he wanted to pull her into his arms to console her, but he had to wait to see how things transpired. No false hopes.

"We'll know as soon as we turn this corner."

"There they are." She lifted her hand in a wave. The same three men sat in the three rockers. One wore overalls with a white t-shirt beneath it just as he had the first time they'd talked with him. The other two wore short sleeve button-up shirts that had seen better days. When they saw their car, the men lifted their hands as well, but theirs were nothing more than small town courtesy.

Bryce chuckled. "I don't think they have a clue who we are."

"No, we might have to start from the beginning, but I have a feeling they know exactly what happened out there at that plantation."

Thirty minutes later Bryce pulled back onto the main street. Jewel sat on her side of the truck holding her hands on her lap, tense. "I can't believe they told us that."

He nodded. "Didn't take much coaxing, did it?"

"It adds up though," she added. "Old man Smyth had this thing going with crooks. They're making who knows what kind of a killing in stolen loot, then the Mallett boy goes missing. Grampa Smyth kicks Jason LeBreaux off the property. The men-4 didn't make any bones about how they thought young LeBreaux had something to do with the possible death of the Mallett boy, did they?"

She shook her head then continued. "No, all three of them couldn't wait to put in his two cents." She shook her head. "Why wasn't something done back then? Why didn't someone keep looking for Mallett? You know if these old men felt something shady had taken place out there, then others did as well."

"When you have a lot of influence, you can make things happen and make things not happen. Whoever led the investigation probably didn't want to mess with someone like Mr. Smyth."

He watched Jewel think about what he'd said. "Looks like someone would've searched harder for a body," she said under her breath. "I feel sorry for the kid's family."

"Well, we're not taking any chances. I've put a call into the local authorities to meet us out at the property today and to the CIA just to make sure."

"Does the CIA have jurisdiction?"

Bryce shrugged. "Jason LeBreaux is in the national spotlight. He's about to announce his candidacy day after tomorrow in Baton Rouge. What better reason for them to get involved?"

"What if the local authorities won't cooperate until the others get here?"

"Oh, I think they will. The Smyths no longer have a lot of pull around here, according to our old men. This is another era." Bryce chuckled. "The old guys couldn't wait for someone to ask them to tell their story."

"I just hope they can keep their story straight if they have to testify."

"I think they will. If we find what they say is out there, they might not need to do any talking."

He looked over at Jewel, who stared out the side window. "Hey, cheer up. You're going to have Ula McDougle's portrait today."

"You're right. I should be happy. It's just—it's like I'm going out there to say farewell to the estate. No wonder the poor spirits were up in arms. There's no telling what's happened out there over the centuries."

"Maybe things will work out." He fought back a smile. "Who knows who'll end up with the property and what they'll do with it. Heck. It might turn out to be the most popular bed and breakfast along the river."

"Wouldn't that be great!" Her voice showed signs of enthusiasm, but the forced smile told him she had about as much hope for that to happen as her living in such a place.

Again he fought back a nervous grin.

The gates to River's Bend were open. "That's strange. Didn't think anyone would be here this early today."

His words were soft, but she'd heard. "Maybe the auctioneer had to set things up?" She too squinted and scanned the property for vehicles. "Do you see anyone?"

He shook his head and pushed away the uneasiness that spread through his body. "Maybe the police got here first."

He pulled into the driveway that now showed signs of a lot more traffic than when they'd been here before. Of course, just his crew on the last visit would have gotten rid of a century's worth of wild grass.

"I'd like to see the caves." Jewel pulled off her shoes and reached for her rubber boots. "I'm scared if I wait any longer, I won't get a chance to ever see them. They'll probably tape them off."

"You sure you don't want to wait for the authorities. They'll be here in a few minutes."

"No, I have to see them for myself. Please?"

He couldn't deny her so after driving as close as he could get to the back of the property, he stopped. There were recent car tracks leading to the caves, but he didn't want to pull up that close.

Within minutes he was leaning next to Jewel on the side of the vehicle. He tugged on his boot. "We can stick our heads in, but to be on the safe side, we need to wait for the authorities to go any distance into the caves."

"I can handle that." For the first time since he'd picked her up today, she smiled. "I'm eager to see the caves, but I'm not completely without a brain."

"Come here, Miss Jewel." He pulled her into his arms and kissed her long and deep. "Damn. You're lucky we'll be having visitors in a little while."

"Really? And what might I have expected if we were alone?"

He just chuckled and let her slide out of his arms.

She pulled away. "Come on. Let's see what's in there."

Bryce hesitated, looked out to the drive, but no one was around. Jewel started toward the river. "Don't be in such a hurry. Those caves have been there for a long time. I don't think they're going anywhere today."

"No, but we are, so I don't want to waste any time."

Bryce grabbed a small backpack from the seat of the truck then caught up with her. A trail of beaten down bushes brought them to a few feet from the opening. Bryce pulled out a flashlight.

"We're not sure what's in there so don't go marching into the dark." He looked down at the ground. "Looks like we're not the only ones who's been exploring." He pointed out several well-defined footprints.

"Probably the auctioneer's crew. Surely everything had to be surveyed and categorized for the sale."

Bryce shook his head. "I don't know. Something doesn't feel right."

"What do you mean?"

"I'm not sure, but I don't have a good feeling. Maybe we ought to do this when everyone else is here."

"I'm so scared this is my only chance to see them."

She looked at the cave and the longing he saw in her eyes pulled at his heart

"I promise," she said. "I'll be careful and won't leave your side."

Reluctantly he nodded. "Here's an extra flashlight." He handed it to her then stepped into the instant coolness of the cave.

"Look, Bryce. There're a lot of tracks in here."

Jewel walked deeper into the cave. He followed, shining the light against walls that showed signs of having had something stacked against them. A few cigarette butts lay along the wall.

Jewel turned to him. "Probably teenagers finding a romantic place to be alone."

"Yeah. Teenagers."

He just wished he believed his own words.

Jewel took several steps in front of him, then stopped. When she turned, her face was white. "I remember something else. Bryce, I saw a teenager boy standing with the shovel in my dream. Here. In this cave."

"That's what the guys were hinting at, I bet."

She crossed her arms in front of her as if to ward off evil. Her face paled even more. "Why didn't I remember that before?"

Bryce stepped toward her to give her a reassuring hug when his phone sang. He grimaced. "I can't believe I'm picking up a signal in here." He pulled it from his pocket and took a few steps toward the entrance to get better reception.

"Hello," he said then listened to his father-in-law on the other end of the line. In the few seconds that Mr. Wilson talked, Bryce felt his world crumbling around him. He looked at Jewel, not believing what he was hearing.

Finally he found his voice. "Are you absolutely positive?"

He listened to Mr. Wilson assure him that his facts were accurate and gave him the names of the different officials he'd talked with.

"Thank you for calling."

Bryce hung up, but couldn't move.

"Come on, Bryce, before the authorities get here."

"Jewel, we have to talk."

She stopped and shrugged. "Okay, but can't it wait?"

270

"No. We have to talk now." He took a few steps closer to her and calmed his breathing, hoping he'd be able to tell her what Mr. Wilson had just told him without showing his anger and hurt.

"What is it?"

"You didn't tell me that Jodi Martin is your mother's sister."

Jewel wrinkled her nose. "What's she got to do with anything? I don't think she knows Jason LeBreaux or anyone in the Smyth family."

"That's not what I'm talking about. Why didn't you mention that your aunt was charged with DUI in the death of my wife Nan?"

She stared at him, and as if a mountain of bricks hit her, she threw her hands up to her mouth and gasped. "No. That can't be."

"Oh, yeah, it can be and it is. Mr. Wilson put two and two together when you said you were from the Boston area and you mentioned your Aunt Jodi. I guess I wasn't around when you two were talking about the rest of your family because that's the first I'd heard of your aunt's name."

"Why didn't he say something? Bryce, I swear, it never occurred to me that your wife was the lady she hit. I wasn't around when it happened. I was at my campus. No one elaborated on it. They told me she'd been involved in an accident and that the lady in the other car died. That's all they said. No one made a big deal of it because I was told the lady in the other car was at fault."

"How could it have been Nan's fault? She wasn't even driving. I was." Bryce's words came out harsh and loud. "It was your aunt's fault. She was swerving from one side of the road to the other because she was so drunk. She ran a stop light and hit us."

Jewel stood in the middle of the cave entrance, her arms wrapped tightly around her body. "I didn't question my family because they said there wasn't even a trial."

"Exactly. Your family used their influence to get her off, and you're right, no one made a big deal about the fact that my wife was killed by a rich drunk."

"I'm so sorry, so, so sorry."

He watched her struggle for words. "Where were they? I don't even know where the accident happened. Were you and Nan in Boston?"

"No, I had a conference in Chicago. We'd taken a couple extra days because Nan hadn't been out of the house with Kevin. He'd been sick and she'd been stuck in the hotel while I was in meetings. We were out sight-seeing and shopping. It was such an innocent and commonplace outing. We were having such a good time. Who could've imagined a day like that could become so tragic."

Tears flooded Jewel's eyes. She trembled. "What can I say? I'm sorry."

"I'm sorry too, but," he turned to go, "I can't be in here with you."

"No, wait, Bryce. Please don't leave. I swear I didn't know there was any connection between Aunt Jodi and Nan or I would've said something. It was too much of a coincidence to think that..." She stopped before she finished.

Bryce felt as though his heart had been ripped out. He left her standing alone as he marched out of the cave, not believing he'd let himself fall head over heels for someone like that. He knew he'd sensed something familiar about her the first day on the island. He just couldn't place it.

Why hadn't he questioned her? Why had he been so stupid as to fall in love with a relative of someone who took his son's mother away?

He got outside in the sunlight, threw his body against the hard rock wall, and let his head fall back. Nausea churned in his stomach. He wanted to vomit.

***

Jewel legs collapsed under her. She braced herself with her hands as she sat on the cool sandy surface of the outer cave. Her flashlight rolled away from her, but she didn't care. Maybe darkness would hide the horror that engulfed her. How could it be possible that Bryce's Nan was killed by Aunt Jodi?

"Oh, God. Please don't let it be." She put her head down in her hands and let the tears flow. Her body shook as great sobs came from deep within her. She thought that finding her David with another woman was the worst thing that could ever happen to her. But no. Nothing compared to what she felt right now.

She'd let herself fall in love with Bryce even though she didn't want to. Her heart didn't listen when she told herself she wasn't ready for another possible heartbreak. Who would've thought this is where it would lead?

For a long time she sat, limp and lifeless, wanting to be swallowed up by the cave's darkness. How could she ever face Bryce again?

Finally, a noise made her pull her head up. Hoping that he'd return, she crawled to where her flashlight had rolled, but when she reached for it, a boot stepped around a sharp curve and stepped on her hand.

"I'll take that, young lady." The man's deep whisper took her breath away.

She pulled herself up and stood facing him, a man barely visible in the cave's darkness. She could see he was short, but well-built, and in his right hand he held a gun pointing right at her.

Another man, much taller, stepped behind him. "Gawd, Lester, couldn't you leave well enough alone. She would've left without knowing we were here."

Jewel's heart beat in triple time, but she tried to talk as if running into these guys wasn't terrifying. "Guys, I'm here for the auction. I'll leave right now and forget I saw you, I swear."

The short guy called Lester laughed. "Sure you will, honey. Faster than a racehorse, you'll run out of here and grab a cell phone and call those blockheads they call policemen around here."

"Hell," she heard the taller guy mutter. "If you had a brain, you'd be dangerous."

"Shut up and get some rope."

The taller man turned around, but as soon as he did, Lester grabbed Jewel and pushed her into a darkened corner. She could hear someone coming into the cave's entrance, and she prayed it wasn't Bryce. As much as she needed him, she didn't want these men to hurt him.

"Jewel, where are you?" Bryce's voice floated through the cave's interior. Jewel's heart sank.

Lester's hand shot up and slammed against her mouth.

"Jewel?" His voice was getting closer. She tried to jerk herself away from the man or to scream, but he held tighter. She prayed Bryce would turn around.

Too late, he stepped around the corner and the tall man hit him over the head with a gun. He fell to the floor.

The man took his hand away from her mouth. She screamed, yanked herself away, and fell down by Bryce.

"Bryce, Bryce. Are you okay?" She grabbed his head and warm blood flowed down her hand.

Bryce moaned, but didn't move.

Lester grabbed her by the shoulders and showed her away from Bryce. She hit the side of the cave so hard she nearly lost her breath. She straightened up and got still. Just enough light showed perspiration dripping from Lester's face. His glazed eyes told her the man was scared or worse, was on drugs. She knew she had to do what they said or they could hurt both of them.

The other man came back carrying one long piece of rope and a roll of duct tape. Lester pointed his gun toward Jewel. "Stay right where you are."

She nodded, not wanting to do anything to startle the

man. Her body trembled as she watched the other man drag Bryce next to her. "You and your sweetie can play 'handsies' when he comes to."

Lester pushed her to the floor and pushed her back against Bryce's limp body and looped the ropes around her wrists and yanked it tight. She bit her lip to keep from yelling as he pulled the rope around Bryce's hands as well. When that was accomplished the tall guy stooped down and helped Lester wrap the rope around their upper bodies, then stretched it to their ankles and tied it there.

The warmth of Bryce's body should've soothed her, but she knew he was in as much danger as she was.

"What a pretty little mouth," Lester said as he kneeled alongside of Jewel.

When the man made a slurping sound, Jewel jerked. "You ape, leave me alone." Her struggles pushed her into Bryce's back.

The other man reached across Bryce and pushed. "Stop it, you idiot. No time for that."

Before he stood up again, Lester leaned over, gave Jewel a sloppy kiss, then slapped a piece of tape across her mouth. He stuck his hand into Bryce's pocket and pulled out the keys to his vehicle before he stuck a piece of tape across his mouth as well.

"You won't be needing these keys."

Lester stood up again. "That ought to do it. Go get that last load and let's get out of here. If his car's not here, no one's gonna search down here. They'll rot before someone finds them out here." He snorted as he followed his partner to the back of the cave.

Within minutes Jewel heard them shuffling back to the outer cave. She opened her eyes enough to see them carry one large box between them. This would be the ideal time for them to be overtaken by the law, but as of yet she hadn't heard anything outside the cave. Maybe no one paid attention to Bryce's call about their newspaper discovery.

"Too bad we don't have time to give her a little taste of a real man."

"Shut up, Lester. Just walk."

Relieved that she didn't have to fight them off, she watched the men back out the entrance.

Silence.

Jewel squirmed against Bryce's back, trying to loosen the ropes, but the only thing she managed to do was have them cut into her flesh. With the tape across her mouth, she whimpered.

Knowing how hopeless their situation was, she felt the bile rise from her stomach and nearly gagged her. Consciously she fought for control and for calm so she could think. She felt Bryce's hand against hers and rubbed a finger along his skin, hoping he'd awakened. She stopped moving and entwined her one finger with his.

How long would they lie here until someone found them?

His SUV had been an indication that they were here, but Jewel had a feeling Lester was right. If the men took it with them, no one would think to look down here, unless the police were convinced something was wrong in the cave and came in. She prayed the law officers of St. Marks were diligent.

What had Bryce told her? Why hadn't she listened closer? Did he say the police were meeting them here or had he simply mentioned a possible problem they should check into later?

She longed for Bryce to wake up. She tried to close her eyes, but that only made her think harder.

Anger shot through her veins. Why hadn't she listened to Bryce and stayed away from the caves?

A shout and several gunshots outside the cave put her on alert. She stiffened. Strained to hear what was going on beyond their sight. She felt Bryce move.

Another gunshot. Jewel flinched.

More shouts, then silence.

Please, God. Please let the gunshots be from the police. At least she knew his call had paid off. Someone was on the property.

Now she and Bryce could do nothing but wait.

Within minutes, two men in uniforms stooped down by them. Had it not been for the tape across her mouth, Jewel would've exhaled a loud sigh of relief.

One of the officers worked with the tape on her face while the other one used his flashlight to check the back of the cave. "Good thing you had enough sense to place that call before coming in here."

He ripped the tape from her mouth. "Sorry. I know that stung."

"Uhhh. Thanks."

She heard the tape pulled from Bryce's mouth. "Owww!" His voice was nothing but a whisper.

With the rope cut, Jewel turned around and threw herself into Bryce's arms. "Are you okay?"

He nodded. "Yeah. What happened?"

Jewel looked into his eyes wanting more than anything to tell him again how sorry she was and how much she loved him, but after his phone call about her Aunt Jodi, she knew when he remembered what had taken place a few minutes before he'd been hit, he wouldn't want to even talk to her much less hold her.

"You two okay?" One of the officers stooped down and took her arm to help her up.

When he reached down to help Bryce, he touched the back of his head. "I think so. Can't thank you enough, but someone needs to tell me what happened here. I'm a little in the dark."

Jewel looked back at Bryce, took a deep breath, then explained what had taken place. The officers in turn explained that they had overpowered the two thugs as they were taking what they assume to be drugs out of the cave.

"You don't have to worry about those two. They're handcuffed in the back of our car. We have more help from the department coming."

"You were lucky," the other officer said. "By the looks of those two, I'm sure they could've put a bullet through your heads and thought nothing of it. We've had some calls about activity out here. We'd checked these caves out before and knew something was going on, but couldn't seem to nab the guys. We're just glad you made the call to us, but sorry you had to be in the middle of it."

One of the officers looked at Bryce's head. "You need someone to look at that. You took quite a blow."

Bryce only nodded.

"I've put a call for medical assistance. While we're waiting, let's go outside and you can tell me more about why you called in the first place."

Bryce looked directly into Jewel's face. She knew she'd have to tell the officers about her dream. Would they believe her? Would they laugh if nothing was found?

With a fortifying breath, she nodded. "Certainly, but I think you'll need to tell your backup to bring some shovels. I think you need to do some digging."

Chapter 20

From her room at a St. Marks's bed and breakfast, Jewel sat alone on a couch and watched the news unfold on T.V. Jason LeBreaux stepped out of his car at the steps of City Hall in Boston, where he was scheduled to announce his candidacy for the presidential election. While he reached across the roped-off area to shake hands with someone in the crowd, three men in dark suits confronted him.

Jewel didn't need to hear their conversation to know what was being said. She watched LeBreaux's reaction. At first his politician's smile and handshake greeted them, but with their first few words, the smile vanished and the robust man on the campaign trail paled. But only for a second. Like a trained actor, he plastered the smile back on his face, waved to the crowd and stepped into the open door of the waiting car.

No handcuffs. No pushing into the back seat. No answering the questions from waiting reporters with cameras and microphones stuck in his face. It was obvious that LeBreaux wanted out of—not in—the spotlight this morning.

Jewel exhaled a long sigh as the news flipped to another story. She was tired. Yesterday had been a blur. Her elation of being back on River's Bend was ended by the unbelievable phone call from Nan's father. Then their run-in with LeBreaux's men and a short trip to the hospital to have Bryce's head stitched would've been enough for one day. But it wasn't.

For the rest of the afternoon, she stood by Bryce and watched hoards of lawmen examine the cave. Very few words were exchanged between them, and what was said was shallow and meaningless. Nothing like what needed to be said.

Just before dark, with cameras recording it all, a shallow grave was uncovered with the skeleton of what was believed to be LeBreaux's friend, Mallett. She couldn't believe her time away from campus had gotten her involved in all that she'd seen. She almost felt sadness for the man LeBreaux. So much about him would've made him a good president, but the side that tried to hide a juvenile mistake came from someplace within him that a president shouldn't allow. Had it not been for his two buffoons dealing in drugs, he might've gotten away with it.

Jewel shook her head, then tried to relax, but she knew it wouldn't happen.

The new owners of the plantation would be disclosed today, a day later than scheduled, and Jewel wanted to be there, even though her insides were being torn out knowing that the new owners might demolish the family home she'd finally found. But worse, she might be visiting the plantation alone. Bryce hadn't talked with her since they came back from the hospital. He'd immediately asked for a second room, got his things from her room and walked out of her life.

Her heart hurt. She'd heard people use that expression before and thought how overdramatic they were being, but she now knew that it was possible for her chest to feel pain.

By ten o'clock she sat behind the wheel of a rental on the front lawn of River's Bend. Signs had been posted but no chairs had been set up as she envisioned. Only a couple of cars pulled into the drive along with her.

Soon the fate of the estate would be decided, but would she know her own fate? Would she and Bryce ever see each again? It was doubtful. He'd made it perfectly clear that her connection with her Boston family overshadowed any feelings he might have had for her.

As much as it hurt, she understood.

Before she could sort through the questions and emotions swirling around her head, she turned to see the silver Towncar pull up beside her.

Disappointment pulled at her insides, but inhaling a deep breath, she stepped out and greeted Mrs. Smyth and her son.

Mrs. Smyth extended a hand to Jewel. "Don't you look lovely today."

"Thank you, ma'am. You look amazingly refreshed to have flown in just this afternoon." *Especially since your grandson is being questioned for goodness knows what.*

"The flight was easy and the rental company had our same car waiting at the door. Very efficient today."

Mrs. Smyth's son pulled a wheelchair out of the trunk. "Mother, would you like to sit here, or do you want to go inside."

"Let's adjourn to the parlor." Mrs. Smyth giggled like a twelve-year old girl. "I just love the sound of that. So Southern, you know."

Her son lifted the wheelchair onto the porch and placed an arm around his mother. She looked up at Jewel. "I'm so sorry your young man couldn't be with us today. He called before we left and said he had to return to the island. He's a doll, you know."

Jewel just smiled.

The group gathered in the parlor under the portrait of Ula McDougle.

Jewel settled her gaze on the portrait, waiting for Ula's presence to be made known to her. She wanted a sign. Anything to let her know if what had taken place affected Ula.

Nothing happened.

Mrs. Smyth rolled her chair next to her. "Do you feel her?"

"No, nothing. Maybe we did it. Maybe she and her captain are both at peace. Together," she threw in.

Mrs. Smyth nodded. "I hope so. They deserve it after all these years. Maybe they'll give us a sign to let us know, but then again, maybe we'll never know. You may have to be content to know you tried."

It was Jewel's turn to nod. "I'm so sorry things worked out the way they did for your grandson."

The old lady nodded. "Yes, I love Jason. My husband had his moments with him. It broke my heart when they parted ways, but that's men for you. Jason is a strong boy. If he did something wrong, he'll admit it and fix it. If not, he'll go on with his life as always. My heart and my love are his. He knows it. It's all I can give him right now." She straightened her shoulders. "Shall we begin?"

Jewel looked around for the expectant bidders to come through the door, scared to know who they would be, but eager and anxious to hear what the fate of her ancestral home would be. "Shouldn't we wait?"

Taking a break from straightening her suit jacket, Mrs. Smyth looked up. "Why? Why should we wait?"

"For the bidders," Jewel answered. "Surely someone is interested in knowing who gets the property? Who would bid on something like this and not come for the big moment?"

Mrs. Smyth pulled her arms up in front of her, rested her chin in one hand. "So you don't know."

Confused, Jewel looked around. "Don't know what?"

Mrs. Smyth rolled her eyes and let out a gasp of exasperation. "Men. I can't believe he's leaving you hanging like this."

At that moment, a well-dressed man came through the door.

"Jewel, this is Mr. Monroe, my attorney. He'll explain everything."

He introduced himself to Jewel, kissed Mrs. Smyth on the cheek, and shook hands with her son.

Mr. Monroe placed his brief case on a small table and pulled out some papers. "Is everyone ready?"

"As ready as ever," Mrs. Smyth said and shook her head. Under her breath, once more she said, "Men."

Jewel listened to several legal points, but mostly her mind wandered from part of the room to the next trying to memorize each detail in the room. She hoped there would be time to take some pictures with her cell phone. She wanted to remember everything about this place.

"Jewel, are you satisfied with that?"

"Ma'am?"

"Mrs. Smyth wants you to have the portrait, but, of course, it will be up to you and Mr. Cameron if it is to be left here on the premise or removed," Mr. Monroe explained.

"I don't understand. Why would Bryce have any say in it?"

Mrs. Smyth and Mr. Monroe looked at each other, but it was Mrs. Smyth who spoke up. "Young lady, your man bought this plantation."

Chapter 21

Jewel stood in front of Ula's portrait, still wrapped in protective paper. It leaned against the living room wall in her small apartment just off campus in Houston.

"Ms. Ula, what am I going to do with you?" she asked as she carefully removed one corner of the wrapping and peeled it down just enough to see the face of Ula McDougle.

She'd considered leaving the portrait hanging in the plantation, but when the attorney contacted Bryce, he insisted that it be given to Jewel and removed from the property.

That hurt.

Bryce now owned her old ancestral home and he didn't want any sign of her in it.

She still wore the necklace around her neck and hoped Ula McDougle was at peace knowing the plantation, the portrait and the necklace were in good hands.

It had been three weeks since she'd left St. Mark, and now it was up to her to find meaning in her old life on campus. Each day she dragged herself out of bed, dressed in her professional attire, and walked the couple blocks to campus. She left the door to her office open, hoping something would take away the deep hurt when anything reminded her of Bryce and his son.

How could she ever forget the hatred she saw in his face when he'd learned of her relationship with Jodi Martin? Even now just thinking about how he must feel toward her, she wanted to curl up on the couch and never get up. From her psychology courses, she knew the signs of depression, and she was about as close to the textbook example as she could get.

Today, she told Ula goodbye and headed to campus, determined to find something to take her mind away from the bazaar happenings on the island and the man who showed her she could love again. "A lot of good that did me."

Just as it had for the past three weeks, the day was torturously long. Fall classes would start soon, and all of her preliminary work had been done. There was nothing to get her mind off the hurt she felt.

By three o'clock, she snatched up her purse and headed for the door.

When she swung the door opened, she jumped back and grabbed her chest. Bryce Cameron stood next to the elevator with his legs apart and his hands in his pockets.

"Bryce! What are you doing here?"

He turned around. "I'm not sure. I've been standing out here at least ten minutes deciding whether I should leave or go into your office."

Jewel stared at the man she'd given her heart to, but words didn't come. What could she say? I love you? I'm sorry? Go away and leave me alone to suffer?

Finally, Bryce took his hands out of his pockets. "Can we go back to your office or do you need to get class?"

"Classes haven't started yet. Come in."

Her heart thumped against her chest as she made her way back into her office. Why had Bryce come all the way to Houston? Fear and hope threatened to take away her voice, but she didn't need to worry because Bryce spoke first.

"Jewel, I've had a lot of time to think." He started talking as soon as the door closed behind him. He stuck his hands in his pockets and paced in front of her desk. "When I left you at St. Marks, I spent a couple days with Kevin at the Wilsons, and when I left there, I was still furious with you and so were Mr. and Mrs. Wilson. We all have every right to be angry with your family for not facing up to what your aunt did to my family, and for you for, well, for being part of it."

"I told you, I knew almost nothing about the accident. I was involved in a huge project in my department during the time it happened. I never even listened to the news or read a newspaper. I only knew what my family told me and that wasn't much. Why should I have questioned them and why should I have connected you with the accident?"

"I know that now." He put his head down and walked toward her window. "I went back to the island and told Marcus. We rehashed everything that had happened since the time we'd found the cloth in the wall of the fort. The more we talked, the more I realized I was right to be mad at your family, but not at you."

Jewel had been standing back, but at his words, she walked up behind him and placed a hand on his back. "Thank you."

He turned. "I had to come up here to tell you that. I couldn't let us part ways with you thinking I hated you."

Jewel nodded, fighting back the tears, but she was determined to tell him how she felt. "Byrce, you know I love you, don't you?"

He squeezed his eyes and shook his head. "No, don't say that. We can't be together. It would be too hard for us."

Jewel refused to take that as his answer. She put her arms around his neck, pulled him to her, and kissed him as hard as she could. At first he tried to turn his head, but then he wrapped his arms around her and pulled her next to him and returned her kiss. Her heart pounded from excitement.

Finally she pulled away. "And I think you love me too."

She watched him search for words. "I do, but I don't see how it'll work."

"We don't have to see how it'll work. We simply have to give it a try. I'm willing to face the Wilsons. I'm willing to try to make it up to Kevin, but I'm not willing to let you walk out of my life without trying to overcome this."

He stared at her a long time.

"You'd be willing to talk to the Wilsons, knowing they'd hate you for what your family did to them and their daughter?"

Jewel swallowed and fought back the tears. "They have every right to hate my family, just as you do, but I think they'd come to see that it wasn't me who caused this to happen. They couldn't hate me forever, and I'm willing to give it a try—give us a try—if you are."

Again Bryce pulled her close to him. "I can't believe this is happening. I love you so much. I didn't think I'd ever love again, and then you came along. Why can't life be easy?"

Jewel looked up into his eyes. "If love were easy, it wouldn't be so powerful. Look at Ula and Hilliard. Nothing was easy for them, but they didn't give up. I love you, Bryce. Let's not give up on our chance to see if we can make it."

Chapter 22

Two Years Later

Jewel stood over the bassinet nestled as close to her bed as she could get it. The tiny head with fine dark hair was almost lost amongst the ruffles of the hand-stitched batiste. Reaching down, she picked up a hand and rubbed her thumb over the soft skin.

"She's perfect, isn't she?" Bryce said as he walked in the door.

Jewel looked up with the smile that refused to leave her face since the birth of their daughter. "She's the most amazing thing I've ever seen. I can't stop touching her."

Bryce walked up and pulled Jewel to him and buried his face in her hair. "And you're the most amazing woman, Mrs. Jewel Cameron, to have given us this precious daughter."

"I've never been so happy," she whispered.

"I'm glad. I like to make you happy." Bryce turned her to face him. "Do you think you're up to taking a little ride on the four-wheeler with me? I know you can't walk across the yard yet, but I'm dying to show you how it came out. Mrs. Wilson said she'd listen out for the baby."

Jewel knew exactly what he was talking about. For the last few weeks, Bryce had a crew out working daily to build a shoo-fly in the very spot on the river that the original one had stood. Jewel was not allowed to go near the spot, not that she could have maneuvered her swollen body that far, but now she was ready to see.

"I'm willing and able, Mr. Cameron." She bent down and placed a kiss on the baby's head. After making sure the monitor was on, she followed Bryce down the stairs.

Getting out of the house felt wonderful. Raising her face to the sky, she inhaled deeply and allowed the warmth of the sun to refresh and rejuvenate her. "Oh, I needed this. I feel as though I've been imprisoned for months."

Bryce helped get on the oversized four-wheeler, the workhorse of the plantation, as he liked to refer to it.

Jewel settled herself in the big seat. "This is fun."

"Tell me if it gets too much for you. We can do this another day."

"Oh no, I've been waiting for weeks to see this. You're not getting me back into the house until I do."

The big four-wheeler eased its way across the grounds of the estate. River's Bend had not been turned into a bed and breakfast as Bryce had first planned. Instead, he and Jewel made it their home as soon as the first stages of the restoration were completed.

Their wedding had taken place on the grounds of the estate with large white canopies spread out under the oaks. For the next year they lived amongst the hammer and dust of rebuilding and restoring the house.

Today, as they rode slowly toward the bend in the river, Jewel thought just how her life had changed since she had first stepped off the helicopter on the island. Just as she'd told Bryce, she'd been willing to face the Wilsons. It hadn't been easy winning them over, but in the end, after they'd come to know her better, they realized she was right for their former son-in-law and their grandson. Bryce couldn't make himself travel to Boston to meet her adoptive family, but that was okay with Jewel. He was her family now, he and Kevin, Sara their new little girl, and the Wilsons. It was all she needed.

As they pulled out of the thicket of trees where the treasures had been dug, Jewel caught her breath. "Oh, Bryce, it's just as I saw it in my dreams. Identical."

There in front of them, standing majestically over the banks of the Mississippi River was a shoo-fly, newly constructed and sparkling white.

"How did you do that?"

Bryce grinned. "We build things, remember? That's my job."

"No, I mean, how did you get it to look like that. It's just as I saw it."

"I've been talking with Mrs. Smyth. She found a picture before the old shoo-fly was torn down. It was in pretty bad shape, but we could see the lines and the dimensions and we used it as a pattern."

"It's amazing that I saw it just like this."

Bryce eased the vehicle to a stop by the stairs that led up to the circular structure. "Think you can make it up there?"

"Even if I have to crawl. Come on."

Climbing the stairs she had seen in her dreams touched her the way nothing else had ever done. Midway up she stopped.

Immediately Bryce put his hand on her shoulders. "Are you okay? Do you want to go back?"

"Oh, no. I'm just so overwhelmed by all of this. Ula really did show me her life. I've done this before. I've climbed these steps." Jewel looked at Bryce. "How could that be?"

"We'll never know." He shook his head, "but we'll always know it really did happen, and I'm so very thankful it did."

"You are?"

"Why sure. Without that stubborn streak in Ula

McDougle to protect what was hers, none of this would've happened. I wouldn't have met you. We wouldn't have our daughter, and we wouldn't be here today."

Jewel snuggled against him, then took his hand and led him to the top of the shoo-fly. The magnificence of the river below, the house peeking through the trees in the distance, and the presence of Bryce next to her—all brought tears to her eyes. She sniffled.

"You okay?" Bryce whispered again.

"I've never been happier. I think Ula must be smiling down on me now."

Bryce looked beyond her at something across the river. "Egrets," he said.

Jewel turned to see a pair of beautiful white egrets soaring together above the trees, then swooping down near the water in search of their dinner. Jewel raised her hands to her chest and locked her thumbs together. "We'll always be together, no matter what."

Bryce placed his hand on her heart and finished for her, "And when we're not together, I'll always be with you right here."

Jewel didn't fight the tears that spilled from her eyes. She looked at her beloved home standing in the distance with Kevin, squealing and chattering, as he ran around Mr. Wilson on the front lawn. This is how she'd always envisioned love.

She looked back at Bryce and placed her hand on his heart. He'd given her the world— forever.

~ THE END ~

About the Author

Fran McNabb grew up along the beaches and islands of the Gulf Coast and uses this setting in FOREVER, MY LOVE. Ship Island, which sits twelves miles off the coast, plays an important part of this book and has played an important part of Fran's life. Today the fort and island that was used in the Civil War is a tourist attraction, but during one memory-filled summer, it became Fran's playground while her family lived on the island to help with a family business. Fran has always loved the water, and now she and her husband live on a quiet bayou harbor and spend as much time as possible boating and enjoying the pristine waters of the Gulf Coast. After taking an early retirement from teaching high school English and journalism, she now enjoys reading, writing, and teaching writing workshops. She loves to hear from her readers at mcnabbf@bellsouth.net.

Made in the USA
Middletown, DE
26 September 2022